THE ROCKSBURG RAILROAD MURDERS

THE
ROCKSBURG
RAILROAD
MURDERS

K.C. CONSTANTINE

With an afterword by the Author

David R. Godine · Publisher
BOSTON

This softcover edition published in 1987 by
David R. Godine, Publisher, Inc.
Horticultural Hall, 300 Massachusetts Avenue
Boston, Massachusetts 02115

First published in 1972 by Saturday Review Press, New York;
subsequently published by David R. Godine, Publisher, Inc. in
1982 in the "Godine Double Detective" series (#1).

Library of Congress Cataloging-in-Publication Data
Constantine, K. C.
    The Rocksburg railroad murders.
    I. Title.
[PS3553.O524R6 1987]   813'.54   86-83178
ISBN 0-87923-662-0

First printing
Printed in Canada

THE ROCKSBURG RAILROAD MURDERS

EVEN WITH THE HAND-TALKIES, it took Chief Mario Balzic a half hour after the game to get the auxiliary police coordinated. Maybe more people were coming to high school football games, or maybe more were coming to Rocksburg High's games, or maybe Rocksburg's narrow streets were never intended to handle this kind of traffic, or maybe there were just too damn many saloons too near the high school field.

Whichever it was, it left Balzic surly, distracted, and thirsting for a beer. He stepped into Evanko's Bar and Grille, hoping for a quick draught, and walked instead into a fist fight between two drunks whose high school football careers had ended at least twenty years earlier and who had started out reminiscing and ended up swinging over the cause of Rocksburg's forty-to-six loss. It took Balzic a half hour to get that straightened out, doing it by buying drinks all around to pacify Mike Evanko to keep him from pressing charges, and by seeing to it that friends of the fist fighters got some coffee into them and gave their word that they'd drive them home.

Back out on the street, traffic seemed worse than before Balzic had gone into Evanko's. Then the auxiliary at the corner of Amelia

Street and Eurania Avenue quit communicating and it took Balzic fifteen minutes to get there to find out why.

"Something's wrong with it," Henry Adamchik, the auxiliary, said, holding the radio up to Balzic's ear and shaking it.

Balzic jerked it out of his hand and fiddled with it. "Here, take mine," he said after an exasperating minute trying to make the other one work. "I'll go back and use my car radio."

On the way back to his cruiser, Balzic looked up at the clear black sky and said, "Bad enough you let somebody invent football, but you weren't satisfied with that. No, you had to let somebody go and invent cars, and then radios, and then, Jeezus Christ Almighty, you had to stick me with auxiliaries yet. . . ."

It was eleven-fifteen before the flow of cars approached the usual level of traffic for that time of night on a Friday, and eleven-twenty before Balzic told the auxiliaries to pack it in. He headed his cruiser down Bencho's Alley and threaded his way through a half dozen more alleys before turning onto Delmont Street to his home. Once inside, he headed straight for the refrigerator and a beer.

On the kitchen table was a note from his wife, Ruth, telling him that she'd given the girls permission to go to Valleta's Drug Store after the game, but that they were to be in no later than midnight. The note also said his mother had had a good time at the Eagles' bingo and won a set of dish towels.

Balzic opened the beer and set out a plate. He cut up some provolone and quartered a banana pepper, filled the plate with them, and went into the living room, taking a long drink of beer before setting the dish on the coffee table and turning on the television. With a little luck he thought he might be able to catch the last inning of the Pirates' game out of Saint Louis.

There was another note on the coffee table with a snapshot beside it. The note said: "Hey, Mario, big shot. What you think this? Next time you holler hippeys, you think this over. You look pretty funny. No?" It was his mother's barely legible script.

The snapshot was of himself. There he stood, grinning with the arrogance only being eighteen can muster, thirty pounds lighter, hair slicked back in a duck's tail, wearing a one-button jacket down to his

4

knees and trousers pulled up by inch-wide suspenders to a point just below where his ribs joined and then ballooning out at the knees and coming to rest in a tight circle on his spade, suede shoes. Completing the outfit were a floppy, polka-dotted bow tie and a key chain that nearly touched his shoe.

"Brother, if I wasn't a mess," he said.

He turned the faded snapshot over and looked closely at the smudged date: June 4, 1942, the date of his senior class picnic. He remembered the date very well. The next day he had enlisted in the marines.

He chuckled ruefully and, tossing the snapshot on the table, drank some more beer, and mused for a moment about taking his mother to the courthouse to give a lecture to District Attorney Milt Weigh about social customs, particularly in matters of dress. Weigh needed somebody to lecture him about that at least as much as Balzic needed to be reminded of it; to Milt Weigh, anybody who didn't wear four-dollar ties and calf-high socks had to be doing something suspicious.

Balzic chuckled again, thinking about all the things Weigh didn't know and about how Weigh managed to sustain the impression that anything he didn't know wasn't worth knowing.

The sound of the television interrupted his thoughts. He got up to adjust the set and then settled back in the recliner the girls had bought him last Christmas to watch the Pirates and the Cards. Instead of the game, he got the last minute of a post-game interview and the beginning of what would have been the eleven o'clock news.

He had just kicked off his shoes and put his feet on the coffee table when the phone rang. He swore in Italian and Serbian and was still swearing as he hustled into the kitchen to lift the receiver before it woke either his wife or mother.

"Balzic."

"Royer, Chief."

"Yeah, Joe—oh, wait. Don't tell me you're sick or something and can't make it tonight. Please don't tell me that."

"What do you mean sick? Where the hell you think I'm calling from?"

"You at the station?"

"Hell yes, I'm at the station."

"Jesus, is it after twelve already?"

"Five minutes after."

"Oh boy," Balzic said, sighing. "I just got back from that damn football game. You never saw such a mess. So what's up?"

"Angelo just called in."

"So? Angelo's always calling in. Angelo can't find straight up without calling in."

"He got a reason this time," Royer said. "He found a guy up on the train station platform with his head caved in. Dead."

"Did he get hit by a train, or what?"

"No. Angelo wasn't making too much sense, but from what I gather, somebody beat the shit out of him."

"I'll be right down. You call Weigh's office?"

"Not yet."

"Well, call him, for crissake. I'll be down the train station."

Balzic gulped down a piece of cheese and some of the pepper as he was putting his shoes back on. He took another gulp of beer, grabbed another piece of provolone to eat on the way, and was starting out the door when his daughters came up on the porch.

"Hi," he said as he hurried past them. "You have a good time? And what are you doing coming in this late? You know you got school tomorrow."

"Tomorrow's Saturday, Daddy," Emily, the fourteen-year-old, said.

"Besides, Mother said it was okay," Marie, the fifteen-year-old, said.

"I'll talk to her about that tomorrow," Balzic said, getting in his car. He got back out to say, "Hey, put that plate of cheese and peppers back in the ice box, will you? And turn the TV off, okay?"

"It's a refrigerator, Daddy," Emily said.

"You know what I mean. And if your mother wakes up tell her I had to go out. Urgent, got it?"

"Yeah, we got it," Marie said with a sidelong glance at her sister.

"Good night, kids," Balzic said, spinning the wheels backing out of the drive.

"Talk about hot-rodders," Marie said.

"Hey, come on," Emily said. "We can watch Humphrey Bogart. He's on channel four."

Balzic had parked his Chevrolet on the State Street side of the Pennsylvania Station when he spotted Angelo Seretti's cruiser. The ticket office was deserted, and he went through the tunnel and up the steps to the platform. Patrolman Angelo Seretti was trying his best to look professional, but the color of his face gave him away. Frank Bennett, the station master, stood beside Seretti, his face more ashen than Seretti's.

"Where?" Balzic said when he approached them.

"Over there," Seretti said. "Under the bench."

Balzic hustled to the bench and went down on one knee. For a second he thought he was going to lose the little beer and cheese he'd gotten down. "Good Christ," he said. He stood up and walked back to Seretti and Bennett. "Get on the horn, Angelo, and tell Royer to get the coroner and the state boys."

"The D.A.'s office, too?"

"He already called them. They should've been here by now. Go on, Angelo."

Angelo, flushing over his hesitation, turned quickly and broke into a run toward the steps.

"Did you know him, Mr. Bennett?"

Bennett nodded, a lock of his gray hair falling over his eye. "So did you," he said, his voice barely above a whisper.

"Who was it?"

"John Andrasko."

"You're—you sure?"

"Yes, I'm sure. John's been riding the eleven-thirty-eight to Knox every night for eight, ten years. I've sold him enough passes. He just bought a new one tonight, as a matter of fact."

Balzic walked back over to the body lying half under the bench. "Good Christ, John, I'm sorry." He was almost going to say he was sorry he hadn't recognized him, but the beer and cheese started

7

coming up, and he just got his face over the edge of the platform in time. He coughed and gagged a couple more times before he wiped his mouth with his hanky. Spitting didn't get rid of the taste.

He was going back to Bennett to ask some other questions when he heard the shoes on the steps coming up.

Milt Weigh, the district attorney, came up, his breath heavy with the smell of gin. He was followed by Sam Carraza, his chief of detectives, and by John Dillman, another county detective. Carraza and Dillman both were raw-eyed and breathing heavily.

"Hello, Milt," Balzic said, nodding to Carraza and Dillman. "I think I ought to warn you guys, be ready to lose all that high-price stuff you been drinking."

"Balzic," Weigh said by way of greeting. "An ugly one?"

"Ugliest one I've seen since Tarawa. Over there. Under the bench."

Weigh, Carraza, and Dillman set off toward the body. The two detectives took a long look, but Weigh recoiled. "My God," he said and immediately turned away and came back to Balzic. "My God," he said again.

"Yeah," Balzic said. "I lost about half a beer, so if you're thinking you're going to lose your gin, don't hold it in on my account."

Weigh took a couple of deep breaths. "What do you have?"

"Just a name so far. John Andrasko. I've known him since I was a kid. Mr. Bennett here had to tell me, though. Says he just bought a pass from him tonight. But I'm really taking his word for it. I haven't gone through his pockets yet."

"Dillman?" Weigh called out.

"Yeah?"

"Check his pockets."

"I'm doing that."

"What's the station man say?" Weigh said.

"Just what I told you. Says he sold John a pass tonight and that he's been riding the eleven-thirty-something every night to Knox for eight, ten years."

"He didn't say anything else?"

"I didn't get a chance to ask him."

"Well, let's go ask him."

8

They walked back to where Frank Bennett was sitting and kneading his palms.

"Mr. Bennett," Balzic said, "this is Mr. Weigh, the district attorney."

"How do you do, sir," Bennett said.

Weigh extended his hand and Bennett shook it feebly.

"I'd like to ask you some questions, Mr. Bennett."

"Go ahead. I doubt that I can tell you much, though," Bennett said.

"How did you learn about this?"

"Fireman from the eleven-thirty-eight came down and told me."

"What time—I mean, was this fellow Andrasko a regular?"

"Yessir. The only one. Been riding for years. Ever since he took the job over at Knox Steel. Eight, ten years at least. Longer, maybe."

"Did you see anybody else?"

"Nossir. Nobody. Of course that doesn't mean anything. There are lots of ways to get on this platform. You can come down State Street Extension from the other side over there, or you could walk up the tracks from either direction. Going past me is only one of the ways. But nobody went past me since eleven tonight except John. He bought his pass and we talked a bit."

"What time was that?"

"Well, on nights when John just comes in, he gets here about eleven-thirty, but on nights when he buys his pass, he generally comes in about eleven-twenty and we shoot the breeze. Nothing important. We just talk. He was a nice fellow."

"How does he usually get here?"

"He walks. John doesn't like to drive. Never has. I guess that's why he's one of the few people left who still ride the trains."

John Dillman walked up then, holding everything he'd found in John Andrasko's pockets: a thin billfold, a ring of keys, a package of chewing tobacco, a pack of twisted Italian cigars, and four dollar bills and three dimes. "This is it," he said.

"Mr. Bennett," Weigh said, "you said he bought a pass tonight. How much money, if you know, would you say he might've had?"

"Well, he paid me with a twenty-dollar bill, as he always does. That money you're holding there is the change I gave him. Should be four dollars and thirty cents. Month pass to Knox costs fifteen-seventy."

"Mario," Weigh said, "I assume your people have contacted the state police."

Balzic nodded. "They should've been here by now."

"Mr. Bennett, are you positive nobody else went past you tonight?"

Bennett nodded slowly. "Yessir. But I've already told you that doesn't mean anything. I mean—no disrespect, Mr. Weigh—but somebody had to get up here tonight, and they didn't come by me."

"Here come the state boys," Dillman said. "Looks like they brought half the barracks."

Lieutenant Phil Moyer, in plain clothes, followed by Sergeant Ralph Stallcup, led a contingent of seven troopers up the steps onto the platform. One of them carried a camera and immediately began photographing the body of John Andrasko from a variety of angles. The rest of them, with no direction from either Lieutenant Moyer or Sergeant Stallcup, fanned out over the platform and began examining it. Moyer ordered them off the platform after about ten minutes, and they started to make their way up and down the three sets of tracks.

Moyer and Stallcup listened as Frank Bennett repeated what little he knew about John Andrasko and the events leading up to the discovery of the body by the fireman from the eleven-thirty-eight to Knox. Moyer went through the effects found by Dillman, verifying the amount of money with the amounts Frank Bennett gave as the price of the pass and the change given.

"Mario," Moyer said, "what's it look like to you?"

"Looks to me probably what it looks like to you. Somebody either had a grudge or else that somebody's off his rocker. Nobody does that kind of job for any other reason that I know of. It sure wasn't for money, unless he was carrying a wad nobody knew about. But a guy like John, well, he was too steady. Too regular."

"You knew him?" Moyer said.

"Ever since I was a kid. Went all through school with him. We were in the same room most of the time."

"Wasn't there anything irregular about him?"

"Not that I knew about. He married a little late, I suppose. No. I can't even say that. He just didn't get married as early as the rest of us is what I meant to say."

"Gambler?"

"Not that I know of. No. He watched his money pretty close even when he was a kid."

"What did he do for a living?"

"He was a millwright over at Knox Steel. Before that I think he worked for one of the big steel outfits down the river. I'm not really sure."

"Ever in trouble?"

"Hell no. John was as straight a guy as everybody ought to be. If everybody was like him, you and me'd be looking for sensible work."

"From what you say, it looks like we can rule out a grudge job."

"Oh, I wouldn't do that. Not just yet anyway."

"Why not?"

"Well, as far as I know, John was a straight, regular guy. But that doesn't mean there wasn't somebody around who thought he was a prick. I just said I've known him most of my life, but I wasn't a drinking buddy of his or anything like that. He may have had a side to him he never showed me. For one thing, I've never even seen his wife. He kept pretty much to himself."

"Where'd he live?"

"He bought a small farm years ago about three miles out of town. North, on 986."

"And you say he rode the train every night to get to work?"

"That's what Mr. Bennett says."

"So how'd he get from his place to here every night?"

"I think I can answer that for you," Frank Bennett said. "John walked. He was a great believer in the virtue of walking."

"Why?"

"Said it kept him in shape."

11

"He had a driver's license. It's right here," Moyer said, pulling it out of Andrasko's thin, black wallet.

"Oh, he could drive all right," Bennett said. "But he hated to. Never drove unless he absolutely had to. Just to go shopping for groceries and for things he needed for the farm."

"So he walked in here every night? More than three miles? In bad weather, too?"

"Yessir. Every night. Rain, snow, whatever. He walked."

"Well, hell," Moyer said. "Look here. He's got two vehicle registration cards. One for a Ford pickup and this one's for a Ford sedan. Why the hell's a guy who hates driving have two vehicles?"

"He said he needed them," Bennett replied. "Many's the time he wished he didn't need them, but then he'd just shrug and say what's the use. America was car-crazy, he used to say."

"Lieutenant?" one of the troopers walking the tracks called out. "Think you better come have a look at this."

Except for Frank Bennett, everybody on the platform set off toward the trooper. He was standing under the State Street bridge, and when they got to him, he flashed his lamp on the gravel near one of the rails between two ties. The light reflected off the fragments of a Coke bottle. Moyer squatted and took a pen from his inside pocket and lifted the neck of the bottle. It was the largest piece.

"Looks like we got the weapon."

"Which means that whoever did it went across the tracks and up the steps to State Street and then dropped it. Or threw it. Must've been thrown. I doubt it would've broken from that height, just being dropped."

"And I'll just bet if somebody took the trouble to throw it, he also took the trouble to wipe it clean," Moyer said.

"One thing's sure," Stallcup said, "he had to have a lot of blood on him."

"Well," Moyer said, standing, "get everything measured off and get the photographer. And get the plastic bags. I want as much of this bottle as we can get."

"Beaten to death with a Coke bottle," Milt Weigh said. "My God."

"Hell of a thought, ain't it?" Balzic said.

12

"Well," Moyer said, "I think that's about all we can do until we get some daylight. The coroner showed yet?"

"That's probably him now," Balzic said. "Behind the ambulance."

"That only leaves one thing," Moyer said. "Who wants the pleasure?"

"What are you talking about?" Milt Weigh said.

"The next of kin, Mr. Weigh. You want to give them the good news?"

"I'll pass that if you don't mind."

"How about you, Mario?"

"Yeah. I guess I'm up for this one. Rather do it alone."

"Hell, be my guest. And see what you can find out."

"Well, I'm not going to ask any questions. I'll nose around, but tonight ain't the night for asking questions."

"Why not?" Milt Weigh said.

"Well, if you want to ask them, Milt, you're welcome to come along and do the asking."

Weigh thrust his hands into his coat pockets. "I'll take your word for it."

"You'll let me know. Right, Mario?" Moyer said.

"Yeah, sure," Balzic replied, clearing his throat and spitting. "See you, gentlemen." He turned to leave the platform as the county coroner, Dr. Wallace Grimes, was placing a stethoscope on John Andrasko's chest, confirming what was obvious.

Balzic had trouble finding the Andrasko place and had to stop at a house to ask directions.

"You passed it," the lady said after she saw Balzic's ID. "It's the next place down."

"You a friend?"

"I know them, if that's what you mean."

"Do you know if Mrs. Andrasko has any close friends around here?"

"Something happen bad?"

"Yes, ma'am. Do you know—"

13

"Oh, I guess I'm about the only one she talks to. You want me to come along?"

"No, but I might have to come back for you. They have kids?"

"Oh yeah. They had two, and she had one from before. It's that bad, huh? Was it to him? John?"

"Yes, ma'am."

"I always said he was going to get hit by a car some day."

"Well, thank you very much, ma'am. If it's necessary, I can count on you to come over there?"

"Sure. That's what neighbors are for, ain't they?"

"Fine. Thanks again," Balzic said and hurried over the grass to his cruiser.

When he found the drive and pulled into the Andrasko place, all the lights were off, save one upstairs. "Damn," he said and sat in the car for a minute after he turned off the ignition. He tried to arrange what he wanted to say. There was no good way he knew. But then there never had been. He just wished they were awake. It always seemed worse to have to wake the people up.

"Just a little help," he said as he got out of the car. He looked up at the stars and said it again and then made his way onto the porch. In the rear, a dog started growling.

He had to knock three times before a light came on downstairs. He took his ID out and waited.

A light came on above him, and he stepped back, so whoever had turned it on could get a good look at him.

"Who is it?" a woman's voice said.

"Mrs. Andrasko? I'm Mario Balzic. I'm the chief of police in town." He held his ID folder up to his cheek so that the badge and his picture showed.

The inside door opened. Mrs. Andrasko pushed open the screen door enough for her to show half her face. Her sleep-wrinkled confusion was already starting to turn to panic.

"What—what's the matter?"

"Mrs. Andrasko, it's about your husband. May I come in, please?"

"Oh God, what happened? What's wrong?"

"Let's go inside, Mrs. Andrasko. Please."

She backed away from the door, her hands covering her mouth.

Balzic stepped inside and took a deep breath. "Mrs. Andrasko, I'm very sorry. I've known John all my life."

"Oh God, God, God," Mrs. Andrasko said and slumped onto a misshapen ottoman.

"He's dead, Mrs. Andrasko," Balzic said, going down on one knee to stop her from falling, in case she fainted. She didn't faint, but she began to sob from deep in her throat, and then she began to wail, rocking back and forth on the ottoman, her hands pressed against her face until the tears ran over her fingers and down her wrists.

"Hey," a boy's voice said behind Balzic. "Are you hurting my momma?"

Balzic stood. "No, son, I'm not. I just had to be the one to tell her."

Mrs. Andrasko threw out her arms, and the boy rushed into them.

"My Billy, my little Billy," she sobbed, pulling the boy to her and kissing him.

"What's the matter, Momma?"

"Oh God, Billy. Daddy's gone, Billy. Daddy's gone."

The boy looked bewildered, but he did not cry. His eyes went from his mother's raw grief to Balzic's somberness.

"He's dead, son," Balzic said.

"Who's dead?" a girl's voice said.

"Oh God, Norma, come to your mother," Mrs. Andrasko said, and the girl, taller and two or three years older than the boy, stepped quickly to her mother's side. She began to cry at once, and in the next second the boy began, too.

Balzic thought his skull would burst. There was no sound like it, and as many times as Balzic had heard it, he had never gotten used to it. This time, because he'd known John Andrasko, he had to bite the inside of his cheeks to stop himself from crying.

He turned away and looked around for the kitchen. He was suddenly very thirsty. He found the kitchen in the rear of the house, and as he turned the tap and looked for a glass, he could hear the dog growling on the other side of the kitchen door.

He drank and let his eyes wander over the kitchen. Aside from a stack of glasses and spoons in the sink, it was tidy and clean. A jar of peanut butter sat open on the corner of the table, and a knife with some peanut butter on it lay beside the jar. It was a small room, but orderly, and there was no smell of grease.

He finished the glass of water and leaned against the sink, and then, just as he was about to put the glass in the sink, he saw the cartons of Coke. They were between the back wall and the refrigerator. Two six-packs contained empties, and the top one in the stack had two empties in it. He stepped quietly to the refrigerator and opened it as gently as he could. Inside, on the bottom shelf of the door were four full bottles of Coke. He closed the refrigerator and shook his head. "What the hell am I thinking about?" he whispered and went back into the living room.

Mrs. Andrasko was still sitting on the ottoman with her arms wrapped around her children. They were all still sobbing.

"Mrs. Andrasko, would you like me to call somebody? A relative maybe. A neighbor?"

She shook her head no.

"A priest then?"

"No—yes. Father Marrazo. Call him."

"Where's the phone?"

Mrs. Andrasko nodded toward the kitchen, and Balzic found it on the wall. He dialed the station and got Royer. "Do me a favor, Joe, and get hold of Father Marrazo. Tell him to get out here to John Andrasko's place to sit it out with the family. It's on 986 North, about three miles. I'll leave my lights on in the drive."

"Rough one?" Royer said.

"Next one I'm saving for you."

"Is this Father Marrazo out of St. Malachy's?"

"Yeah, but he won't be there. He's playing cards in Muscotti's. I'd call myself, but I forget the number, and I want to look around out here anyway. I'll be here till he gets here. And oh—listen. Whoever answers down there might try to give you the noise he ain't there. But tell them I said he is and I need him."

"You do?"

"Almost as much—never mind. Just tell him to get his ass out here. Probably give him the good excuse for getting out of the game anyway. Any calls?"

16

"None for you."

"Good," Balzic said, hanging up, and in spite of himself, found his eyes fixed on the cartons of Coke between the wall and the refrigerator.

He rubbed his eyes and went back into the living room. He watched Mrs. Andrasko for another moment, her arms still pulling her children to her, her sobs now almost a croon, and then stepped quietly through the front door onto the porch.

He lit a cigarette and went down to the cruiser to wait for the priest. He sat for a minute inside the car with the door open and then tossed the cigarette on the ground, got out, and started walking toward the rear of the house.

Set apart from the house about thirty yards was a small barn and beside that was a wide, low building that looked like a garage. The gravel drive forked: one fork led to the barn and the other to the low building. Balzic took the second fork as he heard the dog start growling again.

"Aw, shut the hell up," he said, hoping that the chain he heard being dragged about was both short and sturdy.

The doors on the low building were the sliding kind and without locks. He pushed the nearest one back and stepped inside, taking out his pencil flashlight and shining it around.

Parked near the opposite wall was a dusty Ford pickup. The bay where he had come in was empty, and in the middle bay sat a small Allis-Chalmers tractor. Behind the tractor and hung on the back wall were implements, tools, cans, drums, ropes, chains—most of the things necessary for operating the farm. There was about it all the same care and order Balzic had seen in the kitchen.

Balzic thought almost at once of one of the vehicle registrations Lieutenant Moyer had found in John Andrasko's wallet, the registrations for a Ford pickup and a Ford sedan. He thought also about the woman he'd talked to down the road and what she'd said about the children the Andraskos had—two of their own and one of hers from before.

"Well," Balzic said aloud, "somebody's driving that car."

He was walking back to the cruiser to call the station again when he heard the tires and saw the headlights of a car as it pulled off

17

Route 986. It slowed just briefly, then picked up speed and came on, sliding to a stop scant yards from the rear of the cruiser.

Balzic doubted that it was Father Marrazo—the priest didn't drive like that—and he was sure it wasn't when the driver kept the engine running and the lights on.

"Hey, mister, would you mind moving your car?" a young voice called out.

Balzic walked quickly to the car window and put his pencil light in the driver's eyes. "I'm a police officer," Balzic said.

The driver was a youngster, sixteen, seventeen at most—thin, with a bad case of acne.

Balzic took out his ID and shined the light on it for the boy to see. "Who are you, son?"

"Tommy—Thomas Parilla."

"What are you doing here?"

"What am I—I live here," Tommy said. "What are you doing here?"

"You Mrs. Andrasko's boy?"

Tommy nodded. "What's the matter?"

"I'm sorry to be the one to have to tell you, son, but your father's dead." Balzic knew as soon as he said it that it did not sound right, but he had not prepared himself for telling anybody else.

"My father's been dead a long time, mister," Tommy said. "He went away a long time ago. You must be talking about John."

Balzic tried not to change his expression. "Yes. I guess I am."

"My mother inside?"

"Yes. She's with the kids."

"Well, you still have to—I mean, would you please move your car? I have to put this one in the garage."

Balzic moved the cruiser and then watched Tommy wheel the Ford sedan around him, skidding on the gravel. He hit the brakes hard in front of the garage door, jumped out while the car was still rocking, and opened the door. The boy put the car in, then came out and shut the door, moving, Balzic thought, no differently from the way any other boy his age would move when he'd come home too late with the family car.

Balzic watched the boy go into the house through the kitchen

18

door, then backed the cruiser down the drive and opened the door and turned on his lights so Father Marrazo could see him from the road.

He took out his notebook and made an approximate chronology:

11:20–11:38 killed, not enough noise for Bennett to hear
12–1 with Weigh and state boys
1:15 told wife
1:30–35 kid comes home in Ford sedan, could care less

He put the notebook away and sat wondering whether the boy had left the keys in the car. Or was it key? Andrasko had had a key ring. Balzic hadn't looked carefully at the key ring, but something told him that among the dozen or so keys, there had been three or four ignition or trunk keys. Could it have been about something as simple as that—an argument over taking the car out? Well, he thought, it's happened for less likely reasons.

He was debating whether to check the car for the key when Father Marrazo's car turned into the drive and stopped behind the cruiser.

"Hello, Father," Balzic said.

"Mario, old friend," the priest said, getting out of his car. "Old friend—old nuisance. I was twenty-one dollars ahead when your call came. Why do I love you so much, Mario, can you tell me that?"

"For the same reason I love you," Balzic said. "Nobody loves like one coward loves another."

"Sounds like that came out of a book, Mario."

"If it did, Father, then it was a book you read."

"You heard it from me?"

Balzic nodded, and then told the priest why he'd called him.

"Ah, well," the priest sighed. "The family's inside, I suppose."

Balzic nodded.

"How are they taking it? Very hard? Of course, how else?"

"Three of them are. There's one that could care less."

"Tommy."

"You know him?"

"Yes, I'm sorry to say that I do. Strange kid. He lies in confession just to provoke me. For no other reason. Very full of spite and

19

resentment, but as much as I've tried to find out why, I've never been able to get anything out of any of them. Well," Father Marrazo said, stretching and yawning, "I guess I better get in there. Would you like to join me, Mario? Then maybe afterward, after we get them all to bed, we could find something to drink someplace."

"Muscotti's will still be open."

"The name's familiar. Is it a local establishment?"

"Well, I'm not going in with you, Father, but I'll tell you what. After I go back to the station to check on something, I'll drop in there and save you a seat. How's that?"

"Sounds fine. Depends how quickly I get them calmed."

They said good night, and Balzic could see the priest going inside as he wheeled the cruiser out onto 986 and headed for the station.

Balzic heard the commotion as soon as he opened the cruiser door in the city hall parking lot. Somebody inside was having a shouting match. There was no mistaking Joe Royer's voice, but three or four other voices kept getting mixed up with John Dillman's and Sam Carraza's. By the time Balzic got to the landing outside the station, he was wishing he had just gone on to Muscotti's and had a couple of cold ones.

Inside, at the desk, Carraza and Dillman were trying to herd a crew of the bearded, beaded ones Balzic recognized as the leaders of The Community Store, the local answer to the hippie question. Milt Weigh had been trying for months, ever since he'd been sworn in, and with monotonous failures, to bust them on a narcotics charge. As far as Balzic was concerned, their only crime was that they looked like hell and that they had been naive enough to believe they could open their place on State Street and be left alone. Balzic took a deep breath and went inside.

"What the hell's going on, Joe?" Balzic shouted over the uproar.

Royer motioned him behind the counter and then led him into one of the cubicles in the rear.

"Our hero's done it again," Royer said, lighting a cigarette wearily.

"Weigh?"

"Yeppie. Only this time it's because they gave him a lot of static

20

when he and Carraza and Dillman went in to find out if they saw anybody coming down State Street. So naturally he wants them booked for surety of the peace and Christ knows what all else."

"Naturally they don't know what anybody's talking about."

"Naturally," Royer said. "But that ain't the best part. The best part is, our hero wants us to lock them up down here. He don't have the space out at Southern Regional, he says. Turns out he got four of them in there from a bust he made last night. Sometimes I think he ought to get married, then maybe he'd have something better to do at night than go around busting these goofballs."

"Well, let's go see what we can make of it," Balzic said. "If we're lucky, maybe we can send them all back to their store. The thing that pisses me is, one night Weigh's going to go in there and somebody's going to get hurt."

Balzic went back out to the counter and hammered on it with the flat of his hand. "Sam, you turning these people over to me?"

There was silence for a second as the bearded, beaded ones interrupted their shouting to look at a new target for their rage. One of them started shouting "Pig," and Balzic bounded around the counter and slapped him with a cupped palm so its sound was more impressive than its sting.

"Next person opens his mouth gets the same, only harder," Balzic said, taking in Carraza and Dillman in his warning glance. "Now, Sam, I'm going to ask you again—you turning these people over to me or not?"

Carraza nodded.

"On what charge?"

"Surety of the peace, resisting arrest. Those two'll be enough."

"All right, Sam. You turned them over. Good night."

"Not so fast, Mario—"

"I said good night, Sam. Good night, John."

Carraza looked at Dillman, and they both looked at Balzic. Dillman started to swear under his breath, but he and Carraza left.

Balzic turned to the group now in his charge. None had moved since he'd slapped the one who'd been shouting pig. "Okay, men," he said, "this is my 'Community Store,' and in my store we don't call names, we don't shout, and we don't shove. The sooner you

21

understand me, the sooner I understand you. I already got a pretty good idea why you're here, but I want one of you—and just one—to tell me why you think you're here."

Balzic took off his raincoat and suit coat and sat on a bench near the front door. "I got time," he said.

"Put it on him, Charley," one of them said.

"Yeah, Charley, give him the news," another said.

Charley stepped forward. He was very tall, barechested under a fringed leather vest, and Balzic could see he had spent some time doing something physical, probably playing football.

"Okay, Chiefey, it's like this—"

"I said we don't call names in my store."

Charley looked for a moment as though he would call some more names just to save face. Instead, he said, "Okay, Chief, it's your store. No names, But you know why we're here. That D.A. had the heat for us ever since we set up our place."

Balzic nodded. "But why tonight?"

"I don't know, man. He come in there with his deputy sheriffs looking for Robin Hood or somebody. He don't ask three questions in a row that make sense, man, and the next thing he's telling the deputies to book us. So naturally there got to be a little scuffling. Maybe we did some shoving and bad-mouthing, but that pi—that dude just steady won't let us be, man. He's put the bust on us three times in the last lunar, man, and he still ain't found nothing."

"And tonight he came in and you thought it was going to be more of the same, is that it?"

"You got it, man."

"So you started hollering and shoving before you found out what he was really after?"

"No, man, it wasn't like that. I mean, he really didn't ask nothing that made sense. Like the only thing I heard him ask was did we see somebody coming down State Street at such and such on the clock, man, and I ask you—what kind of shit is that to put down? That's the freakiest excuse for a bust I—"

"It so happens he had a reason for asking that question," Balzic said. "I admit, the chances are probably six to five, he asked it in every wrong way, but he was on the square when he asked."

"Well, hell, man, lots of people come up and down that pavement. Nobody ever told me we were on the payroll to play cops and robbers for his store. What are we supposed to do—check ID's on everybody that trots on by our front door?"

"Think a minute, Charley," Balzic said. "How many places are open on State Street after nine o'clock? Besides yours?"

"None, man. At least I don't think any."

"Okay. So then where else is the D.A. supposed to go to ask if not your store? See what I mean?"

"Yeah, I guess."

"I admit, understand, that Mr. Weigh, if I know him, probably had something else in mind when he came in your place. Maybe he even stood out on the street and told himself that he was only going in to find out the answer to that one question, but when he got inside, other things got into his head. I know brother Weigh a helluva lot better than you do." Balzic paused. "By the way, *did* you see anybody coming past your place, say between eleven-thirty and twelve?"

"Aw, hell, man. I wasn't paying no nevermind. People come, they go. If they don't stop and get commercial in our place, we don't pay them no nevermind."

"Well, if you think of anybody, let me know, will you?" Balzic stood and put his coats back on. "If anybody asks you, I'm releasing you due to a lack of sufficient evidence to warrant arraignment. You want a ride uptown?"

"You letting us go, man?"

"Make sure you put that in the log, Joe," Balzic said. To the bearded ones he said, "Well, I sure as hell ain't letting you sleep here tonight. You go find your own place to sleep. You want a ride or not?"

"No, man. We'll use our feet," Charley said, leading the others out the door.

"So much for that," Balzic said.

"Weigh'll shit," Royer said.

"So? Let him. He makes my ass tired, busting those kids all the time. If he wants them locked up so much, he can just haul them down to the magistrate's himself. He makes half the bust and then expects us to do all the paperwork. I'm tired of that. Then he goes around making speeches to the P.T.A. and the ladies clubs talking about the drug problem right here in old River City. He got so many old ladies fired up now it wouldn't surprise me if they started marching down Main like those temperance biddies used to do. My mother used to tell me about them."

"Your mother told you?"

"Aw, go pound sand," Balzic said. "Anybody wants me, I'll be in Muscotti's. By the way, the coroner call yet?"

"Uh-uh. You want me to call if he does?"

"Nah. I'll hear what he has to say soon enough."

Balzic was finishing his second draught when Father Marrazo, wearing a sport shirt and tan raincoat, joined him in the back room. The poker game was down to four players and, as usual for this stage of the night, had turned moodily mechanical. Nobody invited the priest to play, even though earlier he had taken more than his share of their money.

"You get things calmed down out there?" Balzic said.

"As well as can be expected," Father Marrazo said. "Are you buying?"

"Sure."

They went out to the bar, and Balzic motioned to Vinnie the bartender, who was preoccupied with a crossword puzzle, to bring a round. "Put it on my tab," Balzic said.

"You going to pay that someday?" Vinnie said.

"It's not the end of the month."

Vinnie snorted. "The end of the month. The national debt you're running up." He brought the beers and stood there, grinning at Balzic.

"Put in a good word for me, Father."

"As soon as I see the police department's check for Catholic Charities, I'll be happy to."

"Don't hold your breath, Father," Vinnie said, taking a check out

24

of a cigar box from under the cash register and adding some figures to it.

"Behold the miracle of perseverance, Father," Balzic said, nodding toward Vinnie. "He flunked arithmetic eight years in a row in school, then he drops out, and now he's the richest bartender in the county."

"Quit it, willya," Vinnie said. "You make my chest hurt when you lie like that."

Vinnie went back to his crossword, and Father Marrazo and Balzic drank in silence.

"Anything new?" Father Marrazo said after a minute.

"Nothing much. Our esteemed D.A. made a bad bust and tried to get us to do the pencil work on it, and I sent the people home. He'll be three shades of purple tomorrow, but that's tomorrow."

"Did it have to do with John?"

"Only if you don't know the D.A."

"I don't understand, Mario."

"Well, he figured that whoever did it had to come down State Street, which might make sense if there was only one direction on a map or only one street in this town. The state boys found a broken Coke bottle with blood on it on the tracks under the bridge on State, so apparently Weigh figures whoever dropped it there had to keep on coming down the street. The only place that's open in that stretch at that time of night is the hippie joint—"

"The Community Store?"

"Yeah, so him and his two top honchos, Dillman and Sam Carraza, went booming in there, and before anybody made any sense, the kids were hollering and shoving, so Weigh busts them. Then he remembers his lockup is overcrowded, so he tries to dump them on me. To make the story short, Father, I wasn't in the mood to wake up a magistrate to file the information. I mean, it was his bust, he could take care of the whole thing or nothing.

"But what burns me is, Weigh's got his head full of drug propaganda, and he thinks those kids just naturally have to be pushing something. He's tried three times in the last month to bust

25

them, and he comes up zero every time, and tonight, instead of trying to find out something, he hauls them in. He doesn't even have sense enough to think that whoever did Andrasko in could've gone three other ways after he dropped the bottle off the bridge. Ah, what the hell. So how'd it go with the wife?"

"Needless to say, she's taking it very hard, and the children are upset because she is. I doubt that the truth of what's happened has sunk in as far as they're concerned. But I managed to arrange for the funeral. And that relieved her. Not much, but enough."

"What about the boy?"

"Tommy? He's a puzzle, as I told you out there. But I really know very little about him."

"All I know is he didn't even blink when I told him. I may as well've been telling him it was going to rain. All he wanted me to do was move my car so he could get his car in the garage. That's right before you showed, and I didn't get a chance to look how many keys he had with him."

"What's that have to do with it?"

"John had a key ring on him, but I didn't get a close look at it. Plus, he had the owner's card for the car the kid was driving and another one for a pickup. Then Frank Bennett—he's the station master—he tells me that John hated to drive and didn't really like cars. Told Frank he thought America was car-crazy or something like that. And the way the kid wheeled in there—well, he's like most kids with cars."

"Uh, Mario, correct me if I'm wrong, but I'm beginning to get the impression that you suspect him."

"At this point, Father, I suspect everybody, and if I didn't know you were down here earlier playing cards, I'd be asking you where you were around eleven-thirty, eleven-forty-five."

"Are you serious?" The priest laughed lamely.

"Of course." Balzic laughed and nudged the priest's elbow. "You got that dark complexion, that black hair, dark brown eyes—distinctly a Mediterranean type. Everybody knows wops are the only people who kill other people. What're you—kidding me?"

"For a moment—"

"Ah, come on, Father."

"But then you, uh, you really are serious about suspecting the boy?"

"Well, Father, it's like this. Contrary to what all the law-and-order nuts holler about, most people who kill other people know those other people. In fact, if you broke it down—and don't take my word for this. Write a letter to J. Edgar Hoover—he'll tell you. If you broke it down, you'd find most murders happen in the great red, white, and blue institution, the American home. Break it down even tighter, and most of them happen within twenty-five, thirty feet of the kitchen stove.

"Those ones that hit the front page, the Mansons, the Specks, the Whitmans, they're the exceptions. That's why they're front page. Hell, even the so-called gangland style—to use the newspaper language—even those happen with people who know one another. Not necessarily the guy who pulls the trigger. But the guy who paid the guy to pull the trigger, he knew the guy that got it, otherwise what the hell'd he have him killed for? He picked his name out of a phone book? No way. The guy did something to him, which means they had to be close enough at one time or another to be in a position for something to get done."

"You still haven't answered my question," Father Marrazo said. "You suspect the boy?"

"Well, naturally. But that's just my inclination. I don't suspect him at this point anymore than I suspect the wife. It's a general thing.

"Look," Balzic went on, "I've been a cop here for twenty-five, going on twenty-six years. Now this is here. Rocksburg. This isn't New York or Chicago or Philly. This isn't even Pittsburgh. But right here, in all those years, I only remember four murders where the victim had no connection with the murderer. And every one of them happened in a holdup. There was that old lady in the grocery—Mrs. Manfredi. All we know about that one is somebody heard a shot, we answered the call, and there it was. Cash drawer open, no prints, one twenty-two-caliber bullet. Never even arrested anybody for that one.

"Then there was the watchman out at the Sears warehouse about six years ago. Two thirty-eights in the chest. Whoever did it panicked and didn't even take anything. No arrest on that one either.

"Then about four years ago, there was the Southwest Commercial Bank. You remember that one."

"I do indeed. I gave the sacrament and heard the guard's confession."

"Okay, so there were two dead on that one. Case closed. Then two years ago this July, there was the payroll robbery over at the ready-mix plant. One clerk tries to be a hero, and there he goes. Three arrests on that one, no convictions."

"No arrests were ever made on those first two you mentioned?"

"Uh-uh. How? That's the point. If you don't have some way to connect the victim to the murderer, how you going to grab somebody who just walks in trying to score some money? There's only a couple of ways: either you have a witness or else you get a talker. In the first two we had neither. In the last one, we had six witnesses, but when we arrange the lineups, not one of them puts a solid make on any of the three guys we busted. What galls me about that is I know as sure as I'm standing here those three did it. But they knew we didn't have a make, so we couldn't break them, and I'm here to tell you, Father, I used everything I knew. The only thing I was able to do was get them out of town."

"How did you do that, I mean, if you couldn't prove anything—"

"I'll tell you how, Father. I told them one by one if I ever saw them again, I'd kill them and plant a gun on them."

"You actually told them that?"

"That's right, Father. So even if you and me both know me better than that, these guys must've thought I wasn't just making funny noises. They're not around, Father, that's all I know."

The priest shook his head and sat silently for a long moment, looking wide-eyed at his beer. Then he shook himself and said, "Uh, to get back to what I asked you—"

"Do I suspect the boy, right?"

"Yes."

"In a word, Father, naturally. The way he was driving, the time he came home, the way he reacted when I told him, plus when I was in

28

the kitchen getting a drink of water, I saw a couple cartons of Coke. None of those things by themselves mean all that much. I mean, hell, most kids are car nuts and drive too fast, and who doesn't drink Coke? But it was what he said about his own father that got me."

"His own father?"

"Yeah. I said something like, 'I hate to be the one to have to tell you, but your father's dead,' and he said, 'My father's been dead a long time, mister.' And then he said, 'He went away a long time ago.' Those were his exact words."

"Well, what do you infer from that?"

"I'm not sure. It's just funny, Father. People use all kinds of ways to say somebody's dead. You know that better than I do, but did you ever hear anybody say that somebody *went* away? Passed away, yeah. Passed on. Stuff like that, but 'went away'? I never heard it before, did you?"

"No, I can't recall hearing it put exactly that way, but maybe I have and never paid any attention to it. But I can't see what you're getting at."

"I don't know for sure. There's just something about saying somebody's dead in one breath and then saying that somebody went away in the next. That, plus where John was killed. I mean, a train station is a place where people are always going away. And I'll spare you the details, Father, but John wasn't just killed. Whoever did it literally beat his face to nothing. Like he was trying to wipe out his face."

"You mean so it could look like anybody."

"Yeah. Or coming at it from another direction, like it could look like somebody else." Balzic thought a moment. "It was like, uh, whoever was doing it to John maybe wasn't really doing it to John."

"Mario, you're the policeman, and I'm sure you know what you're talking about more than I do, but from what you've said so far, that is a very fragile connection you're making. I mean, just because the boy used that phrase—'went away'—and because the man was killed in a place where people are always going away, I think you said—that seems a really tenuous association. After all, people are not only always going away in train stations. They're also always coming back in them."

"Oh, that goes without saying. I know it's a delicate proposition. But you asked me, remember? You asked me if I suspected the boy, right?"

The priest nodded.

"Well, if I tell you I do, then I got to give you some reason. And that's what I just did, give you a reason. Hell, I might be ten miles wide. Who knows? It could be anybody for any reason. I'm just telling you that when somebody gets killed, I just naturally start thinking family, and until somebody comes up with something different, I'll keep on thinking family. Speaking of which, what all do you know about them, the whole family I mean?"

"Very little. Mrs. Andrasko and the younger children were very regular in church and confession and catechism and so on, but John was a Christmas-Easter Catholic. The boy, Tommy, came irregularly to mass and was the same about confession. And as I told you before, when he did come, he told me the most improbable lies, and, again as I said before, I had the feeling he did that purely to provoke me."

"Like what kind of lies?"

"You know I can't tell you that, Mario."

"Tell me that when you're wearing your collar, Father. Don't tell me that when you're wearing what you got on."

"Mario, I believe you're serious."

"Damn right I am."

"I'm sorry, Mario, but regardless of the clothes I'm wearing, I can't tell you what was said."

"I remember seeing a movie about that once. Montgomery Clift played the priest, and who the hell was it played the cop?"

"Karl Malden."

"Yeah, you got it. Tell me Father, did you believe Clift?"

"Yes. He was one of my favorite actors."

"Well, I thought Malden came on a little too strong. Course he was playing a Canadian cop. Maybe that's the way they are up there."

"Are they different here?"

"A cop's a cop, is that it, Father?"

"I tend to think so."

"An Irish priest is the same as an Italian priest then, right?"

30

Father Marrazo smiled, but said nothing.

"Okay, Father, have it your way. I can probably make a pretty good guess what the kid lied about anyway."

"You'll not get me that way, either."

"I'm not trying to, honest. But I'll just bet the kid came in and said he was making it with some older ladies in the parish."

Father Marrazo stared into his beer.

"You're a pretty good actor yourself, Father. I'll bet you been studying all the movies Clift was in."

"Never mind that. Where does this theory get you?"

"Same place I was before. It doesn't get me any place. Too much has to be checked out. There's the thing about the car keys, and somewhere there has to be some bloody clothes. The state boys might even come up with a palm print on the neck of that bottle, or they might come up with a witness who saw whoever it was coming or going. There are lots of possibilities, Father. Until somebody comes up with something solid, all I've got are theories."

"I meant to ask this before, Mario, but why aren't you out looking for these possibilities yourself?"

"The state boys are better at that stuff than I am, for one. They got more eyes, more ears, more legs, more equipment. Besides, my tail's dragging."

"Something tells me those aren't the reasons," Father Marrazo said quietly.

"Okay. So I lie," Balzic said. "The fact is when the state boys come in and the D.A.'s in, then I'm out. It's been that way as long as I can remember, and I don't see anything happening anywhere that's going to make it change."

"Bitterness corrodes the soul, Mario."

"You said that in church last Sunday."

"Well, it's still fresh in my mind, I suppose."

"If it's any consolation to you, Father, I was with you all the way in that homily of yours. I just sat back there shaking my head, thinking, yeah, brother Balzic, that's exactly what it does. It corrodes the soul."

"But you got nothing else from what I said?"

"The forgiveness you mean? Sure, I read you on that. I know

that's the way. But my guts don't know it, Father. Only my head."

"Mario, why don't you go home and get some rest?" Father Marrazo stood up as though to leave. "We'll talk about this some other time."

"Are you kidding, Father? I saw him tonight. You only had to deal with the widow, which wasn't any picnic, I know, but I saw him. I won't be able to sleep for two, three days."

The priest nodded. "Well then. How about another beer?"

"Now you're talking. Hey, Vinnie, once more here, and keep them coming."

"Sure, sure," Vinnie said. "And put them all on the national debt, too, I guess."

"How else you going to cheat me?"

"Oh, funny," Vinnie said. "Your friend here's a real funny man, you know that, Father? I'll bet you didn't know that."

"Vinnie, now that this has come up," Father Marrazo said, "I've been meaning to ask you when draughts went up to twenty-five cents."

"They didn't."

"Well, my friend, earlier tonight, I gave you a dollar for a draught and you brought me three quarters change."

"Oh, Father, now wait. I must've been thinking about something. I would never try to hustle you."

"Not so it was obvious," Balzic said, laughing.

"Tell you what, Vinnie. You send me a generous check for Catholic Charities, and I won't remember a thing."

Vinnie shook his head. "My old man told me. How many times he told me. He said you hustle a priest for a nickel, you're going to get hustled for a fin. Don't hustle priests, he said. Be smart. *Be* a priest, he said. *Then* you can hustle. . . ."

Balzic stayed with Father Marrazo until three-thirty and then drove to the station. Joe Royer was alone behind the counter, drinking soup from a vacuum bottle.

"Coffee's on, Mario, if you want some."

Balzic shook his head no. "Coroner call yet?"

"About five minutes ago. Nothing except what you probably know. Said he'd give us a typed report about ten or so today. Only thing he did say was whoever did it was either strong as hell or mad as hell."

"Why's that?"

"Said practically every bone in his face was broken. Must have been—"

"Never mind what it must've been," Balzic interrupted him. "You knew him, didn't you?"

"Andrasko? Yeah, slightly."

"Ever hear anything wrong about him?"

"I never heard anything about him," Royer said. "When I was on a beat, I used to see him hoofing it in. I'd say hello, he'd say hello, we'd both say something about the weather, and that was that."

"Nothing else?"

Royer shook his head and poured himself another cup of soup from his vacuum bottle. "Nothing. John Q. Citizen. Up and down."

"Ever hear about a guy named Parilla?"

"Which one? There's about three dozen."

"I don't know which one. All I know is Andrasko had a stepson named Tommy Parilla. He's about sixteen, seventeen."

"So?"

"So among other things, the kid was driving Andrasko's car tonight. He didn't come home until one-thirty or so, and when I told him about John, the kid didn't say a goddamn word. Just asked me to please move my car. Which reminds me. I got to call the state boys."

Balzic dialed the state police barracks and asked for Lieutenant Moyer.

"Yeah, Mario," Moyer said. "What did you come up with?"

"Not much. Listen, you got Andrasko's effects handy?"

"Right here. I've been sitting here looking at them. Not much to look at."

"Well, take a look at the key ring. How many car keys are there?"

"I count two ignition keys and one trunk key. All Fords. Why?"

33

"His stepson was driving his car tonight. Came home about one-thirty. I wanted to check out the key he was using, but I didn't get a chance."

"How'd the kid look?"

"Like his stepfather died every day of the week."

"Oh? No emotion at all?"

"None."

"How about the wife?"

"Hysterical. I called a priest to stay with her for a while. He said she was all right as soon as he made the funeral arrangements."

"But the kid was a stone?"

"All he said when I told him was his father was dead a long time. Then he said something struck me. He said something like, my father went away a long time ago."

"What do you figure from that?"

"I don't know for sure. Just didn't sound right somehow. But what did you come up with?"

"We verified the Coke bottle as the weapon. I sent most of it off to Harrisburg, but I gave one piece to the coroner and had him take it up to the hospital to check blood types. No question about it. But all we got by way of a quick check for prints was one lousy smudge on the neck of the bottle. I sent it off to Harrisburg purely for routine, because between you and me, I don't think they're going to find a thing."

"You didn't check the houses north on State Street?"

"We didn't, and we won't until after eight this morning. That's all I need to do, is start waking people up. You know what they'll remember—that we disturbed their sleep."

"You want me to spell your men down at the station? Starting with the daylight shift?"

"Not for today at least, Mario. We got a lot more looking to do down there as soon as we get some light. I left a man there tonight. It's roped off. Let's just wait for daylight, okay?"

"Whatever you say."

"Okay, Mario. See you in the morning."

"Right," Balzic said and hung up.

34

"Anything?" Royer asked.

"Nah. Just a confirmation on the weapon." Balzic started looking through drawers. "Where the hell's the cards?"

"By the switchboard. I was playing solitaire a little while ago. You want to play some gin?"

"Yeah. How much I owe you?"

"Four something."

"That much? Jeez, I better start paying attention."

"I got the slip right here in my wallet, if you don't believe me."

"Oh, I believe you, Joe. I believe you. I just don't believe I could've lost that many hands in a row. Not to you."

"Aw shut up and deal. I got to wash out my thermos."

"Shut up and deal. Listen to you. By six-thirty you'll be screaming to play double or nothing," Balzic said, shuffling the cards. "Why in hell don't you guys spring for a new deck once in a while? This deck's been here since time."

"We're waiting on you, Chief—Sir. Nobody around here remembers the last time you sprung."

"Oh, you'll be sorry for that, Sergeant, insinuating that I'm a little close. Are you ever going to be sorry for that."

They played until six-twenty.

"How do we stand now, Joseph, old buddy, old pal?" Balzic said with a broad smirk.

"I owe you two dollars and seven cents, that's how we stand."

"That's what I've always tried to tell you. Straight shooters always win. Well, I got to go. Nice playing against you, Joe."

"Wait a minute. Where the hell you got to go?"

"I got to go home and get cleaned up, for one thing. I been wearing these clothes since yesterday morning, and I'm starting to smell myself. If that's all right with you?" Balzic said, putting on his suit coat and raincoat and heading for the door. "Who's on the desk today?"

"Stramsky."

"Well, tell him what Weigh tried to pull last night, and tell him when Weigh calls to be polite. Polite but dumb. See you."

"You think Weigh'll call?"

"Oh, he'll call all right. You can give twenty to one on that," Balzic said and stepped outside just as the sun was breaking over the roof of the A&P. He stood on the steps for a moment, feeling the cool of the night being burned away, and when he got in his car he indulged himself in a wish to live in a place where every morning of the year he could count on the sun to burn off the night's damp chill.

When he got home, Balzic found his mother sitting at the kitchen table in her flannel gown sipping hot milk.

Balzic bent down and kissed her on the cheek. "S'matter, Ma, can't sleep?"

"Ah, no good last night. All night getting up for the bathroom. Six, seven times. Go back, snooze little bit, then up. Up, down, all night. Where you was last night? I no hear you come home, what's the matter?"

"Something happened, Ma. You make any coffee?"

"Not yet. I no have time." Mrs. Balzic started to laugh. "Hey, Mario, ain't that funny? I'm up half the night and don't think I got time for making coffee. Ah, I don't know, Mario. Every day more, more get tired. Pretty soon die, I think."

"Quit talking like that, will you. You ain't going to die."

"Mario, don't be stupid. I don't raise you up be stupid. Everybody going to die. Soon, late—what the heck you think? I going live forever?"

"I know all that, Ma, but I don't like to hear you talk about it, that's all. Where's the instant?"

"Same place always, Mario. How long you live here?" Mrs. Balzic stirred her milk and watched her son moving around the room, filling a small enamel pan with water, setting out a cup, and putting a spoonful of instant in it, stripping off his tie as he turned up the gas.

"Somebody killed last night, Mario?"

"No, Ma."

"Mario, you my bones and blood and your father's, too, and you can't lie no good ever since you was little boy. Who killed?"

"John Andrasko, Ma," Balzic said, hoping she'd drop it.

"Accident?"

"No, Ma."

"How? Murder? Mario, no. Murder? Say no."

"Yeah, Ma. And now if you don't mind, I don't want to talk about it, okay?"

"Oh, yoy-yoy, that no good, Mario. Who want kill John? My God, I know since little boy. Since born. I know mother, father, grandmother, grandfather, both sides. My God, Mario, you was grew up together, no?"

"Yeah. That's right. I knew him most of my life, I guess. But not too well, Ma. We weren't close. I just knew him."

"That's why don't sleep."

"There was a lot of work to do, Ma. You can't just quit when something like this happens, you ought to know that by now."

"Don't be mad for me, Mario. My ankles hurt too hard already. I'm just old lady talking too much, okay?"

"I'm not mad, Ma. I just don't want to talk about it, all right?"

"Okay, Mario. Hey, kiddo, water's boil."

"I hear it, Ma. I hear it."

Balzic poured the water into the cup, stirred it for a moment, then sipped it standing by the sink, screwing up his face from the heat.

"Wait, Mario. It's too hot."

"I don't have time. I want to get cleaned up before the girls get up. Else I'll never get into the bathroom. Hey, I hear you did okay at the bingo."

"Ah, some towels. Two times I need one more corn for ten dollars once and next time for fifty dollars. But I see lots people. Even friends. Not too much time left for see friends."

"Will you quit talking like that? I can't stand it—never mind. I'm going to the bathroom. If anybody calls, tell them I'll call back. Okay?"

"All right, Mario. All right. No more, okay?"

Balzic gulped down some more coffee, kissed his mother again, and then showered, shaved, and changed clothes just in time. The girls were up and prowling, morning surly, alternately grimacing and giggling in their adolescent conspiracy against the world.

37

Balzic kissed both on the cheek as he passed them in the kitchen. "Why don't you two do something about night football games?" he said to them in passing.

"What's for breakfast?" Emily said.

"Mother wants to talk to you, Daddy," Marie said.

"What's wrong with night football games?" Emily asked.

"Mornings is what's wrong with them," Balzic said. "Isn't your mother up yet?"

"She's awake, but she's still in bed."

"She sick?"

"Uh-uh. Just sleepy."

"I probably won't be around much today," Balzic said, "so have a good day."

"You too, Daddy," Emily said.

"Ditto," Marie said.

"Ditto," Balzic mimicked her, hurrying into the bedroom.

"Come on, sleepy, time to get up. You can't lounge around all day."

"Oh, Mario, I'd like to sleep and sleep," Ruth said. "The girls up?"

"Yeah. Ma's up, too. Said she was up half the night. She okay at the bingo last night?"

"She seemed like she had a pretty good time to me. But I know she had a rough night. That's what I wanted to ask you. Maybe I ought to take her to Dr. Wilson's this afternoon."

"She won't want to go. What do you think?"

"Oh, yes she will. Just let me talk to her a while," Ruth said, pulling the pillow under her chin and turning on her side. "And where were you last night?"

"Ask Ma. I told her already, and I don't feel like talking about it. I'm going to be talking about it all day every place else. I'd like to be able to give it a rest here."

"It wasn't an accident, was it?"

"No. Listen, babe, I got to get moving. I'll call you around noon, let you know about supper, okay?"

"Okay, Mario. If I ever get awake."

Balzic leaned down and tried to kiss Ruth on the mouth, but she turned her head and buried her face in the pillow. "God, Mario, my mouth tastes like yuk. It must smell worse."

"So? What's a little smelly kiss between friends?"

Ruth pushed her face deeper into the pillow, and Balzic kissed her on the neck. "Have it your way, garbage mouth," he said, and squeezed her ear. "See you, hon."

"Bye," Ruth said dreamily.

It was eight-fifteen when Balzic pulled into the train station parking lot on the lower side near the freight office. There were only four other cars in the lot, and one of them Balzic recognized as an unmarked state police cruiser. A man and woman were arguing with the man in the freight office about something; except for them, no one else was around.

Balzic headed into the tunnel and up the steps to the platform where a raw-eyed, yawning state patrolman was rocking on his heels. The patrolman was new to Balzic. He went over and flashed his ID.

"Lieutenant Moyer been around yet?"

"He should've been here. I was supposed to be relieved ten, fifteen minutes ago," the patrolman said. "Damn," he added, "if this isn't the dreariest place at night I've ever seen. You look at this place for a night and you start believing the railroads are in trouble."

"Yeah," Balzic said. "Even when nothing happens it's ugly enough to make you think something's going to."

"There's the lieutenant now," the patrolman said, nodding toward the opposite side of the tracks.

Lieutenant Moyer got out of an unmarked car as three marked cars of the Pennsylvania State Police pulled in behind him on State Street Extension. Moyer waited by his car until eight troopers from the other cars gathered around him. He talked to them briefly, gesturing and pointing. All but two of the troopers set off in different directions, and those two followed Moyer across the tracks toward the platform.

"Morning, Mario. Dunn. See anybody last night?"

"No sir," Patrolman Dunn said. "Only the station master."

"Figures," Moyer said. "You can go."

"Yessir," Dunn said and left, trying vainly to stifle a yawn.

"Mario, something tells me this one is going to be a real corn bender."

"I'm inclined to agree with you. We'll know after your boys talk to the people."

"Yessir, I just got a feeling about this one. We're going to walk and talk and walk some more, and we're still not going to know anything." Moyer walked around the bench where John Andrasko's body had been found. Moyer looked down at the chalked outline and the patch of dried blood that was longer and wider than the chalked outline. "Ever notice, Mario," he said, "how fast the chalk washes away and how long it takes for the blood to wash away?"

"I try not to think about it."

"First rain, this chalk'll be gone. Come back three months from now, you'll still be able to see this blood." Moyer stepped around the blood and came near Balzic. "Any more thoughts about the kid?"

"No. Nothing worth talking about."

"Don't kid me. I can see it in your eyes."

"Well, it's just a feeling. But I still want to run down some papers."

"Mario, I think you're going to wind up chasing your tail about the kid. I can't stop you from thinking, but—well, I can see from the way you're not listening to me that I'm really getting through. Go on and run down your papers. I'm not going to do anything here but get a blister on my brain until my boys get through. Go over the platform again and up and down the tracks, but I don't think we're going to find a damn thing. Why the hell am I getting these blanks about this thing? Can you tell me that?"

"Can't tell you why you are, but if it's any consolation, I feel pretty blank myself."

"No consolation. One pessimist on a job is enough."

"I'll give you a call around noon. Sooner, if I learn anything." Balzic started off the platform with a wave but turned back. "Guess

40

I ought to tell you that Weigh and his horses busted five people over this thing last night, and I turned them loose, so don't be surprised if he comes up and throws a hook in your ear about my incompetence."

"Who had reasons?"

"We both did. He probably thinks he had the best damn reason in the world for busting them, but then he didn't want to do the rest of the work, so I said the hell with him and let them go. I'll settle it with him soon enough, but I thought I ought to warn you." Balzic turned and left without waiting for another question.

He drove through the alleys to the rear of the courthouse, parked in the back lot, and, once inside, tried unsuccessfully to duck the courthouse reporter for *The Rocksburg Gazette*.

"Morning, Chief," Dick Dietz said. "Little early for you, isn't it? I mean especially today."

"What's so special about today, Dietz?"

"Nothing's today. That's just it. It's Saturday. Criminal court session ended yesterday. Civil session starts Monday. You aren't by any chance involved in a civil proceeding?"

"Not likely," Balzic said, looking at his watch.

"Then could it be you're here to find out something that has to do with what happened last night?"

Balzic edged closer to Dietz and lowered his voice, even though no one was close enough to hear what he might have said in a normal tone. "You know something, Dietz? You make my ass tired, and you know why you make my ass tired? Cause you're always trying to chisel information instead of just coming out and asking for it. And as far as last night goes, you got all the information you're going to get when your people made the phone calls they make every night."

"Aw, come on, Chief. There's no need to get touchy now. Not at your age. Besides, I've already got the best news of the day from the district attorney. I just thought you might perhaps be down here to, let's say, reconcile your differences with him. Any possibility of that?"

41

Balzic backed away and headed for the drinking fountain beside the door to the office of the clerk of courts. When he finished getting a drink, he looked up and saw Dietz standing beside him. "Get lost, Dietz," he said, "before I forget what I get paid for doing."

"Wouldn't you like to know what Weigh had to say about last night?" Dietz said, smiling.

"Not particularly."

"Well, among other things, Weigh said that he was upset over the manner in which the investigation was being conducted. He said, in effect, that anyone could see that the murder was the work of either a lunatic or a drug addict."

"Naturally, he told you that in strictest confidence."

"Well, of course, he wouldn't want me to use those words for the record, which is understandable considering his position. He will have to prosecute, and he wouldn't want an adverse-publicity charge to be thrown against him during the trial."

"Naturally," Balzic said, looking again at his watch.

"Do you have any comment about what the district attorney said?"

"Yes. But strictly off the record. You make my ass tired."

"Careful, Chief. This is my beat too, remember."

"Why don't you quote me the Bill of Rights, freedom of the press and all that horseshit."

"If I thought it would do any good, I would."

Balzic looked again at his watch. It was eight-fifty. He left Dietz standing by the water fountain and walked into the lobby of the courthouse. He stepped into one of the bank of phone booths and dialed *The Rocksburg Gazette.*

"I want to talk to the managing editor," he said to the operator.

"Thank you." There was a click, a pause, and then an abrupt voice saying, "Murray speaking."

"Mr. Murray," Balzic said, "you don't know me, and I'm not about to give my name, but I got some information about the parking authority I think your paper might be interested in. Only thing is, I don't want to be seen near your paper. So I'll tell you what. I know your reporter Dietz on sight, so if you want to know what I know, you tell him to meet me at nine-thirty sharp in the Nixon Grille. I won't talk to anybody else, got it?"

"Yes, I've got it."

"Nine-thirty sharp. I'm not going to wait even two minutes."

"What's this all about?"

"I'll tell him. All I'm going to tell you is it's about a conflict of interest in the placement of parking authority funds in a certain bank." Balzic hung up and walked back to the hall outside the office of the clerk of courts. Dietz had moved back across the hall from the fountain.

"A late development, Chief?" Dietz said.

"You might say that."

Just as Mrs. Florence Wilmoth, the clerk of courts, came through the lobby, the phone on the information desk in the lobby rang. The courthouse guard who picked it up nodded a couple of times, and then called out to Dietz. "It's your boss, Dick."

"Probably some late development," Balzic said as Dietz hurried past him to the phone.

"Well, Mario," Mrs. Wilmoth said, "you look cheerful this morning." She unlocked her office door and flipped on the overhead lights.

"Just got rid of an itch." Balzic said, following her inside.

"An itch, did you say?"

"Something like that," Balzic said. "Florence, I don't have much time, and unless you've moved things, I know where everything is I want to see, so—"

"Say no more. Help yourself."

Balzic thanked her and went to the file of death certificates. He began with Parilla and went on through Perilla. He found nothing on any male Parilla or Perilla in the age range he presumed would be the age of Mrs. Andrasko's first husband. When he'd gone through all the possible spellings of the name, he stopped, with his chin resting on his fist on top of the cabinets. He closed the drawers of the death certificates and went to the birth certificates. Among the Parillas, he found: "Thomas John Parilla, male, Caucasian, born 20 September 1953 to Tami Antonio Parilla and Mary Frances Spano Parilla." He ignored the other information and closed the drawer and went back to the death certificates. He could find no record of the death of any Tami Antonio Parilla. That left him with only one other thing to check, but in the file holding marriage licenses he found that none had been made out to John Andrasko and Mary Frances Spano Parilla.

He waved goodbye to Mrs. Wilmoth and went out to the lobby and dialed St. Malachy's rectory.

When Father Marrazo answered, Balzic said: "Listen, Father, I just came out of the clerk of courts' office, and I can't find any record of the death of Tommy Parilla's father, and not only that, I can't find any marriage license for John Andrasko. If you know anything, you can put my mind at rest about these things, 'cause already I'm starting to get a little nervous."

"That's strange, Mario, but I'm sure there's an explanation. Let me think a minute." There was a long pause and then: "Listen, Mario, let me check my records here, and I'll call you back. How's that?"

"Better for me to call you. I don't know where I'm going to be."

"All right. But give me an hour or so. I have some young people coming here in a few minutes, and I'll be with them for half an hour at least, maybe longer."

"Good enough, Father," Balzic said, hanging up.

He rooted through his pockets for another dime and called his home. Ruth answered.

"Hey, baby, is Ma close by?"

"Sure. She's right here. I just made an appointment for her at Dr. Wilson's. He wasn't too happy about her coming in on a Saturday, but—what's the matter?"

"Put Ma on, will you. I need that computer she got in her head for family connections."

A pause. "Mario? What's matter, kiddo?"

"Ma, what do you remember about Tami Parilla?"

"Tami or Tommy?"

"Tami."

"I don't know. Oh, wait. Sure. He's marry to Mary Spano. Then he die."

"You sure?"

"No. Wait. That was Tony."

"Try to get it straight, Ma. This Tami's middle name was Antonio."

"Yeah, sure. But his brother was name Anthony. He's one die. Tami, him, I don't know what happen with. But I know was marry Mary Spano. They have one kid—Tommy."

"You got it. You're sure it was his brother that died?"

"I'm sure. Anthony. Kill in Korea. Tami I don't know what happen for him."

"You know his wife was married to John Andrasko?"

"Yeah, sure, I know. Oh my God, Mario. I forget John," Mrs. Balzic said. "Oh, I feel so bad about that."

"Yeah. I know. But right now I just want you to be sure about them."

"Only thing I sure is they get marry not here. Virginia, Maryland, some place like that."

"You sure?"

"Mario, what's matter—I go round asking people for to see marriage license? How I know they get marry there? That what people say, that's all I tell you."

"Okay, Ma, that's good enough. Hey, how you feeling?"

"Okay, not so okay. Lousy, not so lousy. I go to Dr. Wilson with Ruth today. She make me go. What the heck he's do—give me more pills? I get up and go bathroom all night now. Them pills he give me last time, yoy, God, I can't stop go to bathroom. Who knows?"

"Well, just do what he says, okay?"

"Oh you, Mario, you like all crazy people sometime, think doctors fix them up. Sometimes no can fix, Mario, when the heck you learn? Not everything can fix."

"Okay, Ma, okay. Just do what he says. Promise."

"Okay, okay. I promise. I promise to go all time in bathroom, that's all I promise. Not do in bed."

45

"You're going to be okay, Ma. Don't worry."

"Who's worry? You and Ruth worry. I no worry. I just old."

"Okay, Ma, I have to go now. I'll see you this afternoon maybe." Balzic hung up and stood in the booth fretting. "Goddammit," he whispered, "don't let nothing happen to her."

Balzic drove to the train station, and when he got up to the platform, he found Lieutenant Moyer looking morose and talking glumly with six of his men. Balzic waited until Moyer dismissed them and then followed Moyer to his car.

"Mario," Moyer said, "I hope to hell you came up with more than we did."

"You get shut out?"

"All around. Nobody heard anything. Nobody saw anything. Nobody knows anything. For practical purposes, nobody else was awake or even alive when it happened. I can't figure it. How'd you do?"

"I'm not sure yet. I tried to run down the family, and all I've got so far are loose ends. For one thing, there's the kid."

"What about him?"

"All I found was his birth certificate. Couldn't find anything about his father, and I couldn't find a marriage license for his mother and Andrasko. My mother tells me they were married out of state. Maryland or Virginia. She couldn't remember what happened to the boy's father. I've got a priest checking his records, but something tells me he's going to come up short, too."

"So what do you figure?"

"I'll tell you what I figure, but you're not going to want to hear it."

"Give it a shot."

"What is this place—a train station, right?" Balzic said hesitantly.

"Go ahead. I'm listening," Moyer said.

"So why'd you start to smile, the first thing I say?"

"Well, Jesus Christ, Mario, I mean, we are standing right here."

"Okay, okay. My point is, people are always going away—"

46

"They're also always coming back."

"I told you you weren't going to want to hear it."

"No, no. Go ahead. Give me the rest."

"You saw Andrasko's face last night. Blotted out, right?"

"Yeah. Go on."

"So it could look like anybody or nobody."

"Okay."

"Well, nobody knows what happened to the kid's father, and the fact that he still has his father's name means Andrasko never adopted him."

"So?"

"Well, put it together."

"Mario, put what together?"

"Don't you see any connections? The blotted-out face, the place, the father that ain't around, the stepfather that didn't adopt the kid?"

"Oh, Mario, what the fuck have you been reading lately?"

"Come on, Phil. You ask me what I think, and then you start to jack me off."

"I'm not jacking anybody off. But tell me this: if you're so sure of what you're saying, how come you're not out talking to the missus right now? I mean, let's go. Let's go sit her down and have a talk with her."

"Nothing doing. I mean, I can't stop you from going, but I'm not going."

"And just why not—you're so full of these connections."

"The funeral. I don't get in the middle of any family's funeral. That's enough for anybody to handle. Let us start stomping around asking questions, and it gets shitty, that's all."

"Mario, I've known you for a long time," Moyer said, "and I've always respected your judgment, but sometimes, I swear to Christ, I can't understand the way you operate. You get me thinking about the kid now, and you know whoever did it had to get blood all over his sleeve at least, but you act like you don't even want to go out this guy's farm and look around."

"I don't. But I'll tell you why. Say we get a warrant and we go out

47

there. Hell, man, Andrasko's got about forty acres out there, and from what I hear, he had most of it under cultivation. We could look on that place for a month, and we'd still miss something. And suppose I'm right. Suppose the kid did it. Who's to say he got rid of the clothes out there? There are a helluva lot of roads around here and helluva lot of water—just where the hell are we supposed to start?"

"One thing's sure, Mario. No matter where he got rid of them—if it was the kid, mind you, *if*—he had to go back to that house again for the simple reason that when you saw him coming back he was clean, right?"

"Right."

"So at least we can ask her about his travels last night."

"Well, that takes us right into the middle of the funeral again." Balzic shook his head. "You know, I don't even know for sure if she knows John was murdered. I can't remember whether I told her, and I don't know if the priest did either."

Moyer shook his head and started to laugh. "Mario, you're some cop."

"Ah, it was tough enough just telling her. Christ, she started crying as soon as I said it was John. Who the hell can give details at a time like that?"

"So you didn't tell her?"

"No," Balzic said, looking at the houses on State Street. "I guess I didn't."

"Oh, brother. Well. Just what do you intend to do the rest of the day, I mean, since you don't want to pursue the investigation?" Moyer asked with a slightly mocking grin.

"Fridays I usually go out and shoot, and yesterday I missed. I thought after I checked back with the priest I'd go out to the club range."

"You're full of surprises. All these years I've known you, I never believed you carried a weapon."

"I don't. Not a handgun anyway. If it was up to me, no beat officer would."

"You kidding me or what?"

"No I'm not kidding. Cops kill too many people, if you ask me. Look what happened in Pittsburgh the other day. Two beat officers are checking out a burglary. One goes in the front of a warehouse and the other goes in the back. The burglar comes out a side door, and the officer that went in the front chases him down an alley and starts shooting. He misses the burglar, but he hits a guy painting his porch about three blocks away. That guy's going to be in a wheelchair the rest of his life. Meantime they still haven't caught the burglar, and from where I stand that's bullshit."

"Those things happen, Mario."

"That's just my point. If beat officers don't carry sidearms, they wouldn't happen."

"Then what are we supposed to do when the punks don't give up their guns? Talk them out of it, I guess."

"Hell, man, that's what we've got radios for and tactical squads. You know as well as I do that handguns aren't worth a damn beyond ten, fifteen yards anyway. Good God, I shudder every time I think of some of the men on my force walking around with those thirty-eights. Hell, some of them can't put five shots out of six on a three-foot-high silhouette target at fifteen yards. And that's when they're standing still and all they're shooting at is paper.

"Jesus," Balzic went on, "Weigh's got some people who can't even hit that damn target two shots out of five with those little snub-nose jobs they're so goddamn proud of. You know the worst nightmare I have is the one where my wife and mother and my daughters are walking out of a supermarket and some guy's just held up the place, and he runs out into the parking lot and Weigh's boys just happen to be there with those short-barrelled thirty-eights. Good God, I see people scattered all over the parking lot—ah, what's the use."

"Well, tell me, Mario, just what do you tell your men?"

"About what—about a guy with a gun?"

"Yes."

"I tell them to call me, and I tell them the first officer that returns fire before I get there is suspended without pay indefinitely."

"You're shittin' me."

"What's so hard to believe? You know, I've been chief for eleven

49

years, going on twelve, and nobody in this town has ever been shot by any of my men? Not one, and I'm prouder of that than of anything. The first month I was chief was the closest I ever came. The thing was, the clown who started shooting hadn't fired his weapon in so long he had two misfires out of the first three times he pulled the trigger. Now, at least, my men have got to fire their weapons twice a week, and I've got a man who hand-loads all their ammunition. But it still gives me the creeps thinking of some of the men I've got."

"That sounds like you're contradicting yourself, Mario. First, you say you have them under orders not to shoot, and then, you say you make them shoot twice a week."

"There's no contradiction. I just want to make them aware of that goddamn thing they're carrying around on their hip. I mean if they're going to carry it, they ought to at least find out what the hell it is. But one of these days I'm going to take them away from them. Nobody thinks twice about sending out a meter maid without a gun or a school crossing guard—why the hell do guys doing practically the same job—giving tickets or directing traffic—why the hell does everybody think they need a gun?"

"Not the same thing, Mario."

"The hell it's not. You're just brainwashed, that's all. You just can't picture a man cop without a gun, but you see meter maids without them, and you don't even think about it."

"Okay, so I'm brainwashed. And just what do you shoot?"

"Meet me out the range about two, and I'll show you."

"I'll just do that. Want to make a little bet?"

"Better wait until you get there, Lieutenant, before you go putting up any money. See you later."

Moyer pulled away, and Balzic went to his car and drove to the rectory of St. Malachy's. He found Father Marrazo in the foyer saying goodby to a young couple with marriage in their eyes.

"Mario, I have to apologize. I've been so wrapped up talking with those kids that I haven't had a chance to do what you asked. But come into my office and I'll get on with it."

The priest led Balzic into his small, square office in the rear of the rectory. Father Marrazo pushed some chairs around and directed Balzic to an overstuffed chair covered in cracking black leather.

"Some wine, Mario?"

"No thanks, Father," Balzic said, sitting down and lighting a cigarette.

"Mario, if you don't, then I won't have the excuse," Father Marrazo said, winking broadly. "Besides, it's really exceptional wine. Mr. Ferrara makes it."

"Well, if it's his, Father, then I better have some. I wouldn't want him to hear that I'd turned it down."

"You know him?" Father Marrazo said, pouring the wine, a very clear, light red wine, into two jelly glasses. "It's not Bardolino, you understand, but it is a very good Ferrara."

Balzic took the glass offered him and held it up to the light.

"Sure, I know him. Fact is, I think we're related some way. I been drinking his wine since I was a kid. Fact, one summer when I was about ten or eleven, he paid me two cents for every good bottle I brought him with a screw cap on. I used to go scrounging through garbage cans every morning, and then he paid me another penny for each bottle to wash it and get the labels off. That was a pretty good summer."

"That must have been a lot of money in those days."

"It was. That was thirty-four, thirty-five. On a good day I used to make sixty, seventy cents." Balzic took a sip and rolled it around his mouth and then swallowed it. "Tell you one thing, Father. Mr. Ferrara hasn't lost his touch."

"Agreed. You know, he brings me two bottles every Sunday night. You don't know how many times I've wanted to say to him, 'Mr. Ferrara, what makes you think I drink only two bottles of wine a week?' For a while, I tried to save him three or four other bottles, empties, to give him to take along with his own empties, but that didn't work."

"Didn't you ever ask him about it?"

"No. I couldn't bring myself to ask. Anyway, I got a very clear impression that he didn't approve because he thought I wasn't very subtle or because he thought a priest shouldn't drink more than two bottles a week. So, I went back to giving him only the bottles he'd brought the week before. He seems content now." Father Marrazo lifted his glass. "Salud," he said and drank.

"Salud," Balzic said and drank also.

"So, now to business," Father Marrazo said, carrying his glass over to a row of wooden file cabinets. He set the glass on top and started going through cards and folders. After five minutes he said: "So far, Mario, my friend, all I can find are baptismal and confirmation records for the children. That is, baptismal records for Tommy Parilla and William and Norma Andrasko and confirmation records for Tommy and Norma. There is no record of either of the marriages." He closed the drawers, picked up his glass, and sat on the front of his desk. "Now what will you do?"

"Don't you have any funeral record for Tommy's father?"

Father Marrazo shook his head.

Balzic scratched his chin. "Damn, I forgot to check for a divorce record," he said. "But something tells me I'm not going to find one. What I can't figure is what happened to the kid's father. Not even my mother knows what happened to him."

"Why is that so important to you, Mario? I don't understand."

"Father, I'll tell you straight. I don't know why it is, but it is. The way this thing is going, we're coming up zero every place we look. In other words, as far as a court is concerned, all we've got is a corpse and a weapon. We got no motive, no witnesses, no nothing."

"And you still think because of the way the boy reacted when you told him and what he said—"

"Don't forget the way it was done, Father. We talked about that. Fact, you're the one put me on the idea about the face being wiped out to make it look like nobody or like somebody else."

"If I follow you, Mario, what you're thinking is the boy—if he did it—did it out of some unconscious compulsion."

"Something like that, Father. I mean, my first thought was that it might've been the result of an argument over the kid taking the car, and for all I know that might still be the reason. But again, this is all based on a guess that it was the boy. I mean, we haven't even talked to Mrs. Andrasko yet about where the kid was when it was happening. She might put it all straight about him in two minutes. By the way, Father, did you tell her how it happened?"

"No. I assumed you had."

"Oh, Christ—excuse me, Father."

The priest waved his hand. "Mario, I regard that as a prayer. Not a curse."

"That means she got it from the paper."

"You didn't tell her, Mario?"

"I didn't get a chance. I just started talking, and she took it from there. Then the two younger kids showed up, and what the hell was I supposed to say—ah, Father, sometimes I think I'm the worst guy in the world for this job."

"Mario, have some more wine."

Balzic shook his head.

"Go on. Here, give me your glass."

"I don't want to get a buzz on, Father."

"Nor do I want you to. But there are times, Mario, when Christ offers practical solace for our weaknesses. After all, it was He who turned water into wine. He knew that water may quench our thirst, but wine, Mario—wine helps quench the thirst of our soul." The priest held out the bottle. "Give me your glass."

Balzic held it out, and Father Marrazo filled it. "Drink, Mario. You need it. At times like this, there are no other solutions for our deficiencies."

"You're a damn good talker, Father."

"Not me, Mario. Not me." Father Marrazo made a silent laugh and then grew pensive. "We each made a mistake. Yours was in an omission, and mine was in a presumption. The other, Mrs. Andrasko, now suffers for our blunders. What solace have we left for our blunders but the blood of Christ, eh? Drink up. The newspaper, that epistle of gloom, corrects our mistakes, and where does that leave us. . . ."

"I don't know about you, Father. It just leaves me feeling stupid."

"You're not alone, Mario. I feel stupid ten times a day and twice that on Sundays. Thus . . ." Father Marrazo's voice faded, and he lifted his glass and nodded to it. "Well, what will you do now?"

"Same thing I been doing, Father. Keep checking records to find out if anybody knows what happened to Tami Parilla. Because the way things are going so far, I'm getting closer to the idea that he didn't die. Which reminds me—may I use your phone?"

"Of course."

Balzic put his glass on the priest's desk and dialed the station.

"Rocksburg Police. Sergeant Stramsky speaking."

"Vic? Balzic. Got a pencil?"

"Right here. Go."

"Call the state houses in Maryland and Virginia and see if John Andrasko and Mary Frances Spano or Mary Frances Spano Parilla got married there. Should have been, oh, eight, nine years ago."

"That it?"

"Yeah. Any calls for me?"

"No calls, but your neighborhood district attorney was here about fifteen minutes ago, and was he steaming."

"What did you tell him?"

"What could I tell him? I didn't know anything."

"Good. Let the bastard burn awhile. It'll do him good."

"Where you going to be in case anybody wants to know?"

"Right now I'm in St. Malachy's rectory. In about five minutes I'll be talking to Bill Joyce in the F.B.I. office. After that, I'll call you. Anything else?"

"Not much. Some fenders got bent on Maple, and a missus, lemme see, a Mrs. Scarafolo wants us to do something about some kids cutting through her yard."

"Is that the Mrs. Scarafolo on South Eustice?" Balzic said.

"Yeah."

"Is Ippolitto around?"

"Just walked in."

"Well tell him to go down there and listen to her and see if she needs groceries."

"Oh, it's that Mrs. Scarafolo."

"Now you got her. If that's it, I'll check later." Balzic hung up, shaking his head. "Wish that's all I had to think about."

"Mario," Father Marrazo said, "I couldn't help overhearing. This Mrs. Scarafolo, does she belong to my parish?"

"You'd know that better than I would, Father. She lives in the 600 block of South Eustice. I'll tell you something, though. If you're thinking of doing something for her, don't do it yourself. That woman does not like priests."

"Is it a nuisance to you?"

"No, so far it hasn't been. The thing is, up until a couple of years ago she took care of herself pretty good, but then she broke her hip. So what she does is she calls us and makes a complaint, usually about the kids running through her yard, and then when the officer gets there, she sits him down and gives him some wine and maybe a little pasta, and then she asks him if he's going past Brunetti's Market. She's pushing ninety and got about two hundred years' worth of pride, and she thinks she's foxing us. She only does it once a month, when her Social Security comes. I don't mind it, understand, but there may come a time when I can't let a man and a cruiser go."

"What does she have against priests?"

Balzic shrugged. "Father, when somebody pushing ninety tells me she don't like something, I don't ask questions. Don't you have a committee to work on things like this?"

"Yes, we do. What disturbs me is that if she is in my parish she hasn't been receiving the sacraments."

"Well, that's your department, Father. But if you go down there and get your ears fried, don't say I didn't tell you."

"Oh, there's no problem to that, Mario. I just put on a sport shirt and my raincoat and pose as a detective."

"Let's have another glass of the Ferrara, Father, and then I got to go."

"What shall we drink to?"

"I don't know. How about your career as an actor?"

"Wonderful. To all my frustrations. Salud."

"Salud . . ."

After leaving the priest, Balzic drove to the rear parking lot of the courthouse. He hustled up the back stairs to the regional office of the F.B.I.

A receptionist told him to go right in to the office of the agent in charge, William Joyce.

"Mario," Joyce said, coming around his desk to shake hands. "Where the hell have you been?"

"Oh, around. How about you?"

"Same old things. I hear you've got something."

"I got something all right."

"I also hear you're going no place fast."

"'Fraid so."

"What do you need?"

"I'd like you to run down a couple of names. Here, let me write them down." Balzic wrote the names on Joyce's desk calendar.

"You looking for anything special, Mario?"

"Put it this way. I'm just looking right now. For anything anybody has."

"This Andrasko—wasn't he the victim?"

"Yeah, but I'm looking for anything. Credit records, life insurance, service records. I knew him since I was a kid, but I really didn't know him, if you take my meaning."

"Okay. What about the other one?"

"He's the puzzle. Andrasko was married to a woman who was married to this Parilla, and they had a kid. The kid still goes by his father's name, so apparently Andrasko didn't adopt him, and from what I gathered when I told the kid about John, the kid couldn't have cared less. But nobody seems to know anything about what happened to this Parilla, not even my mother. Ordinarily, I'd put her head up against F.B.I. files anytime."

"You want me to see if anyone put a chaser on him through Missing Persons, too?"

"If you would. You'll get a quicker answer from them than I would. I'll be obliged, Bill."

"No trouble, Mario. Just give me a couple of hours, that's all."

"Good enough. I've got somebody checking marriage bureaus in Maryland and Virginia about Andrasko's marriage. But you'll really help a helluva lot."

"Why are you checking the marriage bureaus?"

"I can't say, really. I just have the feeling that old John never

56

married that woman. Don't ask me why, and don't ask me what difference it's going to make, but I'd like to know about it if it's true."

"All right, Mario. I'll see what I can do."

"Thanks. Say, why don't you and Marge stop up the house some night? Play a little penny ante, drink some beer, and tell each other a lot of lies about the time we captured the James boys."

"Last time I did that it cost me three dollars and fourteen cents."

"It went for a good cause. I had a helluva steak from that money," Balzic said soberly. "I can still taste it. Haven't had one that good since."

"Go to hell," Joyce said.

"Okay, Bill. Take care, and give my best to Marge."

Joyce waved, and Balzic stepped into the corridor and went down the back stairs and out to the parking lot. He got in his car, sat for a moment, and then went back into the courthouse.

He hurried to the office of the clerk of courts. Mrs. Wilmoth looked up from her conversation with a lawyer for whom she was going over some files and nodded approval to Balzic after he mouthed the words that he wanted to check something. He went back to the indexes listing divorces filed and divorces granted and checked the Spano-Parilla marriage both ways. He found what he already suspected: if Mary Frances Spano and Tami Antonio Parilla were divorced, they hadn't gone through the proceedings in this country. "That's that," he said to himself and closed the drawers, waving to Mrs. Wilmoth as he left.

He was almost to the rear exit when someone touched his arm.

"That was pretty cute," Dick Dietz said. "I never gave you that much credit, Chief."

Balzic glared at Dietz for a moment, then let his face go soft. "Not that I give a good goddamn, Dietz, but just what am I supposed to be getting credit for?"

"Oh, you know what I'm talking about."

"Dietz," Balzic said, blowing out a sigh, "why the hell is it that every conversation with you turns into riddles? I mean, if you got something to say, why not just come out with it?"

"I don't have to, now. I know what I want to know."

"Good. I hope you'll sleep better tonight."

"I don't ever have trouble sleeping, Chief. Do you?"

"I haven't slept right since 1943, Dietz, and you want to know something? You know what some of the kids are saying these days about not trusting anyone over thirty? Well, I don't trust anyone over thirty who sleeps good. See you around."

Balzic bounded through the exit and down the steps and across the alley to his car. He drove home but found the house empty. A note on the kitchen table written in Ruth's hand said: "Mario, Took your mother to Dr. Wilson. Ella gave us a lift. Meat loaf in the refrigerator. Have a good day. One of these days I'm going to brush my teeth."

Balzic smiled and whistled all the while he made himself a plate, filling it with chunks of meat loaf, cheese, and olives. He opened a bottle of beer and was just sitting down to eat when he saw the paper. Page one of *The Rocksburg Gazette* bore this story:

FEW CLUES—

NORTH ROCKSBURG MAN FOUND BEATEN TO DEATH

by Dick Dietz

ROCKSBURG GAZETTE STAFF WRITER

Police are still searching today for the killer of John J. Andrasko, 45, of Route 986 North, Rocksburg RD, who was found savagely beaten to death Friday night on the platform of the Pennsylvania Station, where he was apparently waiting for the 11:38 train to Knox.

State police Lt. Philip Moyer, chief of criminal investigation division of the Rocksburg Barracks, in charge of the investigation, said he has few clues to go on and no witnesses. Moyer said, however, the murder weapon had been found but would not reveal what it was. Moyer also said no motive has been determined but did not rule out robbery as a possible motive. He did not elaborate.

Dist. Atty Milton Weigh said the murder was "the most vicious and savage thing I've ever seen." He said detectives assigned to his office were assisting in the investigation, but he had little to add to what Lt. Moyer said.

Informed sources close to the investigation told The Rocksburg Gazette both police departments were working on the theory the murderer was possibly a drug addict.

Balzic threw the paper across the kitchen and finished eating, furious with Weigh and Dietz, tasting little of what he ate, eating too fast, and knowing he was letting himself in for a bout of indigestion.

He washed the dish and set it in the drainer in the sink. He finished his beer and then picked up the paper, restoring it to something like its original shape and putting it back on the table.

He locked the house and drove slowly out to the Rocksburg Police Rod and Gun Club range, keeping the radio open, smoking and looking at the trees turning color, pulling off the road when cars approached from behind to let them pass. He turned into the club grounds and drove in low gear along the half-mile dirt road to the range, stopping on the crest of a low hill, so Moyer could see him from the road. He opened the trunk and then sat on the browning scrub grass and lit another cigarette, looking around at the trees and listening to the squirrels and birds.

Off to his right he saw the tall grass and brush moving and then heard a pheasant calling. He watched the tall grass and guessed there were at least three hens following the cock. Something spooked them, and the parting grass gave the appearance of the wake of a speeding boat.

"Run now, beautiful," Balzic said through clenched teeth, "'cause in a couple more weeks I'm going to be right behind you."

He sat there long enough to finish the cigarette, butting it out carefully on the ground and splitting the paper and letting the tobacco crumble through his fingers, as Moyer's unmarked cruiser came slowly up the road, leaving small clouds of dust that hung for a moment before floating off. Balzic stood and brushed off his seat.

Moyer parked beside him and got out and stretched. "Mario, what's the good news?"

"It's quiet out here, that's the best news I've got."

"Yeah, it is that. God, look at those trees."

"That's all I did, driving out here, was look at the trees. Fantastic, this time of year."

"You know something, though, Mario? I used to think this time of year was the best, because it was so damn pretty, but the older I get the more I think spring is."

"Well, you said it, Phil. It's 'cause you're getting older."

"You think so?"

"Hell, I started thinking spring was better ten years ago."

"Maybe you're right," Moyer said. "Well, what do you say, sport? You ready to make some holes in the paper?"

"I'm ready. Anything new?" Balzic said, leaning into his trunk.

"Not a damn thing. Saw the paper, though. I don't know who's got less between the ears—Weigh or that reporter. You see it?"

"I saw it. Made me forget what I was eating."

"What the hell you got in there, Mario? What's this big secret weapon of yours?"

Balzic unzipped a rifle case that hung from wide leather straps attached to the underside of the trunk back an inch or so from where the lid swung up. He drew out a rifle with a telescopic sight.

"What you got there?"

"This, my friend, is a modified Springfield '03."

"This is what you shoot with? Why, for crying out loud?"

"You grab those profile targets in there and, as we walk along, I'll tell you. Just let me get this box of cartridges."

They set off over the crest of the hill and headed for the hollow of land that lay between it and another ridge more than three hundred yards away. The range extended between the two ridges.

"Hope you brought some way to fix the targets," Moyer said.

"Oh, there're always plenty of tacks on the butts."

"So tell me about the rifle."

"The whole thing is, if I ever do have to shoot somebody—and I hope to hell I don't—then at least I know I can hit where I'm aiming with something that's going to knock him off his feet without killing him or hurting him too bad."

"And just how do you figure that?" Moyer asked.

"Well, I talked to a couple doctors about it, and they said—both of

60

them were hunters, too—they said a two-hundred-grain bullet from a 30.06 would knock any man off his feet no matter how big he was, especially from under a hundred yards. Then they showed me on an anatomy chart where the big veins and arteries were, and they both said that a bullet that size traveling that fast—well, here. Let's put these targets up, and I'll draw it for you."

They fixed four life-sized silhouette targets to the butts, and Balzic took out a pen and drew circles, using a half-dollar piece as a guide, on the shoulders. "There," he said. "That's about a half-inch from the outside of the shoulder and about a quarter-inch from the top of the shoulder. The nearest artery's about two inches away, and the nearest vein's a little less. But that's bone under there. That's right at the socket. I got it from two doctors, as I said. I hit anybody right there, he's going down, he's not going to be able to move that arm, and he's not going to die."

"Well now, Mario, that's just fine if the guy stands up nice and tall and gives you his word he's not going to move."

"Yeah, yeah. I know. That's what everybody says. Okay, I'll show you something." Balzic paced off twenty-five steps. "Would you say this is about the width of a two-way street with room for cars to park and for sidewalks?"

"That's about right," Moyer said.

"Okay," Balzic said. "Let him have it. You got six shots in that thirty-eight or five?"

"This one has six."

"Is that the one you carry?"

"No."

"Where's the one you carry? I'll bet it's one of those snub-nose jobs."

"Yeah, I do."

"Hell, you're as bad as some of my men. Go ahead. Use that one then. All six shots. He's just standing there, and he just promised you he wouldn't move. Go on. Start shooting."

Moyer scowled, then turned, dropped to one knee, held his revolver with two hands and fired six times.

"Damn," Balzic said, "that thing makes more noise than my rifle."

61

"In a pig's ass it does."

"That's your opinion. Well, let's see how many times you killed him."

They walked to the target and Balzic said: "No doubt about it. You're a killer all right. Look there. One got him right in the heart. Those two got him in the lungs, which means he's got maybe twenty minutes before he drowns in his own blood. That one's a real beauty—you got him right in the abdominal aorta and probably through the interior vena cava, which means he's got about ten, fifteen minutes before he bleeds to death, and even if you get him to a hospital in time to stop that, the slug probably hit him in the spine, which leaves him in a wheelchair. That one went through his stomach and a kidney. That's about twenty-to-one against him, and holy hell, Phil. Look at that one. You shot off the guy's pleasure."

"Very funny," Moyer said, frowning more deeply. "All right, doctor, let's see what you do with that piece of equipment you're so goddamn proud of."

They walked off the same distance, and Balzic loaded four rounds into the Springfield. "You got a second hand on your watch?"

"Yeah."

"Okay, time me. I'm going to shoot four times at the right shoulder on each profile. You ready?"

"I'm ready when you are."

Balzic planted his feet and fired, working the bolt, aiming, breathing, and firing in an even rhythm. "How long?" he asked when he'd fired the last round.

"Twenty-seven seconds."

"That's a little slow. But let's have a look."

When they got to the targets Moyer said, "You sonuvabitch, you must come out here every day of the week."

"Only two or three times a week, Phil," Balzic said, grinning broadly. "You want to try it from, oh, say, fifty yards?"

"You got to be kidding."

"Let's just try it. I'm really trying to prove a point here, you know that. Tell you what. You shoot from fifteen yards, and I'll shoot from fifty. How's that? Fair enough?"

"How much time do I get?"

"I'll give you a minute." Balzic stepped off fifteen yards. "When you're ready. Just shoot for the left shoulder."

"All four targets?"

"Sure. That's what I'm going to do. That's what I did."

Moyer grumbled something under his breath and then said he was ready. He went into a crouch, held his revolver with two hands, and fired.

"Forty-six seconds, Phil. That's not bad."

"Aw, go screw yourself," Moyer said as they walked toward the targets. He started grumbling again.

"One out of four's not bad, Phil. Not bad at all. I've seen guys come out here with a handgun and shoot one out of thirty. Don't forget, this is only paper, and he's not doing anything while you're taking almost a minute to hit him once out of four shots."

"You really like to lay it on when you make a point, don't you?"

"Yeah, I do. But only when I'm trying to make this point. But I'll skip the sarcasm. Give you my word, okay?"

Moyer nodded and then, to ease the moment, took a pen and circled the shots on or near both shoulders on all four targets. "Go ahead," he said as Balzic paced off fifty yards. "Just let me get clear."

Balzic loaded four more rounds into the rifle, turned and nodded to Moyer, and then began firing in the same steady rhythm he'd used before.

"I'll be damned," Moyer said when they inspected the targets.

"How long did it take me?"

"Thirty-one seconds," Moyer said, shaking his head.

"If you'll notice, Phil, each one of these is just a shade lower than my first ones were, but they're still on the socket, with plenty to spare."

"You do this three times a week?" Moyer said, as they walked back to their cars.

"I try to," Balzic said. "In all kinds of weather, in all kinds of light. I just want to be sure."

They reached the cars, and Balzic slid the Springfield into the case

63

hanging in his trunk. "I just wish I could be halfway sure about this other thing."

"About Andrasko?"

"What else? The only thing I'm sure about is, he's dead and somebody killed him, and now our district attorney is running his mouth about drugs again." Balzic started to laugh. "Though I'll admit, that part of it kind of tickles me."

"What do you have against him, Mario—I mean, has he ever done anything to you personally?"

"To me? Hell no. Unless you call that kind of thing he pulled last night personal. But that's really stretching it. No. I just don't like small men with big ambitions. They always wind up using a red herring to get where they want to go. With Weigh, it's drugs. He's going to talk himself right into Harrisburg on that pitch. Wait and see. I'll give him five, six years. 'Course by that time, he might have to dream up a new fish to say he knows how to catch."

"Well, Mario, you can't deny that drugs are on the increase."

"Aw, come on, Phil. For every drug bust you've made this year, I'll bet you've made twenty drunk drivers. Hell, Weigh's been in office a little more than a year now, and I don't know of one prosecution he's made involving a death connected in any way with heroin, never mind marijuana, and how many deaths have been caused by boozers behind a wheel? Fifteen? Sixteen? Hell, Phil, there've been eighty-four traffic deaths in this county this year, and I know for a fact that at least ten of them have been because somebody was drunk."

"Can't argue that."

"And where do those things wind up? I think three of them made it to the grand jury, and only one made it to trial. Then our hero blew that one."

"I remember that one very well," Moyer said.

"I know you do."

"Yeah. Second offense for that guy. Yeah, boy, that was the day I wanted to choke Weigh."

"So?" Balzic said, throwing up his hands. "What is all this stuff about drugs? Hell, he's too lazy to file a proper information over a surety of the peace—how the hell can I believe anything he says about drug abuse right here in old Rocksburg? He's the goddamn music man, is what he is. Ah, I've seen D.A.'s come and go. 'Least he's a little smoother than the last one."

Moyer started to howl. "Old Froggy. Jesus, somebody ought to write a book about him."

"Nobody'd believe it."

"Hey, you had to be around for this one. I heard about it, but I was on vacation then. Did Froggy really bust that Greek that runs the newspaper store on an obscenity?"

"Yes, he did. And everybody said he couldn't be that stupid. I mean, they knew a couple days before that he was going to do it, and nobody believed him."

"So he actually did it."

"Yeah. Walked right in there himself with the warrant. That was two weeks before the election. About the dirtiest thing the Greek had in there was the *National Enquirer,* and one block away is Janus's joint. Hell, he had to walk right by Janus's to serve the warrant on the Greek."

Moyer was roaring. "He really thought that Greek was backing Spagnos for judge?"

"No. He thought he was Spagnos's cousin."

"You're kidding."

"So help me."

Moyer laughed until tears ran down his cheeks. "I don't believe it," he sputtered.

"You better believe it. You know where old Froggy finished in that election."

"Who doesn't? Last out of five."

"Last out of five," Balzic said, smiling. "He couldn't have won that one with two million dollars."

"Didn't Spagnos finish third?"

"Yeah. But you know where most of Spagnos's money came from, don't you?"

"I heard. I also heard Spagnos didn't know anything about it, but I kind of doubt that."

"No. It's true. He didn't know anything about it until after. That's when he found out how much money the others got. All those plain envelopes full of tens and twenties. Jesus, they were practically floating around the county. But Spagnos really didn't know where it was coming from. Take my word for it. I've known Spagnos all my life, and if ever there was a guy who didn't believe in an organized book, it's him."

"Well, he's got to believe now."

"Jesus, they must've sent him over thirty thousand. But knowing him, it still wouldn't surprise me if he thought they all wanted him to win 'cause he had a pure heart and knew the law. They were just fed up with paying Froggy, and then, when Froggy busts the Greek, they knew they'd been paying a clown all those years, and they couldn't stand it. Jesus, he embarrased them."

"You tell that to most people, they'd never believe you," Moyer said, wiping his eyes on his sleeve.

"I'll tell you, I'll be the happiest guy around the day they legalize the book," Balzic said. "Then maybe goddamn judges and D.A.'s will get elected 'cause they know the law. Do you know, my mother to this day thinks I don't know she plays the numbers?"

"Honest to God?"

"Every day she calls Vinnie down at Muscotti's and gets her dime down."

"How old is she?"

"She'll be sixty-nine. But the best part is, she tells Vinnie to put her bill on my beer tab, and then she sneaks two dollars into my pants every time she gets her Social Security. She's been doing that for, hell, I don't know, must be twenty years. Long as I've run a tab down there."

"She ever hit?"

"Oh, yeah. That's when the real fun starts. She turns herself inside out with stories about where she got the extra fifty. One time she said she got it from a cousin with a guilty conscience in Italy. Another time she said it was an income tax refund. That was in July or something."

"Vinnie never lets on?"

"Oh, no. He thinks I think he's cheating me."

"You know what you ought to do?"

"What's that?"

"You ought to bring her down there some day, and I'll bust them both on a lottery charge. Be real serious about the whole thing."

"That might be pretty funny just to see their faces. Maybe we'll do it, soon as this thing's over."

"Yeah. There's that, isn't there? Think we ought to be going, don't you?"

"Guess so. Enough fun for today. Maybe I'll see you later on, Lieutenant."

"Okay, Mario," Moyer said, getting into his cruiser.

Balzic watched Moyer drive off, then closed his trunk, and stayed long enough to smoke another cigarette, listening, as he smoked, for the pheasants.

He drove back as slowly as he had come, knowing that sometime today, sooner or later, he would have to run into Weigh, and he wanted to put that off as long as he could.

Balzic parked in the lot in back of city hall instead of in the spot reserved for him on the side. He went in the back door and down the hall leading to the station. At the corner that opened onto the big rooms where the switchboard and teletypes were, Balzic stopped and listened. Sergeant Stramsky was trying to persuade somebody to take his complaint about garbage collection to the sanitation department on the second floor.

Balzic peeked around the corner and was much relieved to see that no one else was in the big room. He walked in and went through the swinging gate, nodding to Stramsky in passing, and continued to the rear of the room, where the coffee pot was. He poured himself a cup and waited for Stramsky to finish with the man, a stoop-shouldered fellow long past retirement, his face flushed with indignation.

"You don't understand me," the man said. "I want those nincompoops arrested."

"Yessir," Stramsky said. "I understand you, but I've told you twice already that you could do a lot better by going upstairs and talking it over with the people who run the department. I know most of them. They're pretty nice people. I'm sure they'll try to get things straightened out for you."

"But those nincompoops spill my garbage all over the place, and last week they didn't even show up. I want them arrested."

"I'm sorry, sir, but your complaint isn't a criminal complaint. It's something that can probably be handled in five minutes if you'd just go upstairs and talk to the right people."

"You're the police, aren't you? You're supposed to arrest criminals, aren't you?"

"Yessir."

"Well, their service is worse than criminal, I tell you."

Balzic took his coffee to a phone and called upstairs.

"Sanitation Department," a woman said.

"This is Chief Balzic. We got a citizen here who wants to have somebody in your department arrested for bad service. How about sending somebody down to hear the gentleman out. I'm sure he wouldn't be here talking to us if he didn't have a legitimate complaint." Balzic turned his back to the elderly man and lowered his voice. "I think the reason he don't want to come up is, he's probably not allowed to walk up steps. Besides, if somebody came down instead of making him come up, that'd be enough right there to satisfy him."

"We'll see what we can do," the woman said and hung up.

Balzic stepped to the counter beside Stramsky. "Somebody'll be down in a few minutes to talk with you about your problem, sir, so why don't you have a seat while you're waiting?"

"I'll stand, thank you."

"Suit yourself. Like a cup of coffee?"

The man shook his head once. "Not allowed to drink coffee."

"I see," Balzic said, nudging Stramsky's elbow and walking back toward the coffee pot.

"Arrest the garbagemen, for crissake," Stramsky said.

"Aw, what the hell," Balzic said. "Got to give the old boy a chance to get in his licks, too, you know. Everybody else is pitching a bitch these days, so why not him? Be glad we ain't in New York or Berkeley."

"Don't think I ain't glad."

"So. There you are. Boy, is this coffee lousy. D'you make it?"

"You never complained before, dear," Stramsky said.

"Nothing tastes right today ever since I read the paper. Before we get interrupted, what did you come up with on the marriage thing?"

"Maryland said no record, and Virginia said they'd call back."

"Weigh been in again?"

"No," Stramsky said. "But I spoke too soon." He nodded toward the side door.

Weigh came through the swinging gate in the counter and said, "I'd like to speak with you, Mario. Alone."

"Certainly," Balzic said, setting down his coffee. "Let's go back here." He led Weigh into one of the interrogation cubicles in the rear of the big room and shut the door behind Weigh.

"Have a chair, Milt."

"Let's skip the amenities, Mario. Just tell me what the hell you think you're trying to pull?"

"You don't mind if I sit down, do you, Milt?" Balzic said, sitting in one of the three straight-backed chairs, so that the small table was between them.

"Sitting or standing makes no difference. I want an explanation."

"About last night, I take it, is what you mean."

"You know damn well what I mean. Cut the coy routine."

Balzic lit a cigarette. "You move too fast, Milt."

"That's it? That's all you have to say—I move too fast?"

"You talk too fast. You think too fast."

Weigh thrust his hands in his pockets and glared at the ceiling. He appeared to be counting ten silently. "You listen to this, Chief of Police Balzic, and you listen to it very carefully. You pull a stunt like that one again, and I'll file an information against you for malfeasance in office and violation of the public trust."

"Easy, Milt, easy. That's a two-way street you're on now."

"Of all the goddamn—who the hell do you think you're dealing with, Balzic? Some ridge runner from Fayette County that took a correspondence course in law. Dammit, man, I was Phi Beta Kappa at Cornell, and I studied law at Dickinson."

Balzic smiled in spite of himself. "I know who you are, Milt. But I know something else. Any time you or your boys make a bust and

69

then expect me or my boys to do the pencil work for you, I'm going to do exactly what I did last night. And since we're in a warning match, I may as well tell you that you file an information against me for what you said, I'll file one against you for the same goddamn reason. And then we'll let a judge decide. You want to chance it?"

"Of all the petulant—" Weigh could not go on. The flesh between his brows and under his eyes was starting to go blotchy. "Mario," he said, stepping to the door of the cubicle and jerking it open, "I promise you, I won't forget this." He rushed out of the big room, sending the swinging gate bouncing and slamming the outside door.

When Balzic came out, Stramsky was directing the elderly man and somebody from Sanitation into another cubicle.

"Looks to me like our hero was a touch unhappy when he left," Stramsky said.

Balzic rubbed his chin. "Aw, the sonuvabitch wouldn't give me a chance to let him save some face. He just started threatening and promising. I can't handle that crap. So I threatened him back, and it was a standoff. Hell of a way to do things. But that's what happens when you go against a guy that won't sit down. I sat down. I sat down for him, but the dummy didn't even know what I was doing. Shit," Balzic said, picking up his cup and going for more coffee. He changed his mind and washed out the cup. "Vic, I'm going up the funeral home and pay my respects and have a look around."

"Which one is it?"

"Bruno's, I think. Maybe I ought to check with Father Marrazo. He took care of it."

Balzic paused in the middle of dialing the rectory. "That's one thing I always liked about Father Marrazo, you know that, Vic?"

"What's that?"

"I've known him for eight, nine years now, and he never once told me where he went to college."

Balzic hoped he would get to Bruno's Funeral Home before the family. He wanted a couple of minutes alone to say the things he thought he ought to say to what was left of John Andrasko. But

70

when he walked in and followed the tiny white arrows on the directory, he found the family already there.

The casket was closed. Mary Andrasko and her two younger children were kneeling before it. Another woman Balzic did not recognize was kneeling on the floor slightly behind and to the right of Mrs. Andrasko. Standing behind this woman and to her right, his hands folded behind his back, was Tommy Parilla.

The other woman got up as soon as she heard Balzic step into the room and came to his side. She was younger than Mary Andrasko, but the family resemblance was unmistakable.

"They'd like to be alone for a little while longer," the woman whispered.

"I understand," Balzic whispered. "But I hope it isn't for too long. I have to talk to her." He nodded toward Mary Andrasko.

"You can tell me," the woman said, and led Balzic outside to the parking lot.

"What I have to say, I really have to say to her," Balzic said.

"You can tell me. I'm her sister."

"I don't know why, but I just assumed she didn't have any relatives."

"Just me. I'm Angie. Who're you?"

"Mario Balzic. I'm chief of police here."

Angie took a small step backward. She was very dark-skinned and wore no makeup. Her long hair was pulled back under a black babushka. Dressed as she was, entirely in black except for her stockings, she gave the appearance of being of an earlier generation.

"Are you the one didn't tell her?" she said. "So she had to find out from the paper?"

"Yes. That's why I came so early. Or why I tried to. I wanted to apologize."

"What good do you think that's going to do? The damage is already done, Mr. Chief of Police."

"Look, Mrs.—"

"It's Miss."

"Spano?"

She nodded.

"Well, look, Miss Spano, I can understand why you're mad about this—"

"You think so, huh?"

Balzic squared himself. "Just a minute, Miss Spano. My first name is Mario. My mother's maiden name was Petraglia. So I know about courtesy. But what I'm trying to tell you is I never got a chance to tell her how it happened, and then I thought the priest told her. It turned out he thought I did, so that's how it happened she had to learn it the way she did. And that's why I came now. You can take that or leave it, but it's the truth."

She folded her arms and flushed slightly. "I'm sorry," she said.

"I didn't tell you that to make you say you're sorry."

"I know."

"All right. So then we understand."

She pursed her lips and took off her babushka and shook her hair. "I hate these places," she said.

"Yeah. They try to make you think what happened didn't happen. Well, not with John. I mean, with the casket closed."

"You called him by his first name. Did you know him?"

"Since I was a kid. I didn't know her, though. Your sister. I never saw her until I had to tell her. She's older than you?"

"Eight years. How did you know John?"

"I just knew him, that's all. Not really very well. I was sort of hoping now, maybe you could tell me more about both of them."

"John and Mary? Or John and Tami?"

"You knew Tami?"

"A lot better than I knew John. I moved from here ten years ago. I've only been back three or four times."

"What happened to Tami?"

"He left her."

"Just like that?"

"How else is there? You leave or you stay. When you leave, what can anybody say, except you left? You can put all the pretty words on it you want, it still comes down to the same thing. He left her."

"You know why?"

"What's to know? Tami was a regular bastard. When he was nice,

72

he was nice. When he wasn't, he was one of those rotten wops that make you sick you're Italian. Then one day he just walked out, and she never heard from him again."

"How did he leave?"

"How? He left. That's all. How many ways are there?"

"Yes, but this is important. If you could remember."

"My God, man, that was eleven, twelve years ago. I don't know. One day she called me up and said he left. I didn't ask her how. I was just glad he was gone. What did I care how?"

"How did she take it?"

"How could she? He stuck her with the kid. No money. After he was gone for a week, she found out he hadn't paid the rent in six or seven months. She moved in with me, and I supported them until she found a job."

"How old was the boy then?"

"Well, he's seventeen now, so he must've been four or five then."

"Did you two—you and Mary—did you talk a lot about Tami? In front of the boy I mean?"

"Sure. For a long time she wouldn't talk about anything else. Every time I tried to talk about something else, she'd change the subject back to him. That's the big reason I left. I got sick of hearing about it.

"After she got back on her feet," Angie went on, "I mean as far as the money went, I left. The son of a bitch made a pass at me once, and then he slapped me when I wouldn't go for it. She doesn't know about that, but every time she'd start talking about him, that's all I could think about. She didn't have to tell me how rotten he was, but after a while I started to feel guilty, you know? Like I had something to do with him leaving her. Which was crap, because I didn't. I couldn't stand to be around him before. Before he made the pass I mean. After, well . . ."

"But the boy heard lots of talk," Balzic said.

"Sure he heard it. Didn't I just say so? I only had two rooms and a bath. We all slept in the same room. How could he not hear it? Anyway, that's history. What difference does it make?"

"Little pitchers have big ears, Miss Spano. I got two of my own, and

73

the biggest education I ever got in my life was watching them get acquainted with the world. You never know how things you do or say affect them until you ask them about it. And some of the answers I used to get from my kids about some things I said really used to set me back. Still do. Let me give you an example.

"I know a family lives a couple blocks from here. They have a son who's allergic to all kinds of things, but especially animal fur. Dogs and cats. He's seven years old now, and as long as he can remember, his parents have been telling him to stay away from dogs and cats—they're bad for you and make it tough for you to breathe—stuff like that.

"So last year, we started getting complaints from people in this neighborhood about their pets getting killed. And not just killed. Mangled. Make a long story short, this kid was going around killing all the dogs and cats he could get his hands on. Six years old and a really bright kid. But in his head, all that talk from his parents about cats and dogs make it tough for him to breathe, well, he figures all he had to do is kill them all and his troubles are over. That's the kind of thing I'm talking about."

"Wait just a minute," Angie said. "If I understand you, what you're saying is Tommy—are you trying to tell me you think Tommy killed John?"

Balzic nodded and then shrugged, as though to apologize.

"But that's crazy. Because of what we said about Tami? But that was Tami. That wasn't John we were talking about back then. My God, she hadn't even met John then. She didn't meet him until about a year or so later."

"I know it sounds crazy," Balzic said. "But that's what I'm talking about. Whoever did it wasn't right. John wasn't robbed. But he was beaten so bad I didn't even know who he was. I had to be told. I mean his face—well, never mind. I didn't recognize him, that's enough."

"Oh, my God, I don't believe I'm hearing this. But wait a minute. If you know this or if you think you know this, how come you don't arrest him?"

"In the first place, I don't know. I'm just guessing. In the second place, even if I did know it, I can't prove it, and in the third place, even if I could prove it, I wouldn't arrest him. Not now."

"Why not?"

"Because I made one mistake with your sister. And I'm not about to make another. When I do—if I do—I'm going to make sure there's a doctor, a lawyer, and a priest standing right there beside me. But to tell you the truth, I can't do anything until I get something solid to go on."

"God," Angie said, chewing her lips, "I used to feel guilty because that creep made a pass at me. Now this. You know what you're telling me, don't you?"

Balzic nodded.

"You're telling me that me and Mary—our big mouths—are the cause of all this. And you're telling me that the kid is so screwed up he wasn't killing John at all. Isn't it?"

"That's the idea. That's why I wanted to know if you could remember how Tami left. If you'd told me he left on a train, I'd be willing to bet a hundred to one the kid did it."

"Well you just go to hell, mister," Angie said. "You're not sticking me with this thing. The rest was bad enough. It took me five years to get over that. So you just go straight to hell." She brushed past him and ran into the funeral home.

"Dummy," Balzic said, blowing out a sigh. Then he kicked at a leaf and said it again.

"S'matter, mister? My aunt make you mad?"

Balzic jumped. He had not heard the boy coming.

"Hey," Tommy Parilla said, "aren't you the chief of police, the one that told my mother?"

Balzic nodded. "That's me." He looked directly at the boy. "And I'm the one that didn't tell her how it happened."

"Is that why my aunt was mad?"

"Yes. She had a right to be."

"She makes everybody mad, and she gets mad at everybody," Tommy said, shoving his hands into his pockets and looking at the sky. "Say, you wouldn't have a cigarette on you, would you?"

"Yeah," Balzic said, fishing in his pockets for his pack. "I keep trying to put them in different pockets so I'll have to think whether I want one or not. It's a lousy habit, Tommy. You shouldn't have started."

"That's what John used to say," Tommy said, taking the pack from Balzic, taking a cigarette out, and handing the pack back. He refused Balzic's offer of a light. "I got a lighter. Zippo. Best little lighter made. Got a lifetime guarantee."

Balzic watched the boy light his smoke and then said, "You don't seem to be too upset about all this."

"About John? Why should I? I didn't like him." Tommy took several deep drags on his cigarette and tried to blow a smoke ring.

"Did you get along with him?"

"I didn't see him that much. In the daytime he was always working around the place, and I'd be in school. Then when I'd get home from school, he'd go to sleep. Then he'd get up around ten, ten-thirty, and go to work. The last three summers I worked, so I didn't see him that much."

"Where'd you work?"

"Out the Blue Pine Driving Range. All day and half the night."

"I take it you didn't help around the farm."

Tommy shook his head. "Nah. I didn't like that. Only thing I ever help with is the canning. I always help my mother with that. But that stuff with planting and running the cultivator—you can have it."

"Is that why you didn't like John?"

Tommy shook his head. "What difference would that make? Lotsa people do stuff I don't like, I could care less. I didn't like him 'cause he wouldn't marry my mother."

"He wouldn't do what?"

"I said he wouldn't marry my mother. They were always having arguments about it. I thought that was the least he could do. But I gave up on him a long time ago. I never said nothing to him about it, but it made me mad."

Balzic blew out another sigh. He tried to read the boy's face. It seemed incapable of pretending. Finally Balzic said, "Well, you know, Tommy, they were married."

"What—what are you talking about?"

76

"Just what I said. They were married. Just as married as if a priest or a justice of the peace married them."

"I don't believe you."

"Well, there's a thing called common law marriage. If a man and woman live together for a couple of years in this state, and they call themselves mister and missus, the law says they're married, and the law treats their marriage the same as any other."

"I don't believe you," Tommy repeated, rolling the cigarette between his thumb and forefinger.

"Believe it or don't. All you have to do is call up any lawyer."

"Well, how come my mother didn't know about that? How come she was always fighting and arguing with him about it?"

"I don't know," Balzic said, "but I can guess. Probably for a long time she was embarrassed about it. I mean what the law is and what social custom is are two different things. There are lots of people who don't give a damn about social custom, but apparently, from what you say, your mother wasn't one of them. I guess it could be pretty embarrassing to a woman to live with a man all that time and think that maybe other people are thinking that what she's doing isn't the right thing, if you get what I mean."

"I still don't believe you," Tommy said, dropping the cigarette on the macadam and crushing it out with his heel. "But I'm going to call a lawyer, all right."

"Good idea. Then you can be sure. Just remember where you heard it first."

"Why? You think you did me a big favor or something?"

"No. I just told you the truth, that's all."

"Boy, you sound more and more like John. He was always walking around telling me stuff like that. 'Honesty is the best policy.' 'Don't take any handouts.' 'If you don't take care of yourself, nobody will.' You and him must've had the same teacher or something."

"As a matter of fact, we did."

"What?"

"I said we did. I went all through school with John. We had a lot of subjects together."

"Did *you* like him?"

77

"I didn't have any reason not to. But then, I didn't have to live with him."

"That's for sure." Tommy looked squarely at Balzic and for a second looked as though he was going to say something else, something Balzic hoped would be significant, but he didn't.

Balzic waited a moment longer and then said, "Think we better be getting back inside. I still haven't told your mother what I came to tell her. You going in?"

"Nah," Tommy said. "Think I'll stay out here for a while. I don't like the way it smells in there."

"All right. See you again sometime," Balzic said, walking away.

"Yeah, sure," Tommy said, spitting between his teeth.

Inside the door, Balzic stopped far enough away from the window to be sure he couldn't be seen and watched the boy in the parking lot. But the boy did nothing. He just stood there with his hands jammed in his pockets, spitting every so often, and looking either at the sky or at the cars and trucks going by on Market Street. If Tommy was disturbed by anything Balzic had said, he gave no indication of it.

Balzic stood a minute longer, waiting for some sign, some gesture, with which to feed a conviction that Tommy had killed John Andrasko. He got none. Worse, everything the boy had said and the way he'd looked when he'd said it, made Balzic begin to doubt everything he'd thought about the reasons the boy would have had to kill Andrasko.

On the other hand, everything Angie Spano had said about the boy's early years fitted perfectly. It was all there: the loss of the real father, the sense of rejection, the feeling of abandonment, the constant harping by the mother about the father—everything, in short, to convince Balzic that the boy was not killing John at all when he'd beaten him to death, that he had been killing his blood father who, in all likelihood, he could not consciously remember.

Yet there the boy stood, having just given Balzic every reason for believing that he was aware who John was. How then was it possible for him to confuse John with his real father? More importantly, Balzic thought with a growing sense of frustration, how was the boy

78

able to act as he was now? Especially when he had a perfectly clear reason for hating John just as John was? It made no sense. Balzic knew he couldn't have it both ways: either what Angie Spano said was right and the boy had killed someone who had come in his mind to stand for his blood father, or—or what, Balzic asked himself. Or the boy killed John because he wouldn't marry the boy's mother? No way, Balzic thought. He would never have said the things he'd just said.

As he walked back into the room where the rest of John Andrasko's family waited, Balzic kept trying to interpret something in the boy's words and manner to keep his conviction alive. It was useless. He had the dizzying feeling that unless somebody came up with solid evidence, the chances were doubling by the hour against proving the boy did it.

Balzic approached Mary Andrasko. She sat in the front row of straight-backed chairs with her son on her right and her daugher on her left. Their eyes were raw, and they breathed through their mouths. Two chairs away sat Angie Spano, her face rigid.

Balzic had to stand in front of Mary Andrasko because she wouldn't look at him. He knew that Angie had told her why he'd come. He hoped she had not told her the rest.

"Mrs. Andrasko," Balzic said, "I came here to apologize. I'm not going to make any excuses. I should have told you."

"All right," she said, her eyes fixed on the coffin. "Now you said you're sorry. Just go away now."

"Mrs. Andrasko—"

"Please just go away now," she said, her eyes filling with tears.

Balzic gave a slight nod. "I'm sorry," he said and walked quickly to the back of the room where he turned toward the coffin and, without kneeling, crossed himself and prayed for the soul of John Andrasko. He crossed himself again and left.

Out in the parking lot, he stopped to light a cigarette and was almost to his car before he noticed that Tommy wasn't where he'd been. Balzic looked around but couldn't see the boy anywhere. He sat in the car thinking a dozen contradictory and conflicting thoughts and then drove to St. Malachy's rectory.

Father Marrazo was in his office typing.

"Don't get up, Father," Balzic said. "Just tell me where the wine is. I need a little something."

"It's right here," Father Marrazo said, turning on his swivel chair and reaching into the bottom drawer of his desk. "The glasses are in the bathroom."

"Want some, Father?"

"Not right now. I want to hear what's caused your aggravation, though."

Balzic got a glass and filled it. Capping the bottle and holding the glass aloft to look at the wine in the light coming from a window behind the priest, he said, "Father, I just made an ass of myself all around. I don't know how many more ways I could've done it today. Something tells me there aren't any other ways."

"You're too abstract, Mario. Concrete problems must be solved concretely."

"You must be working on tomorrow's homily, Father."

"Ah, that's how it goes when you have a one-track mind like mine." Father Marrazo smiled. "But it's not a bad idea, don't you agree?"

"Yeah. I guess. Well. To put them in a row, I made a mess with the D.A., I made a mess with Mary Andrasko's sister, I made a mess with Tommy Parilla, and I really did a job with Mary Andrasko."

"By mess, do you mean you've alienated all of them?"

"That's a fancy word, Father, but I guess that's what I did."

"You learned nothing useful?"

"Oh, I learned a lot. I learned that Tami Parilla just took off one day when Tommy was about four or five. I learned he made a pass at his sister-in-law. I learned that Mary and her sister lived together for a year or so after Tami took off and that they talked almost constantly about Tami in front of the boy. And I learned from Tommy that he didn't like John—are you ready, Father?—he didn't like John because John wouldn't marry his mother."

Father Marrazo's eyebrows shot up and his mouth looked as though he had just mistaken a lemon for an orange.

"Yeah, Father. And when you get that much information and then you manage to turn off your sources all in one hour, well . . ."

"Why are you so sure you've turned off the sources?"

"Take my word for it. I managed to say all the wrong things at exactly the right times. I won't get anything out of the sister anymore. I blew that one about as bad as you can blow it. As far as Mrs. Andrasko goes, well, it'll be a miracle if she tells me which way up is. As for Milt Weigh, he's looking for an excuse to make fried ass out of me. And then there's Tommy. That kid is either the best actor I've ever seen, or else he's the sickest. All I managed with him was to plant one little seed. One lousy little seed. To tell you the truth, Father, I handled myself today as though I didn't know anything about people. Nothing."

Balzic drank his wine and then held up the bottle and looked imploringly at the priest. Father Marrazo waved for him to fill his glass, and then went to the bathroom to get a glass for himself.

"Tell me, Mario," Father Marrazo said when he returned, "This seed you planted in Tommy. What was that?"

"I just told him that legally his mother was married to John. And that was the only time I got something besides indifference out of him. But you see what's wrong with that."

"No. I can't say that I do."

"Well, Father, let me put it this way. If he gets guilty about that, it means he's not sick at all. Or not in the way I figured he was. The way I got it figured, he did it, but he didn't know he was doing it. Or even if he knew he was doing it, he wasn't really doing it to John. John getting killed was just incidental—or at least that was the way I had it figured."

"What makes you doubt it now?"

"The way it bothered him when I told him about John and his mother being as married as anybody else. He said two or three times he didn't believe me. It was as though he had to keep believing they were the way they'd always been."

"If I understand you, Mario, what you're saying is that he would have been unconcerned about whether they were married if he had, in fact, killed John in the belief he was killing Tami."

"Something like that, Father."

"I suppose it would be no comfort at all for me to remind you that the rationalizations of psychopaths are often extremely well

81

conceived and at times even brilliant—would that offer no consolation?"

"Yeah. I've thought about that. That's why I said he's either the best actor or the sickest. But that's not what's really bothering me now, Father. What's really eating me now is we don't have anything on him. Nothing. And I don't think we're going to get anything, either. And that leaves me with a very unpleasant thought."

"Which is?"

"I hate to even think about it, Father, but unless somebody else gets killed, it's all over."

"By that, you mean under nearly identical circumstances."

"Not necessarily identical. But they'll have to be similar as hell, Father."

"Yes, I see. But then, the circumstances of hell are always similar, aren't they?" Father Marrazo filled their glasses again and then frowned at the nearly empty bottle. "I hope Mr. Ferrara comes today. Ah, but what a foolish hope that is. He always comes on Sundays."

"Would you like me to get something for you at the state store?"

"No, Mario—oh, what's the use? My mouth says no, and my face gives me away. Of course. If it isn't out of your way. Here, let me get some money."

Balzic was already at the door. "Forget it, Father. I'm buying." He left then, walking quickly because he didn't want the priest to catch up with him to force the money on him.

After Balzic bought a half-gallon of California Mountain Red at the state store, he stopped in the courthouse to see Bill Joyce.

"Mario," Joyce said. "How goes it?"

"The same," Balzic said in Italian. "You come up with anything?"

"Yes. Much sooner than I expected, too."

"Such as?"

"About Andrasko, he had a top rating from the local credit bureau, had insurance policies at Knox Steel for life, major medical, and hospitalization. He also had a five-thousand-dollar policy on himself and on his wife and two-thousand-dollar policies on the three kids, all with Prudential. He had the farm mortgaged with Knox Savings and Loan and insurance that guarantees payment in full. He would've paid it off in six more years, anyway. The truck was his unencumbered, and he had seven payments to make on a Ford sedan, with insurance on that guaranteeing payment as well. The only time he missed payments on anything was during a three-month period back in sixty-two when Knox was on strike."

"Solid citizen, huh?"

"Down the line."

"What about Tami Parilla?"

"Just as easy. He holds an able-bodied-seaman's card issued in San Francisco in 1959, and since sixty-one he's been working regularly out of Seattle on ships leased to the U. S. government, moving matériel to Vietnam. No indication of any activity even slightly questionable."

"Anything about his family life?"

"The only thing of interest to you is that the government insurance issued to him and the policy he carries through the union both list Mary Frances Spano Parilla and Thomas John Parilla as beneficiaries, in that order."

"Any idea where he is now?"

"Yes," Joyce said, picking up another piece of paper. "Right now he is aboard the U.S.S. *Mondeville* in Manila Harbor, and he's been on it since it left Seattle seventeen days ago."

"Well, that takes care of that."

"I couldn't get anything out of Missing Persons about him. If anybody cared about him leaving Rocksburg, they didn't care enough to ask for a search. And as far as Andrasko's marriage went, well, I didn't press that because your man Stramsky called about an hour ago looking for you, and he said that both Virginia and Maryland replied negative."

"Yeah. I know that. Fact is, they weren't married. It was common law."

"Where'd you learn that?"

"From right next to the horse's mouth. The kid told me. Said his mother was always arguing with John about marrying her, but apparently John wouldn't. Well, he didn't, anyway. What his reasons were I don't know yet, but I'm not sure it's all that important. All I know is the kid didn't like it and didn't like John because of it."

"The kid tell you that?"

"Yup. Matter of fact as all hell. Wasn't the least bit shy about it. Shook him up a little bit, though, when I told him that legally they were married. I can't figure just how much it did shake him. But we'll see. One way or another."

"Anything else I can do for you?"

"Nothing I can think of, Bill. You got what I needed a damn sight faster than I could've. Thanks." Balzic stood and headed for the door.

"Does it help?"

"Well, it narrows things down. And it hasn't changed my mind about anything."

"You think it's the boy."

"Yeah. But put it this way. Even if it isn't the kid, it had to be somebody with a grudge, which means it had to be somebody who knew him. I haven't read the coroner's report yet, but I'm betting that any bruises John had on the back of his head came from bouncing off the platform. And nobody heard anything."

"So he was facing whoever it was and there was no shouting beforehand, is that the way you figure it?"

"How else? Which also leads me to believe that if there was a grudge, John wasn't aware of it, and that's what keeps me thinking it was the kid. But hell," Balzic said, "I might be making the whole thing too complicated. My first thought when I went out to tell the wife and then the kid showed with the car—I thought, hell, it's probably nothing more than an argument over the car. I still don't know where the kid was last night. When he took the car, whether he had permission, where he went—I don't know. All I know is what time he came home in it. The rest, well, you know—that's where we wear out the rubber. I'll see you, Bill, and thanks again."

"Anytime," Joyce said, picking up a phone that had started ringing.

Balzic went down the back stairs and to his car, drove to St. Malachy's rectory to drop off the wine for Father Marrazo, and then went on to his home.

He found his daughters in the living room on the floor, eating popcorn and watching *Dick Clark's American Bandstand.*

"Hi, group," Balzic said, loosening his tie and dropping into the recliner. He got no answer. "Hey," he said, leaning forward, "some guy just walked in and said something to you two. I think it was hello."

"Oh, hi, Daddy," Emily said.

"What's with your friend there—she lose her voice cheering for Rocksburg's lost cause last night?"

"No, Daddy, I didn't lose my voice," Marie said.

"Well, then. Do you think you might trouble yourself to speak to me? Frankie Avalon I'm not, but—"

"Oh, Daddy. Frankie Avalon's ancient history."

"Ex-cuse me. Who's this guy?"

"Tony Joe White," Emily said.

"Guitar, mouth organ, jeez," Balzic said. "All he needs is a couple cymbals on his knees and a bass drum and he's a regular one-man band. What's he singing about? What's that he's saying—pork salad? What's that?"

"That's poke salad, Daddy," Emily said.

"It is not. It's polk with an 'l,' " Marie said. "P-o-l-k."

"Poke, polk—what is it?"

"That's something that grows in Louisiana."

"Does he eat it or smoke it?"

"He eats it," Emily said. "It's a small plant that has berries on it, and people make dye from the berries, and they eat the roots, and it's spelled p-o-k-e."

"Just where did you hear anything so dumb?" Marie said.

"I looked it up, that's where. Nyahhhh."

"I still say it's with an l."

"I'll say one thing for him," Balzic said. "He's sure no virtuoso on that mouth organ."

"That's a harmonica, Daddy," Emily said.

"Do you two mind?" Marie said. "I would like to hear *some* of him."

"Yeah, Emily. Keep quiet. Can't you see the girl's intoxicated?"

"Daddy!"

"Speaking of that," Balzic said to himself, "I wonder if we got any beer left." He got up and went into the kitchen. When he came back with the last cold beer a commercial was on.

"See what happened because of you two?" Marie said. "I didn't get to hear half of him."

"Why don't you go buy the record?" Balzic said.

"'Cause she used up practically all her allowance last Tuesday, that's why," Emily said.

"Big mouth."

"All right. That's enough of that. You're both getting a little too salty."

"Well, she didn't have to tell you that," Marie said.

"It's true," Emily said. "Why shouldn't I say it?"

"And I said that's enough, Emily. Marie, you want to buy the record?"

"I did use up my allowance."

Balzic reached in his pocket and fished out two dollar bills. He handed one to Marie and the other to Emily. "Okay. So now you can both buy a record."

"Thanks, Daddy," both said.

"All I ask is you don't buy any headache makers, fair enough?"

They promised they wouldn't.

"By the way, either of you two know Tommy Parilla?"

Marie shook her head no, but Emily said, "You do so know him. You danced with him a couple of weeks ago. At the P.T.A. dance."

"Oh, him. Yuk."

"What's that mean?"

"Yuk, that's all. Just yuk."

"Come on. Use words that mean something," Balzic said.

"Oh, he's got pimples all over, and he thinks he's really cool."

"You should've heard her two weeks ago," Emily said.

"You keep quiet!"

"All right, you two. What else do you know about him?"

"Oh-oh," Emily said. "What did he do, Daddy?"

"Never mind. Just tell me what you know about him."

"Like what?" Marie said.

"Like anything. Anything you can think of."

"Well, he has to dance with sophomores, and he's a senior," Emily said.

"So? That's nothing. Your mother was a freshman when I was a senior."

"Did you dance with her?"

"Certainly I danced with her. But never mind about that. I want to know about Tommy."

"He doesn't wash his hair very often, I can tell you that," Marie said.

"Come on. Be serious."

"Well, you're asking me what I know about him, and I'm trying to tell you, Daddy. He puts some kind of goop on his hair, and—"

"What else? Skip the hair business."

"Well, he bragged the whole time I was dancing with him."

"About what?"

"About how fast he drives."

"About anything else?"

"No. But I really wasn't paying much attention to him."

"Ha! Get a load of her," Emily said.

"I'm going to belt you one—"

"Knock it off," Balzic said. "Look, Marie, I'm not trying to spy in your private life. But I'm not asking like your father—you understand?"

"You still haven't told us what he did," Emily said.

"As far as I know, he hasn't done anything. I'm trying to find out if he's capable, and you two aren't helping much. Think a little bit, Marie. What else did he brag about?"

"He said he didn't take any crap from anybody, and—and, well, he said if I'd go for a ride with him, he'd show me a better time than any football player could."

"Were you dancing with a football player earlier that night?"

"With a couple of them," Emily said.

"Emily, I swear—"

"Marie, did you ever talk to him before?"

"Oh, sure. He's always talking to all the girls. But nobody talks back. Nobody can stand him. I danced with him that night because I felt sorry for him. Everybody was turning him down all over the place. But the longer we danced—well, it was funny. I mean, I just kept feeling sorrier and sorrier for him, but at the same time I just wanted to get away from him. I mean, I knew why everybody wouldn't dance with him, but then I wished I hadn't danced with him. And then I thought if he'd just wash his hair and do something about his acne he'd be kind of cute—if he'd just quit bragging about how cool he was. He was really a good dancer."

"Yeah," Emily said. "Better than anybody at that dance. Of course Billy Francis wasn't there. And neither was Bobby Ceretti."

"Have you talked to him since?"

"Uh-huh. Couple of times. But since then I've been trying to avoid him."

"Why? Did he say something?"

"No. Just the same routine about showing me a better time than any football player. He feels so inferior, and it's so obvious, but he really got mad when I told him."

"Told him what?"

"I told him he ought to give himself a chance to be nice once in a while and that he didn't have to be bragging all the time. Wow, did he ever get mad."

"Mad enough to look like he was going to take a swing at you?"

"Yeah, boy, did he ever. I really got scared for a minute, but then he got up and left."

"Where was that?"

"In the cafeteria. About a week ago. Last Monday, I think."

"You talked to him since?"

"Uh-uh."

"You have so," Emily said. "You talked to him last night. When we went to get a hot dog."

"Oh that. I just said hi to him, that's all."

"You sure that's all you said?"

"Well, not exactly. He gave me the same routine about a better time and all that, and he said he had his car."

"When was that?"

"That was at half-time."

"And you told him no?"

Marie shook her head yes.

"How did he take it?"

"He—he told me to go to hell. He said he could find lots of girls, and I felt rotten because I know he can't."

"Did you see him after that?"

"When we went back to our seats, he followed us and sat right behind us," Emily said.

"But then he left," Marie said.

"When?"

"I don't know exactly."

"It was the beginning of the fourth quarter. Right after the score was forty to six. Lots of people left then," Emily said.

"You see him leave the stadium?"

"Well, no. But he left and was walking toward the gate with everybody else who was leaving then. But I didn't see him go out, I mean I wasn't watching him. I just saw him go past us."

"How about you, Emily? You see him leave the stadium?"

"Uh-uh. I was just glad he wasn't behind us anymore."

"Beginning of the fourth quarter. That'd be about nine-fifteen or so, wouldn't you say? Had to be, 'cause traffic really started backing up about nine-thirty. Okay, group, thanks."

"What did he do, Daddy? You still haven't told us."

"Wrong. I told you twice he hasn't done anything as far as I know."

"Oh, Daddy," Emily groaned, "you never tell us anything."

"You got it, kid. I wouldn't last very long in my business if I went around telling everything I know to everybody who asked, now would I?"

"We're not just everybody," Marie said.

"I'll buy that, and as soon as I know something, I give you my word you'll be about the tenth or twelfth persons to know. How's that?"

Emily groaned again and buried her face in her arms. Marie rolled on her side and propped her head on her fist as the dance contest started on Dick Clark's show.

Balzic went into the kitchen to finsh his beer and stood by the table, hoping he was wrong about what he was thinking.

Balzic could not sleep. He tried for a time on the bed beside Ruth, and then on the recliner in the living room, and finally on the living room floor. It did not matter where; the moment he closed his eyes he saw Tommy Parilla telling Marie to go to hell and then smashing her face with a Coke bottle. At three o'clock he stopped prowling around the house, dressed, and drove to Muscotti's.

The bar was empty save for Vinnie, who was wiping the coolers behind the bar.

"You closed, Vinnie?"

"Am I closed? What the hell kind of question is that? Crissake, you know the law. I was closed an hour ago. Who's open?"

"I mean are you getting ready to go home, or can I have a beer?"

"Yeah."

"Yeah, what?"

"Yeah, I'm getting ready to go home, and yeah, you can have a beer. How's that suit you?" Vinnie poured a draught. "You paying or you charging?"

"Charging. Anybody in the back?"

"Yeah, they're playing. Nine or ten guys back there. They might even have two games. Before, they had just one. Kokomo they was playing, but now I think they got two games. Go back and see. What do I know about what goes on back there—I'm just a bartender."

"Oh-huh," Balzic said under his breath, "and the Pope's just a Catholic." He picked up his beer and walked down the narrow hall to the door beyond the men's room. He went in and drew up a chair behind one of the two tables and straddled it.

A stud game was in progress at the nearest table; the other table was going with Kokomo. Balzic watched one hand before he noticed Father Marrazo sitting with his back turned, directly in front of him. As many times as Balzic had see the priest in street clothes, the sight always put him off momentarily. He slid his chair closer and said, "How're you doing?"

"Terrible," the priest said barely opening his mouth. Then he threw in his hand and turned. "Oh, Mario. It's you. I wondered who was asking me. What brings you?"

"Couldn't sleep."

"Well, you've come to the right place. This nest of insomniacs beckons us all," Father Marrazo said and then smiled. "Hey, that's pretty good, don't you think? I'll have to think of a way to use that. Can't use it tomorrow, but another time perhaps."

"You really doing lousy?"

"Oh, only fair-lousy. Not lousy-lousy. I'm getting close to my time limit anyway. It's not three-thirty yet, is it?"

Balzic looked at his watch. "You got five minutes."

The priest nodded. "Last hand, men," he said to the other players.

"Last hand," one of the other players said. "Listen to him. Takes all the money, and then it's 'last hand, men.' "

"Frank has a bad habit of exaggerating," Father Marrazo said to Balzic. "Did you ever notice?"

"This is going to be interesting," Frank said, dealing the first two cards. "A priest asking a cop. Go ahead, Balzic, tell him."

"He's too polite," Balzic said. "He calls it exaggerating."

"You'd call it something else, right?" Frank said.

"Right," Balzic said, looking at the up card, a four, in front of Father Marrazo and the corner of the down card as the priest turned it up. It was also a four.

"Ace bets," Frank said.

The player to his left with the ace said, "Check."

Everybody checked with him.

The next round of cards showed no obvious improvement in any of the hands. The player with the ace checked again, and everybody checked along with him.

In the next round, the player with the ace got another, Father Marrazo got his third four, and Frank, the dealer, got another three to go with one he had showing.

"Pair of aces bets two-fifty."

"Call and raise five," Father Marrazo said.

The two players between the priest and Frank dropped.

"Your bet, Frank," the player with the aces said.

"I know it's my bet. I learned the rules this afternoon. Read a book on them." Frank studied the pair of fours in front of Father Marrazo and the pair of aces on his left. "I'm out," he said.

"Your five, Father, and ten back at you," the player with the aces said.

"Hum," Father Marrazo said. "I think I'll just call," he said, laying a twenty in the pot and taking a ten out.

"Last card," Frank said and dealt a five to the player with the aces and a queen to the priest.

"Twenty," said the player with the aces.

Father Marrazo sighed. "I am obliged to call, but something tells me . . ."

"Should've saved your money, Father," the player with the aces said. He turned up his hole card.

"Well," Father Marrazo said, looking at the third ace, "that is the way it isn't done." He pushed back his chair, picked up the bills and change in front of him, and put on his raincoat. "Good night, men. I hope I'll see some of you tomorrow morning." He led Balzic out to the bar and took a stool.

"Vinnie must've gone home," Balzic said, "or else he's in the can. Want a beer, Father?"

The priest nodded and Balzic got two bottles from one of the coolers.

"Now why didn't I believe him when he raised me ten?" Father Marrazo said.

"You want an answer, or you just thinking out loud?"

"Just thinking, I suppose, That's the way I played tonight. I'd play very well for a while, and then suddenly I'd have a lapse like that. I should've known immediately from the raise after he'd been checking like that that he had the ace underneath. Why do I do that?"

"You come out ahead?"

"Oh, of course. I can't remember the last time I lost, but it's as though I have some subconscious limit for winning. It must be my conscience."

Balzic laughed. "You serious?"

"I don't know. Am I? I must be. You know, tonight I was ahead at one point, oh I can't say for certain, but I must have been over a hundred dollars ahead. And what do I have now—I started with twenty-five and, let's see, there's forty, forty-one, forty-two, forty-seven-fifty. Twenty-two dollars and fifty cents. Do you know that the most I've ever won here, and I've been playing here now for eight, nine years, longer, almost ten years, and the most I've ever won is thirty-four dollars. And that night at one point I was over two hundred dollars ahead."

"At least you don't lose," Balzic said. "Tell me, Father, just what do you do with these winnings you take out of here—what is it? Twice a week?"

"That, my friend, is none of your business. Drink your beer, and tell me why you couldn't sleep."

"Bad dream," Balzic said, sloshing his beer around in his glass. "You know anything about dreams?"

"Some. Enough to know that only experts and fools dare to interpret them, and I'm more fool than expert."

"Well, it wasn't a dream really. I mean I wasn't asleep. You'd have to be asleep to have something you could call a dream, wouldn't you?"

"That is something only a very clear-talking psychiatrist could say, and I must say I've met very few of them in my life. What about day dreams, so-called? Or any flight of the imagination? When is one a dream, and when is it a hallucination, and so forth? I'm certain that somebody somewhere has troubled himself to try to define these things, but I haven't read them, and something tells me I wouldn't understand them even if I had. All I can do is offer the consolation that nearly everyone I know suffers from unpleasant thoughts

93

whether awake, asleep, or in any degree of consciousness. Was it about someone in your family?"

"For somebody who claims to be no expert, you're pretty good at guessing."

"No," Father Marrazo said. "That's just the usual pattern of these things, that's all. When we have dreams we don't even begin to understand, we generally dismiss them. But when we have the ones about those we are close to, again whether awake or asleep makes no difference, that's when we start worrying about ourselves, or at least that's been my experience in trying to deal with it when some of my parishioners come to me with the problem."

"Nobody ever comes to you about dreams he just plain doesn't understand? They only come when it's about something bad happening to somebody they're close to?"

Father Marrazo nodded. "And you'd have to admit that it would be naive to assume that those were the only kinds of dreams they had, but that's the only kind they tell me about. To narrow the thing down even more, generally the only time this comes up is when there's been a very superficial article about dreams in the slick sections of the Sunday papers. You know the kind of thing—'your dreams and what they reveal'—articles like that. I dread seeing those things, because by Wednesday I'll get a dozen calls from people who just have to talk to somebody. And when they get into my office, these poor people, all they want is to be told they're not crazy.

"In other words, Mario, what I'm trying to say is, forget about your dream. Admit you can't sleep, and do what you have to do about that. Stay awake as you're doing. Drink, if that helps, but don't worry about your dream. You only compound the problem, and not being able to sleep is problem enough for any man."

"Well, I would forget the dream, Father, but this one's a little different."

The priest started to ask how but changed his mind and waited.

Balzic rubbed his forehead for a moment. Then he said, "First, you have to know that Tommy Parilla has been trying to get my daughter to go out with him."

94

"Marie?"

"Yeah. Then you have to know that the last time he tried was at the football game on Friday night, and when she wouldn't, he told her to go to hell. There's more to it than that, but that's enough."

"That isn't your dream?"

"No, no. That's fact. The dream is Tommy telling Marie to go to hell and then smashing her face with a Coke bottle. That's the thing I saw every time I closed my eyes tonight."

"Well, I said before that only experts and fools dare interpret things like this, but, Mario, this is so obvious I'm wondering why you haven't figured it out yourself."

"May be obvious to you, Father, but not to me. I mean there was something pretty obvious about it to me, but from the look on your face, something tells me what you think is obvious and what I think is obvious are two pretty different things."

"Yes. Well. Tell me what was obvious to you."

"Aw, come on now, Father. I mean what do you think would be obvious to me? What else? I saw my daughter getting hurt."

"What else?"

"Whatta you mean, what else? Isn't that enough?"

"No, my friend. You're talking only as a father now, or rather, as the father you like to think you are. You have a dream such as you describe, and then you forget everything you've been saying about Tommy Parilla."

"Keep going. I'm listening."

"I wonder whether I should," Father Marrazo said.

"Well, don't stop now. I mean, what the hell. You give me this stuff about me being the father I like to think I am, and then you're going to hang it right there?"

"All right, Mario. As the father you like to think you are, you see your daughter in the place of someone else someone who was horribly beaten. Killed.

"But the fact remains that if this were true, if your daughter were in danger, then everything you've said about the reasons for John Andrasko's murder would be completely false."

95

"I don't follow you, Father."

"Yes, you do. What you mean is that right now you don't want to."

"Okay, then you explain it to me. I'll listen."

"You're daring me now, Mario, and I don't like to find myself on the other side of dares."

"Well, what do I have to say?"

"It's not what you say now. It's the way you're looking at me, and the tone of your voice—that's what's making me hesitate now."

"So forget my tone."

Father Marrazo took a swallow of beer and let it go down his throat slowly. "All right, Mario. What you saw in your dream and what you didn't like seeing is Marie having some responsibility for Tommy's act that night. To be sure, it was something completely beyond her control, never mind whether she had any knowledge of what Tommy had in mind. She doesn't know anything at all about this, does she?"

"No. I mean, well, I was going to say that she must know about John Andrasko, but I can't even say she knows that for certain."

"So there is a great possibility that she knows nothing at all of the connection between Tommy and John."

"Probably," Balzic agreed.

"Then any responsibility she may have had in triggering Tommy's act that night is something only you would know about."

"I'm with you so far."

"Something tells me you're not, Mario but . . ." The priest took another swallow of beer. "What I'm trying to say is this: your dream appears to you as a father as a very real danger to your daughter. But to you as a cop, it appears to you that your own daughter is partly responsible for what happened that night, though she is totally unaware of what happened. And please remember your theory about Tommy is that he is also unaware of what he did." The priest paused and searched Balzic's face a moment. Then he said: "Mario, the cop in you is angry at her for that, and she gets hurt in your dream because people who do wrong deserve punishment."

"Now wait a minute, Father—"

"No. You wait. I started this, and I want to finish it, otherwise you're going to go away with some misconceptions."

"Okay. Then finish it."

"Your dream, Mario, is a dream of justice—no, retribution would be closer to it. It's a very common dream among parents. Every time a son or a daughter stays out too late and doesn't call home, the parents begin to suspect the worst, a traffic accident usually, but what they're really acting out in their minds is a way to safely punish their child, because, you see, by staying out too late, the child is causing the parent some anxiety. How does the parent get even for this momentary suffering? By fantasizing suffering for the child, and invariably, when the child comes home safely, the parent starts to lecture him about staying out late and about the dangers on the highways and so forth.

"Mario, I tell you I hear this sort of thing five, six times a week, either from the children or from the parents. The children come to complain about the parents, and they go away feeling contrite for making their parents anxious, and the parents come to complain about their dreams and go away feeling contrite for having such terrible thoughts about their children."

"So what you're saying, Father, is that I really blame my daughter for what Tommy Parilla did, is that it?"

"Not so fast, Mario. It's not this or that. You were anxious about your daughter being anywhere near Tommy. You still are, otherwise you would not have had the dream. So that's a large part of it, but another part of it is because of the cop in you, and still a third part of it is that quite possibly you don't like being a cop where your daughter is concerned. In other words, Mario, the reason you can't sleep is, you don't like yourself for having that particular dream."

Balzic shrugged, as though to accept what the priest was saying, but after a moment he started to grind his teeth.

"Mario, at the rist of stepping beyond friendship as well as beyond my abilities, I have to say that such dreams are very common among people who—people like yourself—people who are always striving to be good."

"I don't know whether I like that, Father."

"Give me a moment, Mario. I'm trying to think who it was who wrote something about this. It was an Irish writer. I'll think of his name in a second." The priest tapped his lips with his knuckles. "The name escapes me, but he wrote: 'The momentary relief from the necessity for being good is a feeling that I suspect most decent men and women have shared'—that's it. Frank O'Connor. That's who it was."

The priest again searched Balzic's face before continuing. "And that's what I'm talking about, Mario. Somebody else wrote that this was the function of dreams—to allow decent people to have indecent thoughts. Dreams give you the momentary relief from being good that you don't permit yourself while you're awake—"

"Goddammit, Father, I was awake."

"Mario, Mario. How did we begin this whole conversation? Didn't we have some doubts about when a dream was a dream and when a hallucination and so forth? You're taking me too literally now."

"Maybe I am."

"Don't be angry with me, Mario. More important, don't be angry with yourself." The priest paused. "If you'll permit me another observation?"

Balzic shrugged morosely.

"I think that you're seeing Marie in more or less the same position you saw Mrs. Andrasko, or at least seeing the potential for Marie. You didn't tell Mrs. Andrasko—nor did I—and she had to find out about John the worst possible way, and now you see the potential for your daughter to find out that she may have had something to do with what Tommy did that night."

"Ah, this is all getting too complicated."

"Certainly it is, Mario. When is anything like this ever simple?"

"At least I'm starting to see what you're getting at anyway."

"Are you?"

"Yeah. About that last thing anyway. For sure I don't want Marie to get burned in this, and I guess I was thinking she was too close to the kid for anybody's good. And you're right that she doesn't know anything about what I'm thinking about him."

"Well, Mario, all your problem with Marie stems from whether you ever arrest the boy, isn't that it?"

"I suppose."

"It seems then that Marie will have to be among the first to know if you do."

"Yeah, Father, but all this depends on whether anybody every gets enough on the kid to make an arrest, and the way it's going, it doesn't look like that's going to happen, not unless the state boys come up with something in the car."

"Are they investigating that?"

"Hell, yes. They probably did already. I mean I told Moyer to stay away from the kid, and I know he'll respect that, at least until after the funeral, but he won't be sitting on his can about the car. Fact is, I'm a little surprised nobody's called me about it yet."

"And if the boy didn't use the car—I mean the car will only help if the boy drove it to and from, isn't that it?"

"You got it, Father. If he didn't take the car, or if he changed clothes somewhere—wait a minute. He had to have the car. Marie said so. That's what he told her at the game. Oh, Father, what a dummy I am. Listen, I got to go. You need a lift?"

"No. I have my car."

"Well, how about marking the beer up on my account in the cigar box under the counter, okay? I'll see you, Father," Balzic said, taking the steps to the side door two at a time.

Balzic found Lieutenant Moyer dozing off on a cot in one of the offices. A desk sergeant directed him to the room.

"I was wondering when you were going to show," Moyer said, sitting up and rubbing his eyes.

"I'm a little slow tonight," Balzic said. "Been a little slow the whole damn day and half the night before."

"We got the car. That's what you wanted to know, isn't it? I mean, you told me to lay off the kid, and I laid off, but I couldn't lay off the car."

Balzic lit a cigarette and waited.

"Mario, you never saw such a clean automobile in your life. You know where we pick it up? Coming out of the car wash on 986. Mrs. Andrasko's sister is driving it, and she just had to clean that car. It was absolutely filthy, she says. Jeezus, that woman must've taken lessons from the people who clean operating rooms. The only thing is, she says she didn't clean the trunk, and the trunk is like it came out of the showroom yesterday—no, make that this morning."

"So now we know."

"Sure. Now we know. And where does that get us? We scraped up a couple of envelopes, and ten'll get you a dime all the lab finds is good old pine tar and Lysol. And brother, that woman, is she something. She didn't buy any of it. We tell her it was just a routine inspection, except we have to keep the car until she produces the registration. We send her back with one of our men, and he's trying to stall, but we didn't get nearly the time we needed, and you just knew she wasn't buying any of it."

"I didn't think she would. Fact is, I may've had something to do with that."

"Yeah? How so?"

"It's not important how. What's important is, she won't be any help to us," Balzic said, looking away from Moyer's steady gaze. "Anyway, we got the circumstantial that somebody took a lot of trouble to clean the trunk, even if the lab doesn't come up with anything."

"And what'll any lawyer worth a pint of cold piss do with that? Can't you hear him? 'Your honor, the prosecution expects this court to believe that the fact that people want to keep their automobiles clean is reason to suspect my client. Why, your honor, if that were true, half the adult population in this country would be suspicious.' Then he'd give the jury a nice little grin, and they'd grin back, and there we'd be with our thumb up our ass." Moyer stood and scratched himself. "What did you come up here to tell me? Anything?"

"Oh, just that I'm almost positive the kid had the car most of that night." Balzic nearly apologized for saying it. "Course, you probably had that figured a while ago."

"Nobody up here was so sure of that. How come you're so sure?"

"My daughter told me. The kid tried to take her out during half time in the school game, and he told her he had the car."

"What time was that?"

"Nine. Nine-thirty, the latest."

"So we got him from nine-thirty until you see him coming home about one-thirty, right?"

Balzic nodded.

"Wonderful. We got John Andrasko from eleven-thirty until that train comes. Wasn't it about ten minutes late?"

"If that's all the later it was, it must've been late from an earlier run."

"Probably won't make much difference, but I ought to get a time-check from that fireman. One of my people talked to him yesterday. He better as hell have asked him about that."

"Well," Balzic said, "there's no use my hanging around, so I'm going to take off."

"Yeah, sure, Mario. Anything comes up, I'll let you know."

"Right," Balzic said and walked to his car feeling less and less useful.

At dawn, after having driven around Rocksburg for nearly two hours, Balzic turned into Delmont Street, where he lived. Halfway down the 200 block a car parked under a street light caught his eye. On its rear bumper was the sticker: "Support Your Local Police." Balzic passed the car, then stopped, and backed up. He sat staring at the sticker for a minute, then got out, went over to the bumper, and peeled the sticker off. "Dummy," he said, jamming the sticker in his coat pocket.

He drove on to his house and fell asleep in his clothes on the recliner in the living room. If he dreamed, he did not remember them when Ruth woke him two hours later.

John Andrasko was buried Monday morning at ten in St. Malachy's Cemetery. Balzic assisted the funeral director with the cars, though so few people came that the last three cars in the procession were occupied only by the drivers.

Balzic kept his eyes on Tommy Parilla throughout, but the boy showed nothing except concern for his mother. He stayed at her side, helping her in and out of the car, holding her arm when she knelt or rose during mass, and leading her gently by the elbow over the uneven ground of the cemetery.

Mrs. Andrasko never looked at Balzic, or if she did, Balzic was too preoccupied with her son to notice. Angie Spano looked at Balzic once, in the parking lot as the casket was being carried from the funeral home to the hearse, a look so intensely hostile that Balzic had to turn away.

After it was over, and Balzic was driving out of the cemetery, he saw Lieutenant Moyer standing beside an unmarked cruiser across the road from the exit. He pulled in behind Moyer's car and rolled down his window.

"See anything, Mario?" Moyer said, leaning with his forearms on the door of Balzic's car.

"The kid's a stone. A good and proper son looking out for his mother, but a stone. He didn't blink. What did you get?"

"Nothing from the lab except what kind of disinfectant was used, and we found that. There were about three gallons in a drum in the barn and a couple more gallons in another drum in the garage. The same kind we'd find in half the barns in the county."

"You go over the place good?"

"Except for the grounds. Barn, garage, and house. We got them good. They just happened to leave the kitchen door unlocked."

"Nothing?" Balzic said.

"Not a damn thing except for the Coke in the kitchen. You saw that."

"Yeah, I saw it. Who doesn't drink Coke?"

Moyer sighed. "I think it's about time we went to work on the kid. Time we told him his rights and put it to him."

Balzic frowned.

"Come on, Mario. What the hell are we supposed to do—give her a six-month period of mourning? What choice do we have? Christ knows, I don't like this any better than you do, but tell me something else to do and I'll do it."

102

"If I had something else to tell you, I would. The only thing I can say is—ah, never mind."

"Let's hear it."

"Nothing. You're right. There's nothing else to do, but you're going to catch another zero. That kid's psycho. He won't know anything, and he'll be telling the truth."

"Don't you even want to find out if you're right?"

"Uh-uh. Right now I'd just like to go get a beer—no, wait a minute. On second thought, you pick him up and let me have him."

Moyer screwed up his face.

"Put it this way," Balzic said. "How long do you think you can hold him before his aunt shows up with a lawyer? She'll be on the phone before you get him out of the house. That means you get at most an hour with him before the lawyer walks in and tells the kid to shut up, period. Then where are we? Just let me have him for a half-hour down at the train station."

"You think his aunt's going to sit still for that any longer?"

"No, but at least I'll have a half-hour alone with him. By the time she shows up at your office with the lawyer, we have the kid on his way home."

"And just what do you plan to say to him down there?"

"Tell the truth, I really don't know. But I told him a couple things already, and I'd like to find out if he's been thinking about them."

"Mario, first you say the kid's psycho and he won't remember anything, and now you tell me you told him some things to make him think." Moyer stood away from the car. "You know I respect you, Mario. Of all the local police in the county I got more respect for you than for half the rest put together. But since when are you a psychiatrist, number one, and number two, just what do you think a lawyer's going to do with you on the stand? I mean, suppose you do get something out of the kid. If the kid's really psycho, what the hell's he going to say that'll do us any good in court?"

"I know, I know. The lawyer asks me where I went to college and where I went to medical school, and I wind up looking like fried ass. But that's not what I'm thinking about."

"Well, what then?"

"I was thinking about setting myself up."

"Ah, Mario, I didn't know you watched those kind of TV shows."

"Okay. So it sounds like bullshit. So what—if it works?"

"Yeah. So what if you stand on that platform every night for ten years waiting for that kid to show up with a Coke bottle?"

"Then do it your way, Lieutenant."

"You're not going to get pissed off about it, for crissake."

"Why should I? This is your case."

"Mario, cut it out. You sound like a rookie."

"So I sound like a rookie. Just promise me one thing."

"All right. I promise. If we come up short with the kid, you get next crack. But psycho or not, we get him going for a couple of hours, he's going to bend some way."

"Don't forget the aunt, Lieutenant. Don't forget that little lady. You're not going to have time to give him the full go-round."

"Well, I'm going to make a damn good start."

"Okay. You want me, I'll either be at the station or else down at Muscotti's."

"Good enough. I'll let you know."

Balzic drove to city hall and busied himself with routine matters for the better part of an hour. He kept looking at his watch and checking it with the wall clock. He was reading a preliminary report of the salary board of the Fraternal Order of Police when he suddenly tossed it aside and told Sergeant Stramsky that he was going out to the club range to shoot.

"Moyer'll probably be calling in a little while, Vic. Tell him where I am, and if it's important, tell him to get me on the car radio."

"Where will you be after?" Stramsky said.

"At Muscotti's," Balzic said over his shoulder as he started out to his car.

"Ah, for the life of a chief," Stramsky said.

Balzic turned back at the door. "You say something?"

"Me? I didn't say nothing."

"You lying Polock. I heard what you said, and I'm going to tell you right now why you'll never be chief. You eat too much kolbassi, and it's starting to affect your brain."

"How 'bout that ginzo crap you eat—what's 'at doing to yours?"

"Making me smarter and smarter. And better looking, too. Hell, just the other day I looked in the mirror, and I said to myself, Balzic, be grateful you weren't born a Polock. Your face'd be a mess today. Just like Stramsky's."

"Hey, that reminds me," Stramsky said, reaching in his back pocket for a book of raffle tickets. "Next Sunday's the big day. You want a couple chances on a bushel of booze?"

"You talking about that corn roast at the Falcons?"

"Yeah. Corn, kolbassi, holupki, kapusta—all for the benefit of the building fund. Two o'clock until."

"I'll take a couple, but I'm damned if I'm going to that thing. Last year I had the runs for a week."

"Buck a chance," Stramsky said, holding out the book of tickets and a ballpoint pen.

"A buck? Last year it was fifty cents."

"So? That's inflation for you. Blame it on Nixon."

"You fill them out. I'll take three. Leave them on my desk."

"Uh-uh. Where's the dough?"

"Aaaw, Vic. You don't trust me?"

"No way. Last year it took me three months to collect."

"There was a rumor it was fixed last year, Vic. I was making an investigation."

"My ass. Dollar a throw. Come on, you goddamn half-breed, get the lock off your wallet."

"Put them on my desk," Balzic said, going through the door. "I'll catch you payday."

"Payday," Stramsky said. "That's shit." He filled out three chances for Balzic and laid the tickets on Balzic's desk, muttering the while about being a sucker.

At the Police Rod and Gun Club range, Balzic fired his usual twenty rounds with the 30.06 and then leaned against the back fender, smoking and thinking about what he would say to Tommy Parilla if he ever got the chance.

The longer he thought about it, the less certain he was about what to say. Other thoughts crowded in: the possibility that Moyer would get something out of Tommy; the possibility that Angie Spano would raise a large stink; the possibility that Milt Weight would start to use the newspaper to ridicule Balzic's part in the investigation and aggrandize his own office; and the most serious possibility of all—that Tommy Parilla had nothing to do with it. "But if he didn't," Balzic said to himself as he drove back into town, "then who the hell did? Some other nut?"

He shook his head as he parked in front of Muscotti's, as much to restore his conviction that Tommy Parilla was the murderer as to shake loose those other possibilities.

Balzic pulled open the front door and hesitated. Standing at the end of the bar with their heads together were Dom Muscotti and Sam Carraza. Balzic knew he could ignore them if he chose, but Pete Muscotti, Dom's nephew, was tending bar, and that immediately set Balzic on edge.

He had been arresting Pete Muscotti for the better part of ten years, the first time when Pete was fourteen, after Pete had decided, because he'd been thrown out of a typing class in high school, that it would be fair to pour maple syrup over the insides of all the typewriters. Dom had bailed him out of that one and every one since: every stupid scheme from the theft of automobile state inspection stickers to trying to run an independent handbook in territory assigned by somebody in Pittsburgh to somebody else's cousin.

All of Pete's troubles with the law had been costly but easy for Dom to set right; the bookmaking in protected territory had nearly cost Pete Muscotti his life, but, fool that he was, he thought it had been his own guts and moxie that had saved him. Dom indulged Pete because Pete's father had been Dom's favorite brother; Balzic, however sympathetic he tried to be to Dom's indulgence, could barely stomach Pete and sometimes not enough to stand being waited on by him.

Still, Balzic was thirsty, and priming himself to ignore the lip Pete would send his way, he went in and ordered a draught.

"You want this on your bill, Chiefo?" Pete said, pouring the draught. At the word "Chiefo" both Sam Carraza and Dom Muscotti looked up.

"Why don't you get a bullhorn?" Balzic said.

Pete smirked and said, "You paying, or what?"

"On the bill," Balzic said, trying not to let his eyes meet Pete's.

"Hey, Mario," Sam Carraza called out. "You seen the paper yet?"

"No. Is there something I should see?"

"Give him the paper, Petey," Carraza said.

Pete reached under the bar and came up with the city edition of *The Rocksburg Gazette.* He glanced at it and then turned it so that when he slid it across the bar in front of Balzic, the story Carraza was talking about was immediately obvious.

Across the bottom of the front page was:

HIPPIE GANG MEMBERS CHARGED IN ANDRASKO MURDER

by Dick Dietz

ROCKSBURG GAZETTE STAFF WRITER

District Attorney Milton Weigh announced this morning the arrest of what he termed "prime suspects" in the murder of John Andrasko, 45, of Rocksburg RD. County Chief of Detectives Samuel Carraza was credited by Weigh for having broken the case.

Arrested were Charles W. Reilley, 24, who gave his address as The Community Store, 616 State St., Rocksburg, and William A. Morrow, 20, of the same address.

The two men were arraigned before Magistrate Thomas Coccoletti Monday morning within minutes after John Andrasko's funeral cortege left St. Malachy's R.C. Church.

Dist. Atty. Weigh said Carraza, acting on a tip from a former member of the hippie-type group which makes its headquarters at the State Street address, arrested the two men early Monday morning as they were in Weigh's words "obviously preparing to leave town." Weigh also said that Carraza and his men confiscated a quantity of marijuana, some pipes, six marijuana cigarettes, and a quantity of pills.

Balzic stopped reading at that point and pushed the paper away.

"What's the matter, Mario," Carraza called out, "you don't like what you read in the paper these days?"

"You guys don't ever give up," Balzic said, sipping his beer.

"Maybe you ought to," Carraza said.

"All right, Sam," Dom Muscotti said. "Be nice now."

"I'm being nice. Friend Balzic is the one not being nice."

"So why don't you tell me how you broke the case, Sam," Balzic said. "I'm not too proud to learn something about my business."

Carraza laughed. "This is one trade secret I think I'll just keep to myself."

Balzic restrained himself until he saw Carraza and Pete exchanging grins. He set his glass down and started toward Carraza. "How 'bout if I tell you how you broke the case. How would that be?"

"You're the one doing the talking," Carraza said.

"That's all he can do," Pete said. "Sure as hell can't make anything stick on anybody."

"Pete!" Dom said, and Pete leaned back against a cash register and folded his arms.

Balzic glared at Pete for a second and then continued toward Carraza. "I'll tell you how you broke this case, Carraza, and you can correct me if I'm wrong."

"You're still the only one talking."

"Well, it went something like this. You picked up some punk on a narcotics, and you scared the piss out of him, and when he was ripe, you put a few hints in his head that just maybe if he could remember a few things you wanted to hear, just maybe you could arrange a lesser charge or maybe even drop all charges. And when he started to make the music, you gave him the words—isn't that the trade secret?" Balzic stopped a foot away from Carraza, who remained seated.

"Easy, Mario," Dom Muscotti said. "Go easy now."

"Tell your flunkey to go easy," Balzic snapped.

"Watch what you say now, Mario," Dom said. "You don't want to be sorry tomorrow for what you say today."

"I won't be sorry for anything tomorrow except maybe that I didn't catch this double-breasted ass-kisser where there weren't any witnesses."

"That's enough, Mario," Dom said.

"Who says so? You? Better think some more, *padrone*. It ain't like

108

it used to be, and I know you from before this flunkey was out of grade school."

"I wish there weren't any witnesses," Carraza said.

Balzic's left hand, his fingers stiff, stabbed Carraza in the throat and Carraza went backward off his stool. He lay on the floor holding his throat, gasping and coughing, his eyes filling with tears.

"You make a move, you sonuvabitch," Balzic said, "and I'll kick you."

"Mario!" Dom said, hustling out from behind the bar with his hands outstretched.

"Don't touch me, Dom."

"I'm not touching you. I wasn't going to touch you. I just don't want you to do nothing foolish."

"Then make sure he doesn't do nothing foolish till I get out of here."

"Okay. All right. He won't do nothing. Just go easy, that's all. That's all I'm asking. Just go easy."

Balzic backed toward the steps leading to the side door. "You keep your hands where I can see them, you hear, Carraza?"

"Mario, quit talking like that," Dom said. "Sam wouldn't do nothing like that in a million years. It's over. You won."

Balzic reached the landing to the side door. "It's not over," he said, "but it will be he ever puts it to me again."

Outside, Balzic swallowed and took a couple of deep breaths. He shook his left hand and pulled the fingers one by one. The middle finger was stoved. "Goddamn," he whispered, as he went around the front to his car. "Goddamn."

He drove back to City Hall. Before he went inside to the station, he went across the A&P parking lot and bought a paper from a machine.

When he got inside the station, Stramsky said, "I see you got the paper already. Hey. You feel okay?"

"Why? Don't I look okay?"

"Hell, man, your hands're shaking. Look at them."

"Ah, I just did something I wanted to do for a long time, and I guess I ain't as young as I used to be, that's all."

"What d'you do?"

"Never mind—what the hell. You'll hear it sooner or later. May as well hear it from me."

Stramsky sat on the corner of a desk. "So?"

"So I laid Carraza out. He started to give me some crap about this," Balzic said, thrusting the newspaper out, "and I took the heat. He said something, I said something, then he said something else, and I let him have it. I wanted to do that to him a long time."

"Where was this—Muscotti's?"

"Yeah," Balzic said, reading the rest of the story he'd begun in Muscotti's. "Look at how these bastards operate. They give you this big headline about arresting the murder suspects, and then you get down to the last paragraph and you find out what they really booked them on was possession of narcotics. Jeezus Christ."

"That's our hero for you."

"Weigh, that sonuvabitch. He makes me want to puke. He's so far up in that tree of his, he don't even know how he won that election, do you believe that? And if that ain't bad enough, he actually thinks Carraza and Dillman were his own choices, the jerk."

Stramsky looked puzzled for a moment. "You really think he don't know what Muscotti sent his way?"

"I know he doesn't. He thinks he made it on his pretty teeth and his country club memberships and his old man's money. Some day for laughs I just might tell him."

"Well, what did Carraza say?"

"He didn't say nothing I didn't back him into. But I have never been able to take him. Ever since the first time I saw him flunkeying for Froggy. I don't know. There's just something about a punk like that—he's so stupid he thinks nobody knows how many corners he's working. Weigh at least thinks he's honest. But guys like Carraza, they work three corners out of four, and they think they're slick-assing everybody."

"What did Dom do?"

"Ah, for a while he tried to come on like he used to before all his goombas went to the Bahamas, but the only thing he really did was tell his nephew to shut up."

"Petey boy," Stramsky said, shaking his head.

"Another weasel. The worst kind: big ambitions and no brains."

"So Dom didn't do anything?"

"Oh, he got between me and Carraza after I put him off his stool, but he knows better than to do anything else. I did him too many favors."

"Tell me something, Mario, just between us girls—did he used to be as big as everybody says he was?"

"Dom? Hell, no. But his old man was. His old man was number three in the county. After prohibition, the old man got every punch board, pin ball machine, and dice game from here east to the county line, never mind numbers and horses. He had those before. He had it all except from here west which numbers one and two had. Then number one goes to Vegas and number two goes to the Bahamas and the old man had a stroke and that leaves Dom. Then there was that thing in the *Saturday Evening Post* or *Collier's* or one of them magazines, and then Kefauver started up his heat, and up jumps old Froggy, who says he's going to clean up the county.

"So," Balzic went on, "Dom makes a deal with Froggy, and it worked okay until Froggy started thinking about his retirement. That's when Dom gets Carraza on Froggy's staff, and all of a sudden, the raids Froggy's making for the benefit of the papers and the little old ladies start to go wrong, and Froggy starts looking like a clown. And the more he looks like a clown, the madder he gets, and the more stubborn Dom gets and, well, you know the rest. Froggy finishes dead last out of five for judge and here comes Weigh riding in on his white horse. Maybe I should invite Weigh and Froggy to a barbecue in my backyard and let Froggy give it to him straight."

"Boy, I'd like to hear that," Stramsky said.

"Ah, that's just wishful thinking. From what I hear, Froggy's so whacked out now, he has three drinks, he forgets where he lives."

"It'd still be worth the price of admission to hear it."

"Weigh wouldn't believe it anyhow," Balzic said, heading for the door. "I'm going up to see Moyer, if anybody wants me."

"Okay," Stramsky said. "Hey, I put the tickets on your desk. How 'bout the money?"

"See me payday," Balzic said and went out to his car.

111

He drove to the state police barracks, pulling on his stoved middle finger at every intersection. By the time he parked in front of the barracks, the finger was throbbing.

Lieutenant Moyer was standing by the desk staring off into space when Balzic came in. His eyes focused on Balzic, and he shook his head slowly. "Should've listened to you, Mario," he said.

"How much time did you get?"

"Just time enough for him to say, and I quote, 'You think I killed him, don't you?' end quote, and in walks Miss Spano with one drunken Greek, and that was that."

"She got the Greek, huh?"

"Himself, and in living color. Myron M. Valcanas."

"Well, you got to admit, he's a hell of a lawyer."

"Sure. If you can stand the bastard."

"Got the kid out of here, didn't he?"

Moyer stared off into space again. "Who would've thought she'd get him?"

"Well, you know, it really didn't make much difference who she got," Balzic said.

"I know that, goddammit. I just thought we'd get maybe an hour anyway."

"You didn't. So that's that. Now what I think we ought to do is—"

"I know what we do. We set you up. Like the movies. It's disgusting."

"What if I go talk to Valcanas?"

"What for?"

"Look, whatever else that Greek is, he isn't stupid. If I tell him what I'm thinking, he might go along with a court order to have the kid examined by a psychiatrist."

"No, he wouldn't. Not as long as we're in on it. He's memorized all the times we picked him up for drunk-driving. He bends over backward and inside out to give us trouble."

"That's probably true, Lieutenant, but I never arrested him for that, and neither did any of my people. He doesn't have any grudge with me."

Moyer threw up his hands. "Go ahead. What the hell've we got to lose?"

"Incidentally, you seen the paper?"

"About Weigh? Yeah, I've seen it. What do you want me to say? That he got his feet three feet off the floor? Okay, so I've said it. Go talk to the Greek," Moyer said, disappearing into one of the offices, his head going from side to side. Balzic could hear the sighs of disgust before the door slammed.

Balzic found Myron Valcanas in the back room of the Rocksburg bowling alleys—Rocksburg Bowl, 24 Lanes, AMF Pinsetters, Good Food and Drink. Valcanas was playing captains gin and losing.

As Balzic drew up a chair beside him, Valcanas said to the bartender who followed Balzic in and was picking up the glasses and taking orders, "For crissake, this time put some whiskey in it."

"S'matter, Mo," Balzic said, "somebody trying to cheat you?"

"All a bunch of goddamn thieves," Valcanas said, lighting a cigarette-sized cigar. "Everywhere you go, thieves and liars in public places. And then there's my countryman, our distinguished vice president."

"Your deal, Greek," Valcanas's opponent said.

Valcanas took the cards and shuffled. "I'd give everything I made last year and everything I'm going to make this year to buy fifteen minutes of prime-time television to debate that lying fake."

"Oh, yeah?" Balzic said. "And just what would you say to him?"

"What would I say to him? Why I'd just ask him about four questions, that's all it would take. Mr. Vice President, I'd say, how do you pronounce democracy in Greek? Then I'd ask him how many political prisoners are being held incommunicado in Greek jails. I wouldn't even bother asking him if he knows what Greek jails are like. Then I'd ask him just what the hell is so subversive about Mark Twain's books—among others—that those goddamned colonels banned them. Imagine it. *Tom Sawyer* for crissake. Now there's a really dangerous book. And the last thing I'd ask him is which side he'll sell guns to when the blood starts to run in the streets over there. The colonels have it all their way now, but I give them about three more years."

"You going to play cards, or you going to give a goddamn sermon?" Valcanas's opponent said.

"What's your hurry, for crissake? You're six bucks ahead right now, and we've only been playing for twenty minutes." Valcanas turned to Balzic and said, "Oh, it's you, Mario. I wondered who the hell I was talking to. A man of common sense, I could tell that. A rare individual these days."

"I only got nine cards, Greek."

"Then pick up another one, and you'll have ten. That's simple enough, isn't it?" Valcanas turned back to Balzic. "Nine and one makes ten, doesn't it? I mean I have always been led to believe that, haven't you?"

"No argument," Balzic said. "Listen, Mo, I want to talk to you about a client of yours."

"Is this an honest inquiry, Mario, or are you trying to find out how I intend to defend him—whoever the hell it is."

"Let's just say this is friendly business."

"Impossible. No business with Greeks is friendly."

"Your play, Greek," Valcanas's opponent said.

"I know that, for crissake," Valcanas said. "Nothing I like better than playing cards with someone who keeps reminding me of the sequence of play." Valcanas glanced at Balzic's hands. "You don't even have a drink, for crissake. How are we to talk about anything—business or otherwise—when you're emptyhanded?"

The bartender returned then with a full tray of drinks for the players.

Valcanas took a long swallow of his drink. "That's more like it, for crissake. And bring my friend here a drink. On my tab."

"Beer," Balzic said.

"Knock with six," Valcanas's opponent said.

"Six! Why, you thief. I have four. Did you actually believe you could get away with six? Who dealt these cards anyway?" Valcanas grinned at Balzic, his gold fillings glinting in the light coming from a window opposite them. "This innocent listens to our vice president, listens to him and watches him on the tube, and he still trusts Greeks."

"I don't mind losing the hand, but do I have to put up with the bullshit, too?"

"The lament of losers everywhere," Valcanas said. "If it's not the wind, it's the rain. It wasn't my fault, coach, the ball was muddy. Deal, for crissake. What's my partner doing?"

"I caught him with half the garage," Valcanas's partner said.

"See there, Mario. Justice, that blind and virginal beauty, triumphs again. Good conquers evil, the world spins on, rectified," Valcanas said. "Now who's this client of mine you want to discuss?"

"Here?"

"Where else? I'm behind, for crissake."

"Okay. The one you left about a half-hour, forty-five minutes ago."

"I'm listening."

"He did it."

"Mario, from a policeman's point of view, I've never heard of one who had not done it. Say something else."

"He's sick. I mean I think he's so sick he doesn't even know he did it."

"Oh? And how many hours have you had him on your couch, doctor? And where did you say you went to school?"

"Come on, Mo. This isn't for a jury."

"Then say something intelligent."

"Honest to Christ, Mo—"

"No appeals to saviors. I said say something intelligent."

Balzic squirmed about on his chair. "Give me a chance."

"I knew a whore used to say that," Valcanas said, grinning. " 'Give me a chance, sailor, that's all I ask. Just a chance to make a couple of honest dollars.' And the next morning there'd be a conciliatory note pinned to the pillow explaining about the flat condition of said sailor's wallet. It was very touching."

"Okay," Balzic said. "Put it this way. There's nobody else."

"There's always somebody else."

"Not this time. No way, no reason."

"But a moment ago you said my client had a reason. A reason he doesn't understand but which you do, and again I ask, Doctor, where was it you said you interned? Was that the Menninger Clinic or was that with the Mayo brothers?"

"Mo, let's go someplace else. I can't make any sense in here."

"I'll drink to that," Valcanas said, draining his glass in three swallows. "Innkeeper!" he called out. "Another round for my friends and enemies—whoa, that card gives me gin, I believe." He spread his hand on the table. "That is gin, is it not?"

"No shit," his opponent said.

"I'm still listening, Mario. But get to the point. I have nothing doing in court for four or five days, and I intend to let my liver know who's boss."

"Okay. Right to the point. I want you to go along with a court order to have your client examined by a psychiatrist."

"On what grounds?"

"On what—Mo. Not a half-hour ago, you got him out of a session with Moyer and his boys. They were ready to turn him inside out."

"That's all they were—ready."

"Well they'll do it again. If not tomorrow, then the day after."

Valcanas turned on his chair and faced Balzic. "Get some things straight, Mario. Number one, nobody does anything to any client of mine without adhering to the letter of the rules and procedures. The letter. Not the rules and procedures as they would like them to be, but *as they are.* Number two, Moyer picked my client up today and got him into one of his back rooms and had not—I repeat—had not even made a notation in his log about ever having picked him up, never mind making a notation about informing him of his rights. Number three, those two little facts are a direct violation of rules and procedures for proper arrest and interrogation from Washington to Harrisburg to little old Rocksburg. Number four, that such violations occurred and that such improper, not to say crude, methods were tried—tried, I said—indicates a clear attempt at coercion. And there's only one reason for police coercion. The same one there's always been—they have nothing else to go on that would stand up in court for two minutes. And number five, I get almost as

116

much pleasure from making Moyer and his boy scouts uncomfortable as I do from scratching my hemorrhoids."

Balzic hung his head and sighed. "Mo, do I look like Moyer?"

"No to that. Ask another."

"Do you want to see somebody else get it the way you know who got it? 'Cause that's what's going to happen."

Valcanas thought for a moment. "You that sure of that?"

"I am."

"Then go talk to a judge. I won't interfere. But do it right. And I mean everything. If there's one comma out of place, I'll stuff it down your throat in the hearing."

Balzic blew out a deep breath. "Thanks, Mo. I appreciate it."

"Save your gratitude. Your war's just starting. I read the paper, you know. Just what do you think little Milty Weigh's going to do when he hears about what you're up to? That's for openers. For callers, court's recessed until Thursday, and there's a bar association meeting tonight honoring that fat fart that got himself appointed to federal district court. All the judges will be there, which means they'll all get loaded, which means, furthermore, you'll be lucky to find one of them willing to listen to anything before Thursday. Maybe not even then."

"Well, thanks anyway."

"It's your deal, Greek."

"For crissake, don't you think I know that? Why is it that of all the card players in the world I have to play the ones who can't quit telling me when to deal. There," he said, shuffling the cards, "satisfied now?"

"I want to cut."

"Cut then. Shuffle them if that makes you happy."

"See you, Mo," Balzic said, starting for the door.

"Won't you be lucky," Valcanas said without looking up.

Balzic turned back, "Just one more thing, Mo."

"Yeah?"

"Try to keep the sister out of it."

"Sweet little Angie? That shy violet? Why, she's a wonderful person. I could tell that after five minutes with her."

"Yeah, sure. Just do everybody a favor and keep her quiet."

"Mario, if I didn't know better, I'd say you were afraid of her. Now what gives me that impression?"

"Say whatever you want. This thing's a big enough mess without her stomping around in it."

"All I can guarantee is to tell her the most agreeable lies. If that doesn't work, well . . ." Valcanas shrugged.

"Gin," Valcanas's opponent said.

"Gin! Let me see those cards. Take your hands away, for crissake."

Balzic left while Valcanas was making some sort of oration in Greek.

Balzic covered the judges' offices in the courthouse in twenty minutes. Each of the six secretaries gave him more or less the same response: "The judge is out," or "The judge has left word he will not be in until Thursday."

He went down to the lobby pay phone and dialed their residences, and one by one, either by recorded message or from a member of the family, heard the same story.

Whispering curses in Italian and Serbian, he used his last dime and dialed again."

"State police. Sergeant Stallcup speaking," came the answer.

"This is Balzic. Let me talk to Moyer."

"He's not here, Mario."

"He say where he'd be?"

"Yes, he did. He said he was going out to see Mrs. Andrasko."

"What? What the hell for?"

"That he didn't say."

"How long ago'd he leave?"

"About five minutes."

"Oh Jeezus Christ," Balzic said. He slammed the receiver on the hook and ran through the lobby down the back stairs to his car. He tried for nearly a minute to get Moyer on the radio. Nothing. He squealed rubber out of the alley and left a trail of horns blowing behind him as he bullied into traffic on Forbes Street.

In three minutes he bounced off Route 986 onto the driveway of the Andrasko farm and skidded to a stop behind Moyer's car, just in time to see Angie Spano doing everything short of actually shoving Moyer off the porch. Balzic did not bother to get out of his car.

Moyer came over and said, "You say one word, Mario, and so help me . . ."

"All I'm going to say is, I talked to the Greek."

"And?"

"And he said he wouldn't interfere if I got a court order authorizing a shrink to examine the kid."

"What else?"

"I can't find a judge, that's what else."

"You know what, Mario? We're a couple of geniuses, that's what we are."

Balzic fiddled with his keys.

Moyer looked at the sky and then down at his shoes. "Okay," he said, "I was in the office wearing out the seat of my pants, and I kept getting more steamed by the minute, so I broke my own rule."

"What rule's that?"

"It's one I made about six, seven years ago when I made lieutenant. I told myself then that whenever I didn't know what to do, I'd never make the mistake of doing something."

"That's a damn good rule, Phil."

"Yeah. I always thought so. What do you suppose made me break it today?"

"You got me."

"What say we get the hell out of here? The longer I stand here, the more embarrassed I get. I can feel the woman looking at me."

"You going back to your office?"

"No," Moyer said. "I think I made enough mistakes for one day. Think I'll go home and take a nice, long shower and read some old *National Geographics*. Stimulate my mind. And don't look for me tomorrow either, 'cause I'm taking tomorrow off. Tomorrow I'm not even going to make the mistake of getting out of bed except to take a leak. You want anything, call Stallcup."

"Okay, Phil. I'll do that. See you Wednesday, maybe."

"Don't bet on it. Maybe tomorrow night I'll get lucky and die."

Balzic backed the car and turned around. He could see Moyer

following him as he pulled onto 986, but soon he quit looking back and when he looked back again Moyer had turned off.

At city hall, when Balzic walked into the station, Stramsky gave him a quick nod. Balzic looked in the direction of the nod and saw Milt Weigh, Sam Carraza, and John Dillman with their heads together by the large window fronting Main Street.

"Something I can do for you, Milt?" Balzic said, approaching them.

Weigh turned with a start. He cleared his throat and said, "There is. You can turn over your weapon to Detective Dillman."

"*Detective* Dillman," Balzic said. "It's going to be like that, is it?"

"It is," Weigh said. "I'm placing you under arrest. I have the warrant here. I don't think I have to inform you of your rights."

"Mind if I read the warrant, Milt?"

"First, your weapon."

"I don't have one."

Carraza's eyebrows shot up. "You don't have one?" he said.

"You want to search me?" Balzic said, opening his suit coat and lifting it and turning around slowly. "Maybe you better search me. Maybe I carry it in a holster sewed to my skivvies." He put his arms down and took the warrant Weigh extended to him. Before he started reading, Balzic said, "I can hear your wheels grinding, Sammy boy. You think your boss can hear them, too?"

"What's he talking about, Sam?" Weigh asked.

"Ask him," Carraza said. "What do I know what this crazy man talks about?"

Balzic glanced over the warrant. "Not bad, Milt. Assault, assault and battery, assaulting an officer of the law. The last one's pretty funny, but I guess the other two are okay."

"There is nothing funny about any of them," Weigh said. "Evidently you're forgetting a few things."

"Like which few things?"

"Like your conduct following the arrest of certain persons for surety of the peace last Saturday night. For instance, in the plain view of these two detectives you struck with your hand one of those persons. For another instance, you're forgetting our conversation the day after that incident. And for another instance—"

"That's enough instances, Milt. I get your drift," Balzic said. "Well. What are we waiting for? Let's go."

"Go where?" Weigh said.

"To the magistrate's—where else? You plan to file the information by proxy or something?"

"Not so fast, Balzic."

"Sergeant Stramsky," Balzic called out, "I think you better come over here. I don't want you to miss any of this. Something tells me the district attorney is about to make some sort of an offer."

"You stay where you are, Stramsky," Dillman said.

"It's okay, Mario," Stramsky called back. "I can hear okay."

"Well, Milt, what's it going to be?"

"I want your resignation, Balzic."

"My what? And just what the hell am I supposed to be resigning for?"

"Your health," Carraza said. "What else?"

"So either I resign because my health's gone bad all of a sudden or else what—you're going to prosecute?"

"That's the idea," Weigh said.

"Milt," Balzic said, "I never realized until this minute what a real amateur you are. And to think that in, oh, say, twelve, sixteen years, you'll be down in Washington, after you do the bit in Harrisburg, of course. What are you thinking about, Milt—you going to hustle for state's attorney general, or you going right after the governor's house? Will it be the House first and then the Senate? Course, it'll all depend, won't it?"

"The joke's over, Balzic. I want an answer."

"Do you now? Okay, I'll give you a couple. Number one, I'm not sick. Number two, you file this information against me, and you won't even get re-elected to the office you're sitting in now, never mind those other places, and I'll tell you why, Milt. 'Cause you don't know your territory. You don't know who is who around this county, and most of all, you don't know who was who in Muscotti's when I allegedly assaulted friend Carraza here. Why don't you ask him what would happen if Dom Muscotti and that little prick nephew of his had to testify against me? Go ahead. Ask him."

"What's he talking about, Sam?" Weigh said.

Carraza shrugged nervously. "What do I know what he's talking about?"

"I'll say one thing for you, Sammy boy," Balzic said. "When you told your boss here what happened, I'll bet it never even occurred to you he might try to pull this, and then I'll bet you started thinking it might not be such a bad idea, but right now I can see from your face, dumb as you are, it's starting to sink in that it's a pretty shitty idea."

"Sam, if there's something you haven't told me," Weigh said, "I want to hear it right now."

"Well, while you girls are talking it over," Balzic said, "I think I'll just give my lawyer a call. You know him, Sam. Mo Valcanas."

"Hold it, Mario," Carraza said. "We can work this thing out."

"What's going on here, Carraza?" Weigh said.

John Dillman started walking for the door.

"Where are you going?" Weigh shouted.

"Outside," Dillman said. "I don't want to hear none of this."

"What is this?" Weigh snapped. "He mentions that drunk's name, and you two fold up. What the hell's going on?"

"Tell him, Sammy boy," Balzic said. "Tell him what a good memory that drunk has. Tell him who was Froggy's campaign manager sixteen, seventeen years ago. And then tell him how come Mo Valcanas wasn't Froggy's campaign manager the next time around."

"Listen, Milt," Carraza said, "I think we better forget this. No kidding, Milt. I think we just better forget the whole thing. I'm sorry I said anything. I don't know what I was thinking about. He never hit me. I mean, he hit me, but I called him a name. Dom heard me. So did Pete. It didn't happen the way I said. Honest."

The veins in Weigh's neck started to swell. He stormed past Balzic and out the door. Dillman and Carraza trailed after him, and for a long moment, Carraza's pleas and excuses filtered in from the parking lot.

Stramsky laughed until tears flowed. "Since when is Mo Valcanas your lawyer?" he said after he stopped laughing.

"What the hell's so funny?" Balzic said. "What other bluff you want me to use? That bastard was out to put me on unemployment, and you want me to play nice?"

"Yeah, I know all that," Stramsky said. "But what the hell does Valcanas have to do with anything?"

"Remind me to tell you some other time," Balzic said. "All you need to know right now is, Carraza is scared shitless of Valcanas 'cause one time Carraza got wise with the Greek and started running his mouth about who he was and what he could do. So Valcanas told him he had it all written down about how many times Carraza tipped off Muscotti about state police raids back when Dom was still number three. And in the meantime, Valcanas is still Muscotti's lawyer, so Carraza knows that Valcanas knows a hell of a lot from that side. But what Carraza doesn't know—and neither does anybody else—is whether Valcanas wrote anything down or not, and Carraza may be dumb, but he's not dumb enough to get on the stand with Valcanas asking the questions. Especially not when the only witnesses are Dom and that dumb-ass nephew of his.

"Hell, Vic, if I could handle half my problems as easy as this one, I'd be thinking about running for public office myself."

"What the hell would you run for?"

"What else? Clerk of courts. Pays close to nine thousand a year and you work about as much as the average Polock desk sergeant."

"Well, up yours, too. And where's the money for those tickets?"

"Payday I told you. How many times I have to say it?" Balzic said, starting for the door. "Man, you're getting mercenary in your old age. I remember when you were on a beat, Vic. All you used to think about was God, flag, mother, and kolbassi."

"Hey, where you going to be?"

"Home," Balzic called back. "And if anybody wants me, tell them I went south."

"Hey, baby," Balzic said as he came into the kitchen. "What's for the stomach?" He put his arms around Ruth's waist from behind.

"Lasagna," Ruth said. "But it's going to be sloppy. I had to use cottage cheese. Louis was out of riccotta."

Balzic kissed her on the neck. "So. It won't be all that bad. Where's the girls?"

"They said they were going to Theresa Androtti's house. To do their homework, no less. God knows where they'll wind up."

"Where's Ma?"

"Laying down. She doesn't feel so good."

"Those pills not helping her?"

"Oh, Mar, you know what she says. All they do is make her go to the bathroom. Half the time I don't even think she takes them."

"We got any wine? I feel like some wine."

"That's not all you feel like."

"Oh, yeah? And just what do I feel like?"

"Well, I know you don't carry a gun, and even if you did, you wouldn't be carrying it there."

"Oh. That. Funny thing about that. That always happens when I catch you alone cooking."

"Big deal. When I'm cooking."

"I notice you're not trying very hard to get loose."

"As much as I've seen you in the last week . . ."

"Keep talking. I hear you."

"If it's not football games, it's an accident, and if it's not that, then it's—never mind. Look out, Mar, I have to get the sauce."

Balzic let go and backed up. "Where's the wine? We got any?"

"There's a whole gallon under the sink."

Balzic got the bottle and poured a water glass full. He loosened his tie and sat at the kitchen table. He took a couple of sips and then a long drink. "This is pretty good. How much?"

"I don't remember. Three something. Three-forty, I think."

"Not bad."

"Mar, there's something we have to talk about."

"Go ahead."

"It's Marie."

"S'matter with her?"

"She's been acting funny for the last couple of days."

"Maybe it's her time of the month. You act pretty funny when it's your time."

"No. It's not that. I thought of that, too. She hasn't said beans for, I don't know, since Saturday."

"Yeah. Well then, I know what it is."

"You do? Then tell me—would you mind?"

124

"It's something I told her. I didn't tell her. I asked her, and she must've put two and two together."

Ruth put down her spatula and turned around. "Well, what did you ask her?"

"It was about this Parilla kid."

"And?"

Balzic took another drink of wine. "Look, Ruth. It's nothing to get all worked up about. I mean it is, and it isn't. But I've already talked it over with Father Marrazo, so I know what needs to be said when the time comes."

"Okay. So you know. Now, would you mind telling me?"

Balzic recounted the conversation he had with Marie and Emily about Tommy Parilla and then the one he had with the priest.

"Well, at least now I know," Ruth said. "The way she was acting I thought I'd done something. Or forgot something."

"Nah. No chance. But she's no dummy. She had to add it up. The thing Father Marrazo said was, if I ever do arrest the kid, I have to be sure to tell her what's going on. Otherwise, she might jump to all kinds of wrong conclusions. But don't worry about it."

"Are you going to arrest him?"

"Toss a coin on that one, baby. Right now all we have is a lot of ideas. They all fit, but that's all they do. I mean if we took it to court, it'd get tossed out in five minutes. I'm just waiting on the judges to come back from wherever the hell they are so I can get the kid examined."

"What if you can't?"

"Ruthie baby, you still got a hell of a pair of legs, you know that?"

"Boy, are you ever subtle."

"That's me. Old smoothie. Smoothest guy you ever knew."

"So what are you going to do in the meantime?"

"Well, for one, I plan to spend the hours between ten and twelve down at the station."

"Mar! Not tonight."

"What's tonight?"

"Tonight we're going to the Joyces' house—how could you forget that?"

"How could I forget what I didn't know?"

"Oh, Mar, honest to God."

"Okay, we can still go, but from ten till twelve I won't be there, that's all. Ruthie, Jeezus, who better than them would understand?"

"It's just the idea. I mean, it was the first date we've had in weeks."

"We'll have the date, okay? No problem. Now finish with the lasagna and come here."

"Nothing doing. Just when we'll get started, the girls'll come bouncing in or Ma'll wake up."

"Ah, where's your guts? Press your luck a little."

"Press my luck a little. Ha. Keep quiet and drink your wine. Go in the living room and have a daydream—press my luck a little. What do you think I've been doing since I married you? If I'd've married a doctor I would've seen him more."

"Okay for you," Balzic said, filling his glass again. "Think I will go have a daydream. Let me see, today I think I'll have one about Anna Magnani—how's that?"

"Good. Have two. Bet the first thing she says is, 'Where the hell you been for the last two weeks, big boy?'"

Balzic left Ruth at the Joyces' house at nine-fifty. They had played penny ante for about an hour, and when Balzic left, he was sure Ruth believed that when he'd said he was going to the station, she understood that to mean the police station.

That he meant the train station turned out to mean nothing very much at all. He stood on the platform from ten until after midnight, and except for the arrival of the eleven-thirty-eight to Knox, which was ten minutes late, he saw nothing else.

Balzic spoke briefly with the fireman and a porter and a man in the mail car, but he learned nothing from them he didn't already know. When the train pulled away toward Knox the uselessness of what he was doing crowded in on him and left him with a sour stomach and a bad taste. He tried to blame that on the cigarettes he'd smoked, but it didn't work, and he drove back to Bill Joyce's house filled with a rising irritation that he might be wrong about everything and that if he was, then somebody else had to be right.

The only somebody who had an alternative was Milt Weigh, and that thought caused Balzic's stomach to erupt in a volley of flatulence, a series of belches and burps both loud and sour.

He made his apologies to the Joyces and took Ruth home at about a quarter to one.

On Tuesday night and again Wednesday night he was on the train station platform. The result both nights was the same.

On Thursday morning, when he went to President Judge Arnold Friedman's chambers to get the order to have Tommy Parilla examined by a psychiatrist, Balzic had to reconvince himself that he knew what he was doing. He started into the judge's secretary's office twice before he finally summoned the nerve to ask her to let him in to see the judge, and then nearly lost it all in the middle of his request to her when the door to Friedman's office opened and Milt Weigh walked out.

Only the expression on Weigh's face when their eyes met kept Balzic from leaving. Weigh looked as though he had spent long hours talking with people who knew more than he and had come away from the talks racked with mistrust of his own ability to judge anything.

For a moment, Balzic felt obliged to console Weigh, or, if not that, then at least to whisper his sympathy that Weigh had to learn certain things the way he had.

Balzic, for his part, could not remember a time when he did not know that public officials were used in ways they did not recognize until it was too late. Weigh, from his slouch, seemed never to have considered the possibility that he could be used as easily as he used others, and the slackness in his mouth when he spoke confirmed how much the learning had shaken him.

"Morning, Milt," Balzic said.

"Morning," Weigh said. "If you want to see Judge Friedman, you can now."

"Yes, thanks," Balzic said. "Maybe you ought to know, Milt, uh, I'm here to get an order to have the Parilla kid examined."

"I know that," Weigh said.

"You do?"

"Yes. I had a long talk with Mo Valcanas yesterday. That was just one of the things he told me."

"You don't—you have no objection?"

"Why should I?"

"I just thought you might."

"I don't," Weigh said. "As a matter of fact, I've already talked to Friedman about it, and you won't have to do much talking. Just tell him what you want. I'll follow it up."

"Okay, Milt. Okay. And thanks."

Judge Friedman appeared in the doorway. "Mario, did you want to see me?"

"Yes, I did," Balzic said and then said so long to Weigh, but Weigh was going through the door of the outer office and didn't hear.

"Come in, Mario, and have a seat," Friedman said. "Before we get to business, tell me who you like in the National League."

"Oh, Cincinnati all the way."

"You don't think the Pirates have a chance?"

"Who doesn't have a chance? But they don't have the pitching or the catching."

"You know, Cincinnati's pitching is wearing a little thin."

"Yeah, but that won't hurt them until the Series."

"You think the Pirates will win their division?"

"I don't really think it'll make too much difference who wins. Cincinnati has too much."

"So if someone offered you, say, five to seven, you'd take the Reds?"

"I'd take them against the Pirates at one to five."

"Really?" Friedman said, leaning back in his chair. "Well, what can I do for you?"

"Well, I want a lot of red tape cut in a hurry. I want to book a kid on a general charge of murder, and then I want him examined by a psychiatrist, but the thing I want to make sure of—well, two things, really. First, I don't want any problems with the charge, and second, I want to make sure the kid gets the works from the doctor just as fast as possible." Balzic looked at his fingernails. "Least that's what I wanted, and that's what I thought I was going to have trouble getting. But Milt Weigh just told me he already said something to you about it."

"He has," Friedman said. "You file your information, Mario, and I guarantee to move this thing for you as fast as possible."

"How soon would you—I mean, how long do you think it'll take?"

"Well, Mario, if I declare no bail, what difference does it make?"

"Can you do that on a general charge?"

"That depends on who his lawyer is, and how much pressure is put on him."

"His lawyer's Valcanas."

"Oh."

"And he has an aunt."

"Why not make it first degree then?"

"That means premeditated, and I don't think this kid had the faintest idea of what he was doing."

"A technicality, Mario. You can't have it both ways. Make it first degree, and he doesn't get bail. It's that simple."

Balzic cleared his throat and rubbed his chin.

"Mario, don't be so cautious. I should say, rather, detach yourself from this. What does it matter if you have your man examined?"

"Nothing, I guess."

"Of course not," Friedman said, standing up. "Give his name to Elaine. She'll take care of the papers. Then you go get him."

"Right. Okay." Balzic stood. "And thanks, your honor."

"Mario, about this other thing?"

"What other thing?"

"You'd give one to five on the Reds?"

"Sure. But nobody'll need to. I would, though."

"You think the odds will come off much lower?"

"No question about it. I'd say they'll go off at six to five or even eleven to ten. It'll be way down."

"So you're suggesting that a fellow should wait?"

"Sure. He'd be foolish not to." Balzic turned for the door and then turned back. "One more thing, your honor."

"What is it?"

129

"I don't want to put this boy in a lockup. I want to take him right out to Mamont."

"Go ahead."

"Well, what I mean, could you give me a name out there, so I can be sure they'll go to work on him right away."

Judge Friedman walked past Balzic and called out to his secretary: "Elaine, get me Mamont State Hopsital. Dr. Lester."

Elaine looked through her desk directory and started dialing. "Is he the only Lester out there?"

"First name is Lou, Elaine. Louis G., I think." The judge went back to his desk to wait. "Good man Lester," Friedman said. "But they've turned him into an administrator, and I'm afraid he's being wasted."

A button lit up on the judge's phone. He picked it up and said, "Lou? Arnold Friedman here . . . Oh. fine. You? . . . Good, glad to hear it. Listen, Lou, I've got a problem. Trying to cut through channels and so forth . . . Yes, well this one's a little different. The chief of police here . . . Yes, that's the one. Balzic. He has a suspect in a case and he has reason to believe the suspect may not be in control of himself. I don't know all the details, but from what I gather, the suspect has some members of his family who are trying to interfere. . . ." Friedman looked at Balzic questioningly.

"And Chief Balzi wants a complete examination done on the suspect as quickly as possible . . . Well, Lou, I'm not going to say what the case involves. I don't want you looking for things that may not be there . . . Now you've got it. That's the idea. Just make a complete examination . . . Right, but don't wait on the paperwork. It will be along in a couple of days . . . Yes, I'm certain he'll have his man out there today." The judge again looked at Balzic for confirmation. Again Balzic nodded.

"Fine, Lou. And thanks. Bye," Friedman said, hanging up. "There, Mario. Done."

"Can't thank you enough, your honor."

"Thank me for what? A little while ago you gave me some information that's going to help me skin a couple, shall we say, friends of mine? I've been waiting ever since last year's Series when those Mets were my undoing. I hate to tell you how much that cost me."

"Didn't cost me a thing," Balzic said.

"Well, then, I'll save you from some other trouble."

"How so?"

"Keep that damn Greek informed of what you're doing. Better yet, see if you can't get him to go along with you."

"You mean through the whole thing?"

Friedman nodded. "If he's free, it would save everybody a lot of grief. Have him with you when you pick your man up—I keep calling him a man, but he's a juvenile, isn't he?"

"Yeah. I don't think he's seventeen yet. Might be, but he's not eighteen. That I know."

"Well, see if you can't talk Valcanas into going along for the ride. If he's there to see that everything's done properly, he'll—well, he'll be able to deal with the family better."

Balzic doubted the reasoning of that, but he wasn't about to question it. Instead he thanked the judge again and went out to give the facts to his secretary. She filled out a warrant for him, which he shoved in his inside coat pocket. He thanked her and went downstairs into the lobby to inquire about Valcanas. There was no telling where Valcanas might be, and Balzic began to fret that Valcanas had made good his promise of letting his liver know who was boss. The more he fretted over that, the more he thought about Angie Spano, and the better he thought Judge Friedman's idea was to have Valcanas along.

"Try Muscotti's," Jimmy Rullo, Judge Scarpattie's tipstaff told Balzic. "That's where he usually winds up. He's probably over there right now half bagged and making speeches."

Balzic hesitated about going back to Muscotti's so soon after his trouble with Sam Carraza. He knew Dom Muscotti would expect an apology, and he knew just as clearly that he didn't feel like making one. With luck, Dom wouldn't be there.

He went in through Muscotti's back door and could hear Valcanas singing along with the juke box. Balzic came down the steps as Iron City Steve came shuffling in the front door, sawing his hand across his mouth and diving into his pockets for money for a muscatel and beer.

"Stevie boy," Valcanas called out. "Man of the world, raconteur, man about Rocksburg. Tell me, Steve, how did it all begin?"

"It all began in the beginning," Steve called back, "and it was all a mistake." He fished a wadded dollar bill out of his pocket and unfolded it slowly, holding it out at arm's length finally for all to see. "A wine and a beer," he said to Pete Muscotti behind the bar.

"Put the money up," Pete said without moving.

"Put the money up," Steve mimicked him. "What do you think I'm going to do with it? The next time you give anything away'll be the next time I get a hardon."

"When you put the bread on the bar, I put the wine in the glass," Pete said.

"Give him a drink, for crissake," Valcanas said. "Can't you see the man needs respite from the world?" He staggered to the juke box and put another quarter in and punched some more buttons. "Mario! How goes it? What brings you to this quaint and humble septic tank? At this time of day—you must be drunk."

"I'm not, but you are," Balzic said.

"No shit. Am I really? How can you tell?"

Peggy Lee began to sing "Is That All There Is," and Valcanas shouted to Steve, who had emptied the glass of muscatel Pete had finally served him and was waiting for a refill. "Hey, Stevie boy. Iron City Steve! Are you listening, old compadre?"

"I'm listening," Steve said. He turned his head and pointed to his ear. He had half a match pack rolled into a horn stuck in his ear. "See? Got my hearing aid all wired up. I can hear anything. Go ahead. Say something."

"The music, Stevie boy. Miss Peggy Lee right here for your listening pleasure, coming to you live in absentia from high atop the Hotel Septic Tank, formerly the Hotel Muscotti, from downtown Rocksburg, P. A."

"Is that all there is," Steve croaked in a monotone that vanished behind the back of his hand as he wiped his lips and took aim on the full glass of muscatel.

"Mo," Balzic said, "I'd like you to do a favor."

"A favor? Hell, yes. Innkeeper, a drink for my friend here. What's your name again? Oh. Mario. Mario—don't tell me. I'll think of it in a second."

"What'll you have, Chiefo?" Pete said.

"Nothing. A big glass of ice water. For him," Balzic said, nodding toward Valcanas and pushing Valcanas's glass of whiskey away.

"Hey. Just what the hell do you think you're doing?" Valcanas snapped.

"You had enough."

"I'll be the judge of that. I don't need any goddamn instruction from you or anybody else in how to run my life. Do I tell you what to drink? Or when? Or how much?"

"I said I needed a favor."

"And I said I'd buy you a drink, for crissake. I know they don't pay you cops enough. Don't you think I know that? What the hell do you think I am? Stupid, like that wise-mouth dago behind the bar?"

"I need you sober to do this favor."

"Sober! Why you can go take a flying trip to the moon. Sober. Shit. What the hell could you possibly want done that I couldn't do practically comatose? Name it. Name one thing I could do for *you* I couldn't do standing on my elbows whistling the Dartmouth alma mater."

"Sober up. I bet you couldn't get sober."

"How much?"

"Five bucks says you can't."

"You're on, you bastard. Innkeeper, a glass of ice water and keep them coming till I tell you otherwise."

"There's one in front of you," Pete said.

"Oh. So there is. Imagine that. A mind reader. Knows what I'm going to order before I do. Have to apologize. You're not as dumb as the ordinary wop."

"Watch it, Greek," Pete said.

"Okay, forget it," Balzic said.

"What are you going to do about it, you overstuffed prosciuttini? Come around from behind that bar, and I'll lay you out."

"Okay, Mo. That's enough."

"I come out from behind this bar, counselor, you'll wish you were back in Greece," Pete said.

"All right, goddammit, that's enough. Both of you. Can it."

"Well, who the fuck's he think he is?" Valcanas shouted. "Primo Carnera? Tony Galento?" He jumped up from his stool and nearly fell as his ankles turned inward.

"That's what started it all," Iron City Steve said. "Abel said to Cain, 'Who the fuck you think you are—Tony Galento?' And Cain said, 'Joe Louis, that's who,' and he knocked him out. Boom. Abel hit his head on the ring post. That's what happened. Ever since people been arguing about who was the best boxer. Some say Abel. Most say Cain. Can't prove it by me. I wasn't there. How the hell would I know?" Steve looked deeply into his muscatel.

"Drink the water, Mo," Balzic said.

"Keep your shirt on, for crissake," Valcanas said. "You still haven't answered me. Who the fuck's he think he is talking to me like that?"

"Forget it. No harm done."

"Take the advice, counselor," Pete said. "For once Chiefo's making sense."

"Quit calling me that, goddammit."

"What's the matter with that? That's what you are, ain't it?"

"I'm a lawyer. A tradesman, that's all. That name you're calling me—that's pretentious horseshit."

"Some say Abel could move better," Steve said. "Had a better left. But there ain't no doubt who could hit harder. Cain all the way. Big right hand. Boom. Course, some say Cain butted him. How the hell would I know? All I know is what I read in the papers. Where's my beer?"

"Give my friend Steve his beer, for crissake, you goddamn chiseler," Valcanas said.

"If you was twenty years younger, Greek . . ." Pete said, going down the bar to pour a draught for Steve.

"If I was twenty years younger, what?"

"Drink your water," Balzic said. "We got a bet, remember?"

"So we have. How much time you giving me?"

"Half hour."

"Fair enough."

"Going to show a rerun on TV," Steve said. "Wide world of sports. Computer fight just like Clay and Marciano. In this corner, weighing one-seventy-three-and-a-quarter, in the purple trunks, from Eden—Cain! In this corner, wearing the white trunks with the black stripes, weighing one-sixty-nine even, also from Eden—Abel! And right here at ringside to bring you the blow-by-blow account—Howard Cosell! Hey, Mo, I'm taking Cain seven to five. Who do you like?"

"I'm a sport,"Valcanas said, wobbling over to the juke box. "Make it nine to five, and I'll take Abel."

"You got twenty-five minutes left, Mo."

"What the hell you worrying about? It's only five bucks, for crissake. Listen to this song. It breaks me up."

Balzic could see he had no choice. But twenty-five minutes later, and after six tumblers of ice water and two trips to the lavatory, Valcanas was walking with only a slight tilt.

"Okay," Valcanas said. "Where's the five?"

"See me next week. That's payday. Right now we got more important things to think about."

"Crissake, payday's always next week with you," Valcanas said. "See ya, Stevie boy. Don't do anything I wouldn't do, but make sure you get a good lawyer anyway."

"In the beginning was the word," Steve chanted, sawing his hand across his mouth, "and on the seventh day, 'long about eleven o'clock, the word was muscatel. God knew he had something there. . . ."

On the sidewalk Valcanas stopped Balzic. "Just where the hell are you taking me anyway?"

"To the high school," Balzic said, hurrying on.

"Hey, what's the big rush?" Valcanas called after him. "At least give me a chance to go to the state store to get a pint."

"No way. Come on, get the lead out."

"To the high school?" Valcanas muttered.

Balzic tried his best to explain to Valcanas in the car on the way, but Valcanas stared glumly out the window and said nothing.

"I'm just taking Friedman's advice, that's all. You're along to see that everything gets done right."

"I suppose you think that's a compliment."

Balzic parked the car and got out. "Listen, Greek, I can think of at least two hundred people I'd rather compliment. You want to come in, or you going to sit out here and sulk?"

"I'll sulk, thank you. Unless you think you need assistance apprehending your suspect."

Balzic was back in five minutes. "We got problems," he said.

"Where's the kid?"

"That's the problem. He hasn't been in school since last Friday, which, in case you've forgotten, was the day Andrasko got it."

"Whatta you mean, *we* got problems? And just where the hell are you going now?"

"Out to their house."

"Then you can just drop me at Muscotti's."

"Nothing doing. You're with me all the way on this one."

"And just what am I supposed to do out there—sanctify your little plan, or protect you from little Angie?"

"Little of both," Balzic said. "But something tells me what you're really going to have to do is get little Angie to 'fess up and tell us where he is."

"You're starting to sound like a ridge runner, for crissake," Valcanas said. He blew his nose, and after he pocketed his hanky, he said, "And what makes you think I'm going to get her to tell me where he is—what do I look like? A priest?"

"Nothing makes me think it. I know she sure as hell isn't going to tell me—if she knows. But I think she does know, and I also know the first person she called when the state boys picked the kid up was you. You add it up."

Valcanas snorted. "We'll see how far either one of us gets."

Balzic pulled up to the Andrasko house and said, "Well, let's just go see."

Angie Spano answered the door. "What do you want?" she said to Balzic, but before he could answer, she glared at Valcanas and said, "Which side of the street are you working?"

136

"Relax," Valcanas said, "and listen to what the man has to say."

"Mind if we come in?"

"Sure, I mind. Do I have a choice?"

"Not really. But it would be more comfortable inside."

Mary Andrasko came up behind her sister. "Who is it?"

"Guess," Angie said, holding the door open for Balzic and Valcanas to come in.

"I have a warrant here for the boy," Balzic said, taking it out of his coat pocket. "He's not in school."

"What? What for?" Mary Andrasko said. "For Tommy? What did he do? My God, don't I have enough . . ." She sank into a chair. "What's going on? The day we buried John, the state police came for him. They didn't say a word. They just took him. Now you. What's going on?"

"Go ahead, big shot," Angie said. "Tell her."

"Mrs. Andrasko—" Balzic started to say and then looked nervously at Valcanas.

"Mrs. Andrasko," Valcanas said, "I've known this police officer for a long time, and I've never known him to do things without good cause. Furthermore, your sister retained me the day of your husband's funeral to act in your son's behalf. Chief Balzic here, in my judgment, has the best interests of your son in mind. That is a warrant he's holding, and it is a murder warrant charging your son, Tommy, with the murder of your late husband."

"Oh, my God," Mary said, her hands flying to her face.

"Mrs. Andrasko," Balzic said, "I don't think Tommy knew what he was doing. I think he's sick—"

"Sick! What do you think I am? You're telling me this—first, he murdered my John. Then he's sick! Do you know what you're telling me? My God, don't I have enough grief?" She was shouting and tears streamed down her face. "You're saying he killed my husband—his own father! My God, my God, I can't stand any-more. . . ."

"You son of a bitch," Angie said.

"You keep quiet," Valcanas snapped. "Mrs. Andrasko, get hold of yourself and listen. Mrs. Andrasko!"

Mary Andrasko's wailing turned to short bursts of sobs and then abruptly to coughing, sending violent tremors through her shoulders. She gripped the cushion of the chair and looked up at them.

"Now, listen to me," Valcanas said, going down on one knee in front of her and taking her hand. "This is not what it sounds like."

"Sure. Give it some fancy names," Angie said.

"I told you to keep quiet," Valcanas said, "and if you open your mouth once more I'm going to ask this police officer to restrain you with all necessary force. Do you understand that?"

"I'd like to—"

"You'd like to what?" Valcanas said.

Angie turned and walked to a chair in the corner near the television and dropped into it.

"Mrs. Andrasko," Valcanas said, "listen carefully to me. In the first place John Andrasko was not Tommy's father."

"I know that," she said. "My God, don't you think I know that?"

"A moment ago you said he was. I wanted to make it clear that you knew that. At this moment, I want to make sure you know the things you know, and I want to tell you the things you need to know.

"Chief Balzic here has already got the word of a judge to order a psychiatric examination for your son—is that correct, Chief?"

"That's correct, Mrs. Andrasko."

"And this whole business about the murder warrant is strictly a matter of legal procedure, Mrs. Andrasko," Valcanas went on. "It's a way of making sure that your son is properly arrested, properly charged, and properly remanded—I mean, properly turned over to the psychiatrists who will examine him. That's all this warrant does. That's what the whole procedure is about. Mrs. Andrasko, are you still hearing me?"

She nodded.

"This warrant does not mean that Tommy murdered your husband. This warrant is not a conviction. It isn't anything but what I've said it is. That is, to be more explicit, it isn't anything more than the legal means necessary to have Tommy examined. The fact of the matter is that no one has the least substantial evidence to indicate that Tommy had anything to do with it. Am I right about this,

Chief? Am I leaving anything out or attempting to make something appear to be something else?"

"He's right, Mrs. Andrasko. Everything he's said."

"Believe me, Mrs. Andrasko, it's a way of protecting your son," Valcanas said.

"But why?" she asked. "What in God's name makes you even get such an idea about Tommy. . . ." She buried her face in her hands.

"Take your hands away and listen, Mrs. Andrasko. Mario, tell her."

"Mrs. Andrasko, in anything like this, we have certain things to go on. We look at the way a thing was done, at where and how. We look at all the circumstances and possibilities. Your husband wasn't robbed, and your son didn't come home until one-thirty that night."

"Is that all? On that, on those two things you think my Tommy did it?"

"Not only on those two things, Mrs. Andrasko. There are others. Things Tommy said to me that night. The fact that somebody took a lot of trouble to clean your automobile, not just clean it, but clean it with disinfectant. The same kind of disinfectant that was found in your barn. Then there's the way—the way John was killed. He wasn't just killed. He was beaten beyond recognition. Mrs. Andrasko, I knew John all my life, and I had to be told who he was. All of these things put together don't mean for sure that Tommy did it, but these things give me reason for thinking that he might have, and I'm trying to find out whether I'm wrong as much as I'm trying to find out whether I'm right. You have to understand that."

"So tell her the rest," Angie said. "Tell her what you told me down at the funeral home. Go ahead."

"What's she talking about? Angie, what are you talking about?"

"Don't worry about what she's talking about," Valcanas said.

"Don't I have a right to know if it's something about this?"

"Damn right you do, honey," Angie said, looking defiantly at Balzic. "Well? What's the big problem? You didn't have any trouble telling me. Tell her now. What you said in the parking lot."

"Tell me what, for God's sake?" Mary pleaded.

"The rest of his nice theory," Angie said. "The rest of why he's after Tommy. Go ahead, cop."

"I will," Balzic said. "When the time comes. But if you make me tell her that now, then you're going to have to tell her what you told me. About a certain somebody making a pass at somebody else. How would that be? Fair enough?"

Angie flushed. She jumped up and ducked between them into the kitchen. Cupboard doors started banging, and then the refrigerator, and then came the sound of ice cubes and a bottle scraping against glass.

"Are you going to tell me?" Mary said.

"Mrs. Andrasko," Balzic said, "right now I don't think any good would be done if I told you what your sister wants me to tell you. Later on, if my idea is right—mind you, if—then I give you my word I'll tell you. But if I'm wrong, well, I don't see any good reason for you to know what your sister's referring to. You'll just have to take my word for it."

"Oh God, if John was here, he'd tell me who to believe. He would. John was always so sure. . . ." Mary leaned forward with her elbows on her knees and covered her face. "I don't know what to think."

"For right now, Mrs. Andrasko, just tell us where Tommy is."

Her head snapped up. "He's in school—isn't he?"

"No, he's not. We just came from there. The people there said he hasn't been in school since last Friday."

"That's crazy. Sure he's in school. I pack him a lunch every day. He won't eat the cafeteria food. He makes me pack him a lunch. I know I packed him a lunch on Friday. And since the—well, my God, I know I packed him a lunch today. And he left the house at the same time he always does."

Angie came back from the kitchen and stood in the doorway. The drink she'd made herself was deep amber. "He's gone," she said.

"What does that mean?" Balzic said.

"Just what it sounds like. Gone. Phfttt. Bye-bye."

"And just what did you have to do with that?" Valcanas said, advancing on Angie.

"Who said I had anything to do with anything?"

"Don't get cute with me, dearie. I've been dealing with liars too long," Valcanas said. "Do you know what you're fooling with, withholding material evidence?"

140

"I don't know what you're talking about."

"Then I'll spell it out for you. Let's try obstructing justice for openers. Then how about aiding and abetting the flight of a fugitive from justice? How about accessory after the fact? Those good enough for you? You know what I'm talking about now?"

Angie stiffened. "I gave him some money, and I told him to take off," she whispered.

Mary stood and confronted her sister. "Angie! What are you saying?"

Angie gulped her drink. "I didn't stutter," she said.

She was starting to turn away when Mary slapped her, the blow glancing off the back of her head.

Angie whirled around. "All right. All right, goddammit. Do you want to know what that cop's talking about? He's thinking Tommy killed John all right, but he wasn't really killing John—am I right, cop?" She squinted furiously at Balzic and then turned her rage on her sister. "He was killing Tami, that's who he was killing. And you want to know why? 'Cause we put the idea in his head. You. And me. Us. Do you remember, sister dear, all those bitch sessions we had in my place after Tami took off on you? I remember them. Oh God, do I ever. And we didn't have sense enough to shut up around Tommy. And what we said stuck in his head, and he grew up on that, and he waited and waited, and finally he went after John.

"You think I'm crazy? Ask the cop. I thought he was crazy, too, the son of a bitch. But then I thought about it some more. And I remembered all those nights. Night after night after goddamn night. You and me sitting around bitching about what a bastard Tami was and there was little Tommy, sitting there and crawling around and taking it all in."

"But he was so little," Mary said. "He was only so little."

"Sure. Just a baby. But he heard it all—ain't that right, cop? Am I telling it right?"

Balzic nodded in spite of himself. He wanted to tell her to shut up. He wanted to choke her, but he kept on nodding.

"And it all stayed there in his head," Angie kept on. "And then one day he couldn't handle it anymore, right, cop? One day—last Friday he got everything mixed up. . . ." Angie turned abruptly and darted into the kitchen. First there was the sound of the bottle and the ice cubes. Then there came the sobs.

Mary turned glazed eyes on Balzic. Then she brushed past him into the living room and sat on the edge of a chair. She chewed her little fingers and began to rock on the edge of the chair.

Balzic went into the kitchen. "Where is he?" he said. When he got no reply, he said, "Do you want a hanky?"

Head down, Angie said, "No."

"No, you don't want a hanky, or no, you're not going to tell me where he is?"

"No I don't want your goddamn hanky, and no I'm not going to tell you where he is, because I don't know where. I gave him every cent I could spare. Sixty-two dollars. He took the car this morning, and that was the last I saw him. Satisfied?"

"No," Balzic said, sighing, "are you?"

She told him in Italian to fuck himself.

"That's not going to help. You got any ideas?"

"You're the one with all the ideas," she said. "How many you got?"

Balzic left Angie Spano in the kitchen and went out to his car. He got Stramsky on the radio.

"Vic, get out an A.P.B. on Thomas Parilla, male, Caucasian, age seventeen. Got that so far?"

"Hold it," Stramsky said. "Okay, go."

"Height five-nine, weight approximately one-thirty-five, slender build, hair black, eyes brown, complexion dark with bad acne."

"Okay, go."

"Driving a 1967 Ford Sedan. Maroon. Check with Moyer on the license."

"Anything else?"

"Yeah. Murder warrant on same. Probably psycho. Probably not armed, but approach with caution anyway. Never can tell. I don't know what he's holding."

142

"Roger. You want me to call Moyer first?"

"Yeah. Tell him I'd like everybody he can spare—as a favor to me." Balzic hung the speaker on the hook and sat back to light a cigarette. "Goddamn you, woman," he said. He sat smoking for a minute and then went back into the house.

Mary Andrasko was still sitting on the edge of the chair, her hands still pressed against her face. Her eyes were clouded over. Mo Valcanas was looking anxiously at the kitchen.

"Where's Angie?" Balzic asked him.

"Still in the kitchen."

"Why don't you go bum a drink? That's what you want, isn't it?"

"Best idea I've heard in the last hour," Valcanas said, heading for the kitchen.

"Mrs. Andrasko," Balzic said, "do you have a recent photograph of Tommy?"

"What?"

"I said, do you have a recent picture of Tommy?"

"What for?"

"It would make things a lot easier."

"For you."

"Yes, ma'am."

"What's going to make it easier for me?"

"Nothing," Balzic said. "I'd be lying if I said anything would."

She continued to stare. "Was Angie telling the truth before?"

"It's still just a theory."

"I don't care what you call it. Was she telling me what you told her?"

"More or less, yes."

"So then you think it's my fault. Mine and hers."

"Mrs. Andrasko, I'm not a judge. I—"

"Oh, how easy for you to say that. But you don't mean it. Listen to the way you say it. You *are* a judge. You already decided whose fault it is. But let me tell you something, mister, it wasn't easy when my first husband left me—"

"I'm sure it wasn't."

143

"How would you know what it was like? How would you know? You probably never did nothing wrong in your whole life. Baloney, mister. Ba-loney. All you people that think you never did nothing wrong, you're always the ones making mistakes, only you never see any of them—"

"It may look that way, Mrs. Andrasko, but it isn't that way, believe me."

"Who're you to tell me that? You know what I say to that? I say bullshit. You people, people like you, you make me sick. Always looking down your noses at me 'cause John never . . ." Her eyes, which has focused angrily on Balzic, clouded over again and then disappeared behind her hands. She began to sob.

"Mrs. Andrasko, it may come as a surprise to you, but everybody I know who knows you thinks you and John were married. What's more, as far as the law's concerned in this state, you two were as married as anybody gets."

"No, we weren't!" she cried out.

"Yes, you were, Mrs. Andrasko. And any shame you feel about your marriage with John is shame you brought on yourself. If you don't believe me, ask Mr. Valcanas. He knows the law better than I do. He'll tell you. There can be no shame about your marriage."

"Marriage, marriage. Quit it! We weren't married—how many times do I have to tell you? I was never divorced from Tami."

"Well, the law covers that, too." Balzic turned toward the kitchen. "Hey, Mo, come in here a minute."

"I don't care what any lawyer says. We were living in sin, and now God's punished us for it."

"I heard that, Mrs. Andrasko," Valcanas said, "and I wouldn't presume to tell you how your religion looks at your marriage—"

"Quit calling it that, for God's sake! It wasn't a marriage. It was sin."

"All right, Mrs. Andrasko. But will you answer a couple of questions? Will you tell me how long it's been since you've lived with your first husband?"

"Thirteen years. Tommy was four when he left."

"All right. The law here grants what amounts to a divorce without proceedings after desertion by one of the spouses after seven years.

That's common law. So you were in fact divorced from your first husband."

"No, I wasn't."

"Believe what you will, but tell me this: how long had you lived with John?"

"Eight years."

"Again, common law says you were married. No question about it."

"What about all those years in between? What about them?"

"Mrs. Andrasko, all those years you're worried about become hypothetical in the eyes of the law. The fact that your first husband never returned after deserting you is all that counts. That, plus the fact that you presented yourself to the world as Mr. and Mrs. John Andrasko. That's all that matters."

"Maybe to you. Maybe to some judge. But you don't know how many times I didn't go out of this house because of what people were saying about me."

Valcanas shrugged. "Madam, I can only tell you about the law. Social custom is something I merely witness, like any other citizen. I gave up trying to understand it long ago. Now, if you'll excuse me, I have a drink in the kitchen." Valcanas nodded at Balzic and motioned with his head for Balzic to follow him out to the kitchen.

When they got there Valcanas said, "Let her alone, for crissake. She'll never take your word for anything. What she needs is a priest. She's Catholic, isn't she?"

Balzic nodded.

"Well, for crissake, if you know a priest, then get him the hell out here. She doesn't want a legal explanation. She wants absolution. The best thing you could do is tell her to confess her sins. She'll love you for understanding what an evil woman she is. Hell, anybody can see she's got sins a mile wide, and she's been working them for twelve or thirteen years. If she works it right, they'll be good for another fifty thousand miles."

"How smart you two guys are," Angie said. She was sitting at the table, running her fingers over the condensed vapor on her glass. "You two know all the answers."

"Quit crying in your sauce, for crissake," Valcanas said. "Neither one of us pretends to know all that much, but I know when a man's wasting his breath trying to explain a very simple thing, and I also know when somebody doesn't want to be explained to. That doesn't take any goddamn genius on anybody's part. Where'd you hide the bottle?"

"Go get your own," Angie said. "You lawyers make enough. You don't need to freeload off of me."

"I'll subtract the price of two drinks from your bill, how's that?"

"Come on, Mo. I'll drop you at Muscotti's," Balzic said, tugging at Valcanas's elbow.

"Fine," Valcanas said, bowing to Angie and lifting his hat. "And a good day to you, madam. Your generosity is exceeded only by your looks, which wouldn't be half bad if you knew how to make up your face and bought some decent clothes."

"Come on, Mo, before you get us into more trouble than we can handle."

"You better get him out of here, the two-faced son of a bitch," Angie said.

"Temper, temper," Valcanas said, grinning.

Balzic led him out of the kitchen and into the living room. "Mrs. Andrasko," he said, "if Tommy should come back, it would be better all around if you called me."

Mary Andrasko did not look up.

"You're wasting your time," Valcanas whispered. "Besides, I'm really getting a thirst on."

In the car on the way to Muscotti's, Valcanas asked, "What now?"

"Now? Now I wait and hope I don't do anything dumb like get drunk while I'm waiting."

"An admirable ambition. If you plan to wait in Muscotti's, I hope for my sake you don't succeed."

"Since when do you need company?"

"I don't, but it would bother me to be having a good time knowing I was standing beside someone who was waiting to avenge an injustice."

"No more. You make my side hurt."

"Can't you make this thing go any faster, for crissake?"

"Patience, Myron. Nobody's threatening prohibition."

"You call me Myron again, and you're going to have to defend yourself, goddammit."

"All right, counselor," Balzic said, restraining his grin.

"Don't call me that, either—hey, you just passed up two parking places, for crissake."

"There's one ahead, Mister Valcanas. Don't get excited."

Balzic parked, and the two of them went into Muscotti's, Valcanas going at something faster than a walk.

Iron City Steve was at one of the tables, looking impatiently at an empty beer glass and an empty wine glass in front of him. "No drilling, no well," he said, sawing his hand across his mouth. "Let's not scratch the surface, let's pick the surface up and throw it away. . . ."

"Let's have a drink," Valcanas said.

"Best idea anybody had all day," Steve said, rising unsteadily and following Valcanas to the bar.

Vinnie was working behind the bar.

"Since when did you start working daylight?" Balzic asked him.

"Since about an hour ago," Vinnie said. "Since the state cops walked in and grabbed Petey boy."

"Pete Muscotti?" Balzic said. "What for, this time?"

"Give us a drink, for crissake," Valcanas said. "You girls can talk later."

"What happened, Vinnie?"

"What do I know what happened? They walked in and put the grab on him. So what's it going to be?"

"C-C and water for me," Valcanas said. "A muscatel and beer for my compadre Steve. Mario can speak for himself, but I'm buying."

"I, too, can speak for myself," Steve said.

"That'll be the day anybody can get you to shut up. What's for you, Mario?" Vinnie said, pouring the drinks.

"Nothing. I just want to know why Pete got busted?"

"A buck even, Greek," Vinnie said. He rang it up. "What do I know? Last I heard he was trying to hustle furnaces. You know him. He's pulling crap like that all the time. Probably some old lady smelled something and got on the phone. What do I know?"

"Was he alone?"

"What—are you kidding? He's too dumb to have a partner," Vinnie said. "Meantime, I got to go on daylight now for who knows how long."

"Dom pissed off?"

"Pissed off! He can't even see. He told Pete the last time was the last time. He ain't about to put him to work no more, blood or no blood. So it's me from now on, pal."

"You never had it so good, for crissake," Valcanas said.

"Then there's the wind," Steve said. "What good is the wind? But there it is. . . ."

"You're the wind," Vinnie said. "You're a goddamn hurricane. Shut up for a minute. Just try and see if you can do it."

"You know," Balzic said, "I never could stand that weasel."

"Pete? He sees too many movies, that's all that's wrong with him," Vinnie said. "He's harmless."

"He is like hell harmless," Balzic said. "He just never had the right opportunity."

"What would he do? Nothing," Vinnie said.

"He just hasn't seen the chance," Balzic said.

"Opportunity knocks several times," Steve said, "but chance never knocks. Doesn't have to—here's to you, Mr. Mo, and a lucky day it was for me when you walked in."

Balzic walked to the end of the bar nearest the front door and motioned for Vinnie to follow him.

"So what's up?" Vinnie said.

"You telling me everything you know?"

"What's to hide?"

"Come on, Vinnie. What was that prick into?"

"Furnaces I'm telling you. You know the bit. He walks in and wants to inspect the furnace, all that shit. Only he picked the wrong old lady. She listens to his hustle, and then she gets on the phone to the better business people, and that was that. Turns out he made about four phony contracts for replacements—after a substantial down payment, understand. Why? What did you think he was into?"

"He's been into so goddamn much, nothing would surprise me,"

Balzic said. "He was no good when times were good. He's been looking for a big score for I don't know how long."

"Come on, Mario, who ain't looking for a big score? Look at me. Last week I got ninety-six bucks on my house number. You going to arrest me for hoping?"

"That's different. Petey boy's been a mean prick since he was a kid."

"Since he was a kid? He's still a kid, for crying out loud. He can't be twenty-three, twenty-four at the most. I'm telling you, he sees too many movies, that's all."

"That's what I mean. He sees those movies, he believes them. He's been trying to get close to Dom now for how long?"

"There again, how many people you know been trying to get close to Dom? What's that mean? Jesus, if I wasn't around to keep all the figures straight, Dom would be dead. He can't remember who he's laying off for. He can't remember from last week. But all the creeps that come in, who do they go for? Me? Or Dom? But without me, Dom's history. But the hot dogs still go for Dom. So?"

"Okay, we both know all that. But think a minute. Of all the people that come in here, all the ones that know Dom, all his relatives, who's been trying longer and harder to get close to him than Petey boy?"

Vinnie scratched his stubble. "You got a point there. He's been hanging tight for a long time now."

"That's what I mean."

"But so what? What the hell are you worrying about him for?"

"I don't know," Balzic said. "I just got a funny feeling. Give me a draught."

"Hey, Vinnie boy," Valcanas called out. "Why don't you have the baseball game on?"

"It's over, that's why."

"Who won?"

"Who do you think? Cincinnati. Who else—the Pirates?"

"Is that the playoffs already?" Balzic said.

"Sure it's the playoffs," Vinnie said. "Where you been?"

149

"What was the score?"

Vinnie shrugged. "All I know is, the Reds won. I wasn't watching."

"Sometimes the Reds win," Steve said, "sometimes the Blues. Mostly it's the Blues. . . ."

"Did it get a lot of action?" Balzic asked Vinnie.

Vinnie screwed up his face and came to where Balzic was and leaned over the bar. "You wouldn't believe how much. Dom had to call Pittsburgh," he whispered. "All Cincinnati. Nobody was buying the Pirates. Christ, he couldn't cover a third of it."

"Between that and Petey boy, he's going to be rare for a while."

"Everybody takes a bath, brother. It was his turn, that's all. What pisses me is I told him to stay away from it soon as I saw how it was going, but you know him. He says nothing doing, the action got to go the other way. I tell him it ain't, and he tells me to tend the bar and keep the numbers straight, and I tell him, okay, don't say I didn't tell you. But you better believe it didn't go the other way. And he got it for two more days yet, and don't you know Cincinnati's going to kill them. Hey, he's so fuckin' smart, sometimes he makes my head hurt."

"Give us a drink here, for crissake," Valcanas said. "Is this a saloon or a bridge club?"

"Bridges and clubs," Steve said, "clubs for doing business and bridges for the getaway. . . ."

Balzic tried to call Father Marrazo, to get him to talk to Mrs. Andrasko about her marriage or sins or both but couldn't locate him. He called his own station every fifteen minutes and the state police as often. Not only was Tommy Parilla nowhere to be found, but the desk man at the state police barracks couldn't say where Lieutenant Moyer was either.

Balzic called home and told Ruth it was going to be another long night.

"Mar, we have to do something about Marie," Ruth said.

"More of the same?"

"She's getting worse. She came home from school and went straight to her room. That's the second day she's done that. Yesterday, she didn't want any supper, and—oh, I'm just getting worried, that's all. You sure you know what you're doing about her?"

"No," Balzic said. "But I don't know what else to do. Anyway, I can't do anything about it tonight. But maybe this will all be over tonight."

"Are you just saying that?"

"I guess I'm just saying that 'cause I want it to be that way."

"Well, will you at least say something to her tomorrow?"

"Uh-uh. I told you before, I'm not going to say anything to her about this until I know for sure that the kid did it. It looks almost a hundred per cent certain he did, but I still won't be satisfied until I hear a psychiatrist say so. But that's all beside the point now. Now we got to find him."

"You mean he ran away?"

"You got it, babe. His goofy aunt gave him fifty, sixty bucks, and he took John's car. Something tells me he isn't going far, but you can't tell. Hell, he might be halfway to Florida by now. I got to go, babe. I'll call you soon as I know something. And quit worrying about Marie. She'll be all right."

"You always say that."

"'Cause it will. See you later," Balzic said, hanging up. He rooted through his pockets for another dime and called the state police again. This time Moyer was in.

"Balzic. Where the hell you been?"

"I had a meeting with some boys from the Washington barracks. What's up?"

"Didn't anybody tell you? The Parilla kid's gone."

"That? Yeah, they told me. What do you want to do about it?"

Balzic felt suddenly foolish. He had no answer for what he wanted to do about it. "I was hoping you might have some ideas," he said.

"Well, look, Mario. You're the one's had a theory about this from the start. Where would you guess that kid's going to be—that is, if your theory is right?"

"At the station."

"Don't know why it took you so long to think of it. You sure as hell have been spending enough time down there at night."

"How would you know?"

"How do you think? I've had two men down there right beside you. You didn't see them?"

"No," Balzic said. "They must be pretty good men."

"Well, hell, Mario. You've been out there under the lights. They just been where you would've needed a spotlight to see them, that's all. Anyway, my suggestion to you is just to go on back down there tonight. I think that's where the kid is going to be."

"Yeah," Balzic said. "Hey, one other thing. What about young Muscotti. Pete, Dom's nephew. What did you pick him up for?"

"I don't know anything about it. That's Stallcup's case. He's been working on young Muscotti for a while, but I didn't even know he picked him up. Wait a minute."

Balzic could hear Moyer calling out to someone in his office.

"Mario?"

"Right here."

"Stallcup booked Muscotti on four counts of fraud and one for attempt to defraud."

"Where is he?"

"He's down the Southern Regional. Looks like nobody wants to take a chance on him, not even the professional bondsmen. Why?"

"Just curious. I heard about it from the bartender here."

"You in Muscotti's?"

"Yeah. Shouldn't I be?"

"I'm not telling you where to be. Just don't get a load on, that's all. I like my guinea pigs to be sober enough to help out—in case." Moyer thought that was very funny.

"Well," Balzic said, "that'll be me under the lights tonight. See you afterward if nothing happens by midnight or so. Maybe we can catch a couple beers."

"Good enough," Moyer said and hung up.

"Shit," Balzic whispered, going back to the bar.

"You look like somebody poisoned your dog, for crissake,"

Valcanas said. "Have a drink. A real drink. Not that lousy green beer."

"What I need doesn't come in bottles," Balzic said, walking past Valcanas and Iron City Steve, and staring through the triangular window in Muscotti's front door.

"Who needs to know what they need?" Steve said, his hand going back and forth under his nose.

"Exactly," Valcanas said. "And what we need right now is a little music." He went to the juke box, dropped in a quarter, and punched some buttons.

"Why don't you two form a club?" Vinnie said.

"A form I don't need," Steve said. "A club I don't need either, not unless I meet somebody with a bigger form. . . ."

"Riddles," Vinnie said, emptying the ashtrays and wiping the bar. "More bullshit."

Balzic locked his hands behind his back and started to rock impatiently on his heels and toes. Through the window, he could see the traffic starting to pick up. He didn't have to look at a clock to know it was near four-thirty, and there he was, he thought, wearing out his shoes going nowhere.

It was six minutes past midnight when Balzic, heaving out a sigh, crushed out the last cigarette he had, and, taking one last fruitless look around, stalked off the platform of the Pennsylvania Station. He wanted to call out to the two troopers he knew had been covering him on Moyer's orders—the ones he still hadn't spotted—to forget the whole ridiculous business. It was all stupid. Tommy Parilla was probably asleep somewhere, probably wishing he hadn't let his aunt talk him into running away, probably wishing he was home drinking a nice, cold Coke. Which is where I ought to be, Balzic thought. Home, drinking a nice cold beer and reading the want ads looking for sensible work.

He went down to the lower level. Frank Bennett, the station master, was dozing in his swivel chair, and Balzic continued past to the parking lot and his car. He stopped with his hand on the car door and reached for cigarettes he knew weren't there and debated whether to go back and bother Bennett for a smoke.

"This is really getting to be a drag," someone said, and Balzic's head spun.

The two troopers were not fifteen feet from him, but he hadn't heard them coming. "What the hell you guys got on your shoes—soft boiled eggs?"

"S'matter, Chief? You getting careless?" one of them said.

"Yeah," Balzic said. "Every time I start to think these days."

"Guess that cuts it tonight," the other trooper said.

"Yeah," Balzic said, patting his pockets. "Say, either one of you got a smoke?"

They both reached for their blouse pockets. Balzic turned to face them and saw something move behind them. "Hold it," he said.

"What's up?"

"Behind you. Under that baggage cart. Am I seeing things?"

Both troopers turned and looked. "I'll be damned," one said.

The other sprinted to the cart, drawing his revolver as he ran. Balzic and the other trooper bolted after him. "Easy now," Balzic called out.

"Come out of there," the first trooper said, bending down and motioning with his free hand and pointing his revolver at the squatting figure.

The figure didn't move.

Balzic went down on one knee. "Come on out, Tommy," he said.

Tommy Parilla suddenly started to giggle and stopped as suddenly, the sound catching in his throat. His head dropped and he looked at the tire iron between his feet.

"Oh, Jesus," Balzic said, seeing the slick look of the tire iron. "Tommy, we're not going to hurt you. Come on out, son."

Tommy started to giggle again, and stopped again as quickly.

Balzic held out his hand. "Come on, son. It's okay."

Tommy stared at him. There was a hissing sound and then a dripping.

"What's he doing?" the second trooper said. "Pissin' himself?"

"Yeah, Jesus," Balzic said. "Come on, Tommy. It's all right."

"No," Tommy said. "Bad, Bad Tommy."

Some seconds passed. Tommy lurched forward on his hands and came crawling out. "I make pee-pee," he said. "I make pee-pee."

"It's okay, Tommy," Balzic said, helping Tommy to his feet.

Tommy crossed and uncrossed his legs, standing each time with the heel of one shoe on the toe of the other.

"God, look at him," the trooper with his revolver drawn said.

"Looks like we been watching and waiting in the wrong place," the second trooper said.

"Where is he, Tommy?" Balzic said.

"Who?"

"Daddy," Balzic said. "Where's Daddy?"

Tommy stopped crossing his legs and pointed with his right hand to the back edge of the parking lot. The maroon Ford was parked beside a black Chrysler Imperial. Tommy started to chew his left thumb nail, and, as he pointed again, his thumb slipped into his mouth.

"Who'd believe it?" the second trooper said, trotting off toward the cars parked at the extreme edge of the lot. In a moment, he called back: "He's still got a pulse!"

The first trooper broke for his unmarked cruiser and called for an ambulance.

Balzic led Tommy to his own car. "Better pick up that tire iron," he said to the trooper who'd called the ambulance and was now trying to get Lieutenant Moyer.

The second trooper came trotting from between the Ford and the Chrysler and got a blanket from the trunk of his cruiser. He ran back with it, and, after a moment, came back shaking his head.

"Get in the car, Tommy," Balzic said, holding open the back door.

Tommy crawled in and curled up on the seat, his thumb still in his mouth. He glanced back wildly at Balzic, but when Balzic closed the door, the boy put his head down and closed his eyes.

"You think he'll be okay like that?" the second trooper said.

"Right now he's four years old," Balzic said. "He ain't going nowhere. Let's have a look." He started for the cars at the edge of the lot.

"I'll wait for the ambulance if it's all the same to you," the second trooper said.

"Suit yourself," Balzic said. He found the man between the cars near the front fender of the Imperial. His breathing had an ominous gurgling sound. Stretched above his head in his left hand was a doctor's bag. Balzic had to pry his fingers off the handle.

Balzic set the bag down and went through the man's pockets, doing that as much to keep from looking at the man's face as to find out who the man was. He found a considerable stack of bills in a billfold and a set of keys in a leather case. Balzic took the small key and hesitated. Something told him he wouldn't find medical equipment or supplies in the bag.

He got out of the way when the ambulance came and was still hesitating about the bag when it pulled away. He didn't unlock the bag until he saw Moyer pulling in, leading two other cars of troopers.

"Look at this," he said when Moyer approached him. "Poor bastard, he thought he was being robbed."

"How much you think is there?"

"Well, Phil, it's a little more than you or me'll make in a couple of paydays."

"I'd say so," Moyer said. "You get a name?"

"No cards in the billfold. Just more paper. Maybe he has some cards in the car. The Imperial."

"Check it," Moyer said to one of the troopers who had come with him. "Well, Mario, how's it feel to be right?"

"Shitty."

"Where is he?"

"Back seat of my car," Balzic said. "Sucking his thumb."

Moyer looked doubtful.

"See for yourself," Balzic said.

Moyer went and looked and came back with the vaguest trace of a smile. "Mario, you're in the wrong business," he said.

"Ain't I though," Balzic said. He looked at the doctor's bag. "I sure as hell don't like this."

"So he hit somebody's bag man. So what? He's a psycho. He's not a robber. What does it matter anyway?"

"It matters that Dom Muscotti was taking a real bath on the

National League playoffs for one thing. It matters that this bag is still full for another." Balzic shook his head. "Why the hell did this have to get into it? I don't like this even a little bit."

"Mario, quit acting like we got a gang war on our hands or something. You forgetting who you got in your car?"

"No. I'm also not forgetting that Dom Muscotti was waiting for this money."

"Why are you so sure it was for him?"

"I know, that's all. He got caught in a lot of one-way traffic."

"Well, pity poor Dom. He doesn't know the chances. Hell, for that matter, you want to worry about something, think about whoever sent this guy out here. Seems to me that whoever that is is going to be a little distressed about it, too." Moyer threw up his hands. "Mario, we could go on worrying about things all night. For what? You got your man. What does it matter how the book gets burned?"

"It matters. It also depends how things go."

"What things?"

"Well, I got it set up to get the kid out to Mamont, but I still don't know if the paperwork's taken care of yet."

"So what's the problem? We book him and take him out to Southern Regional. They isolate him and that's that."

"I still don't like it."

"What's not to like? Mario, sometimes I swear I don't get you."

"For things not to like, take a look at who's coming."

Moyer looked over his shoulder. A car pulled in behind his, and Dick Dietz, *The Rocksburg Gazette* reporter, got out and came striding toward them.

"Mario, old friend, he's all yours. I got work to do."

"Your people know what to do."

"At moments like this, they have to be supervised," Moyer said, walking off toward the Chrysler Imperial.

"Bastard," Balzic said under his breath.

"What's up, Chief," Dietz said, trying to look everywhere at once.

"Not much. Case of assault, that's all."

"That'll be the day. I count seven state cops plus you and Moyer. Come on, let's have it."

"You got it. Assault. Victim's on his way to the hospital.

157

Assailant's in custody and on his way to the magistrate's for arraignment. What else do you want?"

"Some names for a start," Dietz said, taking out his notebook and pen. "And then you can tell me what the money has to do with it."

"What money?"

"The money in the bag you're holding," Dietz said, smiling.

"This, you mean. This is my bingo winnings. Had a hell of a night at the Eagles. Just couldn't keep the corn off the cards tonight."

Dietz let his hands drop to his sides. "Chief, I know you don't like me. I know you never have. Yet everywhere I go in this town, in this county for that matter, I keep hearing what a fair man you are."

"You must talk to some real winners."

"Winners or not, that's what I hear. So what I'd like to know is why you can't be fair with me. What have I ever done to you?"

"To me personally? There's nothing you could do."

Dietz shook his head. "Then, what the hell is it? Hell, man, I have a job to do the same as you."

"I don't like the way you do it."

Dietz looked at the sky in disgust. Then he started to laugh. "Well, just how should I do it—I mean, considering that you've never asked me whether I like the way you do yours?"

"Dietz, don't make me laugh. You got the whole alphabet and a whole lot of space six days a week to tell me and everybody else what you think of the way I'm doing my job. Go back and read the stuff you've written about me and my men ever since you landed in this town.

"You want specifics? Go look at the headline you wrote about those two kids Weigh's boys busted on a narcotics. Go back and read everything you wrote about John Andrasko. And try, while you're reading it, to read it like you was me."

"I was just reporting what Weigh told me, that's all. *You* wouldn't tell me anything. I had to get it from somebody."

"Wrong. Maybe I'm dreaming, but my idea is you get the right stuff. You don't just get any stuff from the first jerk with a loose jaw. Or is that too much to hope for?"

"No."

Balzic searched Dietz's face. "Maybe I'm a real dummy," he said, "but I'll give it to you—on the condition that you tone it down and bury it in the back somewhere. And I mean tone it down so low I can hardly hear it. You read me?"

"Yes."

"Because there's a lot of people mixed up in this. One of them is very close to me. And I've already made a couple of mistakes in this thing. I mean some real beauties. You with me?"

"So far."

"Okay. Here it is." And Balzic told him as much as he thought Dietz could handle, which was most of it. He told him about Marie with Tommy at the football game and about his blunders with Mrs. Andrasko and with her sister, and he even explained Dom Muscotti's bath on the Cincinnati-Pittsburgh playoffs.

"So that's where the money comes in," Balzic said. "And that makes things different. Now come here. I want you to see something."

He lead Dietz over to his car and pointed at the back seat. "Take a look."

Dietz peered in and saw Tommy Parilla still curled up on the seat, his knees drawn up to his abdomen, his thumb still in his mouth, his eyes wide and unblinking.

"That him?"

"That's him. So when you start typing, just remember him. And his mother. And my daughter. I'm not trying to tell you your job, Dietz. I'm just trying to tell you to do it with sense, 'cause if you fuck this one up, you'll never get another word out of me—not even about the weather. Understand?"

Dietz stepped back from the car and nodded slowly. "What can I say, Chief? I'm sorry, I guess."

"Stick the sorries up your ass. Just use a little sense, okay?"

Dietz nodded.

"Now if you wanted to finish doing your job," Balzic said, "you'd go ask Moyer if he found who the guy was. And then you'd check with the hospital. I don't think the poor bastard will last an hour. He was as bad as Andrasko. Worse. He got it with a tire iron."

"Where you going?" Dietz asked.

"Take the kid down and get him booked and put away someplace safe until I can get him out to Mamont. See you around, Dietz."

Balzic got in his car and started it.

Tommy lurched upright, sucking furiously on his thumb.

"It's okay, Tommy. We're just going for a ride. It's all right. You can lay back down. Go to sleep if you want. I'll wake you when we get there, okay?"

" 'Kay," Tommy said around his thumb, dropping back on the seat.

"Atta boy," Balzic said, backing out of the lot. He stopped after he got the car fronting the right way and rolled down his window. "Hey, Phil," he called out to Moyer, "you want to come along?"

Moyer left the troopers he was talking with and came trotting past Dietz. He got in.

"Get a name?"

Moyer held up two cards, a driver's license, and a vehicle registration. "Vitale Joseph Ducci. 2627 Washington Boulevard, Pittsburgh."

"East Liberty," Balzic said. "It gets worse."

"Yeah. They're not going to think it's Christmas. Ah well, their loss is the commonwealth's gain—isn't that the way it goes?"

"Something like that," Balzic said dourly. "Ready?"

"Hell, yes. Let's get out of here before Dietz comes up with another question. What did you say to him anyway? He looked pretty subdued."

"I gave him the story, and I told him to play dead. He must've got the message for once in his life. I hope so, 'cause the extra attraction here really turns things."

"I still don't know why that's got you so worried."

"Phil, you got to understand. I've lived in this town all my life, and—never mind. You want to know what would really ease my mind?"

Moyer looked at him and waited.

"You're going to think I'm nuts, but it would really ease my mind if Dom Muscotti got this money."

"Are you shittin' me?"

"No."

Moyer shifted about on the seat. "Mario, this is your territory, like you say. I'm due for a transfer. You want to give it to him, I won't remember anything."

Balzic grunted and turned up the street toward Muscotti's.

"Was that supposed to be an expression of gratitude?"

"What?" Balzic said, parking across the street from Muscotti's.

"That noise you made."

"Yeah. Be back in a minute. I'm going to get the priest if he's in here, so it might take a couple minutes. Maybe you can talk to the kid."

"Thanks a lot. What am I supposed to talk to him about?"

"Well, you might verify his present condition and state of mind for one thing. Then—I don't know. You're the lieutenant. Tell him about the benefits of civil service."

Balzic grabbed the doctor's bag and hurried across the street into Muscotti's. Dom Muscotti was behind the bar, looking sour. One man was asleep at one of the tables and two community college students were arguing about something at the front of the bar. Balzic walked quickly back to where Dom Muscotti was standing and said, "Got something that belongs to you." He set the bag on the bar.

"What's this?"

"You know. But there's one thing. The messenger's in the hospital."

"What?"

"He got beat up pretty bad. I don't think he's going to make it."

"Acey?"

"I don't follow you."

"Was it Ducci?"

Balzic nodded.

"Oh, my God."

Balzic waited for Muscotti to say something else, but Dom just picked up the bag and stared at it. He made the slightest move as though he was about to throw it against a wall.

"My God," he said. "Acey . . ."

"Father Marrazo in the back, Dom?"

161

"What? Oh yeah. He's back there. You sure it was Acey?"

"Vitale Ducci was on the license and owner's card. I forget the middle name. Washington Boulevard. That him?"

Dom nodded slowly, his face going slack. "What hospital? On the hill?"

"Yeah. Better call somebody quick if he has anybody, Dom. He—I'll tell you what, Dom. It'll be better if he don't make it."

"Go on back and get the Father," Dom said. "I'll make the calls. And take the Father up there, okay, Mario? Acey was a real religious guy, know what I mean? A real religious guy."

Balzic said he would and went on to the back room. He found only one game going on. Father Marrazo, dressed in his poker clothes, was frowning a loser's frown.

Mo Valcanas was sprawled in a chair by the other table, his head rolling and his mouth agape. His lips trembled with the silent words of a dream.

"Sorry, Father," Balzic said, "but I need you for a while."

"Mario," the priest said. His frown turned to a look of reprieve. To the other players, he said, "Cashing in, gentlemen. You understand how it is."

"Do what you got to do, Father," Balzic said. "I'm going to try and get this Greek on his feet." He shook Valcanas's shoulder.

"I told you I don't need a haircut goddammit," Valcanas bellowed, his face pinching into a rage, his eyes fiercely shut. He tried to jerk away from Balzic's hand and fell off the chair, coming awake when his hip and elbow hit the floor. "Hey, Jesus Christ . . ."

"Come on, Greek. Time to go."

Valcanas focused bleerily up at Balzic. "For crissake, don't you have anything better to do? Why don't you go solve a felony? Earn your pay, for crissake."

"Let me help you up."

"I can get up." He put his hand out and tried to push up, but his hand slipped, and he bumped down on his seat. "If you laugh, you would-be J. Edgar Hoover, I'll show you how Greeks take care of their traitors."

"I'm not laughing. You want some help or not?"

"What the hell for?"

"I got a client of yours outside."

"Screw him, whoever the hell he is. Let him get his own goddamn lawyer. Well don't just stand there—give me a hand, for crissake."

Balzic and Father Marrazo got Valcanas up, put his hat on him, and steered him out to the bar. Valcanas wanted to have a drink. "Just one, for crissake. What's one going to hurt?"

Balzic ignored him and said to Dom: "You call the people?"

Dom nodded. He put his head down and pinched the bridge of his nose. His shoulders began to quiver and he turned away.

"What's the matter with him, for crissake?"

"Never mind. Let's go. You got a good hold, Father?"

"As good as I can manage. I'm not used to this sort of thing, you know."

"No shit, Father," Valcanas said. "Aren't you really? How do you think I feel? Me, poor little me, between a priest and a cop . . . all I need now is a crown of thorns. . . ."

"Aw, shut up," Balzic said.

"Hey, Dom, how about a couple of draughts here?" one of the two college students called out.

"Go home," Dom said. "I'm closed."

The students looked at each other and then at the clock above the cash register. "Hey, Dom, it's not even one o'clock."

"I'm closed," Dom said. "Go on. Hit the bricks. Go study something." He picked up their glasses.

They were still protesting when Balzic and Father Marrazo got Valcanas through the door and across the street. Moyer got out to lend a hand. They wedged Valcanas into the middle of the front seat and then Balzic took the priest aside.

"In case you're wondering, Father, that's Tommy Parilla in the back. The worst happened."

"There's no doubt?"

"Not this time, Father. But you better go get what you need and get on up the hospital. The victim's name is Vitale Ducci and Dom says he was a religious guy. Better hustle, Father. He ain't going to last too long."

"I have my things in my car," Father Marrazo said. "Will you need me later on?"

"Yeah. Soon as we take care of the kid. I'd like you to be with me when I tell his mother. I don't want to screw it up this time. Meet you back here in about an hour, how's that?"

"All right," Father Marrazo said, turning toward his car parked around the corner.

Balzic got in behind the wheel. "Come on, counselor, give me a little room. We're going to book your client. Try to sober up, too, will you. So you can make sure we do it right. You hear me?"

"I'm just drunk, Marshal. I'm not deaf. Drive on."

After Magistrate Angelo Molanari got over the sight of Tommy Parilla, splashed with blood, smelling of urine, and sucking his thumb, the arraignment went off smoothly enough to suit Balzic. Valcanas, drunk as he was, functioned sufficiently to correct two procedural mistakes Molanari made, and, to Balzic's surprise, did so with a measure of tact.

Tommy Parilla played with a plastic apple throughout, tossing it up and catching it with his left hand while his right thumb stayed firmly in his mouth, coming out only to wipe his nose. When they were getting ready to leave he asked if he could keep the apple. Angelo Molanari shook his head, and Tommy started to cry.

"Keep it then, kid," Molanari said. "You want to take something else too? An orange, maybe. How about a banana?" Molanari held them up from the basket of false fruit on his desk.

"Apple," Tommy said, wiping his eyes on his sleeve. The drying blood from the sleeve left an ocher smear across his brow.

On the way to Southern Regional Detention and Correctional Center, Balzic started to relax. Nobody said anything, and Balzic was thinking that the first thing he would do tomorrow would be to arrange for Tommy's transfer to Mamont State Hospital. The only hitch he saw in that was that maybe some pencil pusher would want to ship the boy back to Southern Regional as soon as the tests were completed, and Balzic planned to see Judge Friedman about that. After that, he would take Marie for a drive and tell her how things were and how she ought to take them. With a little luck, she'd believe him.

As he pulled up to the gate, Balzic said, "Well, I hope he's only here until tomorrow morning."

"Mario," Moyer said, "you worry too much. I thought you said you had a court order to get him out to Mamont."

"No, I didn't say that. What I said was, I'd talked to Friedman about it and he called somebody out there, but I don't have any court order transferring the kid."

"You didn't get any paper?" Valcanas said.

"No. He told me to give the information to his secretary. Which I did. But the only paper I got then was the warrant. Then the kid got lost, and all I was thinking about was finding him. I guess I should've made sure about the paper."

"Don't worry about it," Valcanas said. "Friedman's all right. He's one of the few judges we've got with any guts. And if he said he'll do something, he'll do it. Not like those other shits."

"What's to worry about anyway, Mario?" Moyer said. "Nothing's going to happen to the kid here. Besides, it seems to me you got things a little twisted. I mean who killed who?"

"That's right," Valcanas said, "restore my faith in the state police. Retribution is what we want. Fuck justice."

"Ah, you're just sore 'cause you don't have the sense to stay out of your car when you're loaded," Moyer said.

"Yeah? And you're still sore 'cause you dummies couldn't even prove that. This man's interested in the welfare of another human being, a sick, bent kid—schizophrenic I'd say from the looks of him and the things he's done—and all you give a good goddamn about is getting rid of him. Putting him away, that's all. Forget him, what the hell? That's your attitude. They must make you guys memorize that down at that imitation of a school you call the state police academy."

Moyer coughed and said, "I'll call the gate man."

"Thanks," Balzic said. After Moyer got out, Balzic said, "Lay off, Mo. He's been backing me on this thing all the way with only one exception."

"Which only proves that even idiots are capable of clear thought once in a while. So give me another reason I should lay off him."

"As a favor to me."

"Bribery again, for crissake. Is that all you cops understand?"

"Aw, go piss up a rope."

Moyer got back in, the automatic gate opened, and they passed through. It closed behind them, and they made their way up the half-mile-long drive to the inner compound, waiting briefly for that gate to open, and then going on to the administration building.

Valcanas began to sing, "Miss Otis Regrets."

"Very funny," Moyer said.

"A cheerful song for a cheerful place," Valcanas said. "You try to put them in, Lieutenant, I try to keep them out. We're both in the same game. But the best-looking cheerleaders are on my side."

Balzic stopped the car in the gravel by the front door. "Tommy? Come along, son."

Tommy sat up and rubbed his eyes. He looked at the building, and his lips began to tremble. Balzic had to call him again before he slid out of the car and walked beside Balzic into the building. Moyer followed, but Valcanas stayed in the car singing the rest of "Miss Otis Regrets."

Inside, a bony man with long arms and a lower lip puffed full of snuff came out from behind a partition. His uniform was crumpled, as though he'd been sleeping, but his face gave no evidence of it.

"Where's Hartley?" Balzic said.

"Transferred," the bony man said. "Who're you, and what you got?"

"I'm Balzic. Chief in Rocksburg. This is Lieutenant Moyer, Troop A, state police."

"You got ID's?"

Balzic and Moyer produced their cards.

"Who's the mess?" the bony man said, looking at Tommy Parilla.

"Name's Parilla. Booked on a general charge of murder."

"Sure looks fucked up," the bony man said, walking to the side of a desk to spit in a coffee can on the floor.

"He's got problems," Balzic said.

"Don't we all," the bony man said, spitting again. He picked his teeth and wiped his fingers on his hip. "Well, all you got to do is sign him over, and I'll take care of him."

"I want him isolated," Balzic said.

166

"Do you now?"

Balzic shot a glance at Moyer.

"You're new here," Moyer said.

"You catch on quick," the bony man said. He went to a drawer and took out a pad of forms and a ball point pen. He laid them in front of Balzic. "Write him up, cowboy."

Moyer reached in his coat pocket and brought out a pen and a small black notebook. He stepped close to the bony man and peered at the badge on the man's shirt pocket.

"Hey. What're you doing?"

"What's it look like?" Moyer said, writing the badge number in his book.

"I can see what you're doing. What the hell for, is what I want to know."

"Do you now?" Moyer said.

"Damn right I do. Anytime somebody starts taking my number, I want to know what for."

"For not knowing your job," Moyer snapped. "You don't know who's supposed to fill out the forms?"

"I—I am."

"Then do it. And make a note on there, and print it big, the prisoner is to be isolated."

"Yessir."

The man slid the pad of forms and pen around and sat behind the desk.

"Just a minute," Balzic said.

"Huh?"

"What's your name?"

"Derr. R. C. Derr."

"You don't sound right, Derr. Where'd you come from?"

"North Carolina."

"What did you do down there?"

"Same as I'm doing here."

"What did you do before that?"

"Same thing. I always done it. Always been in correctional work."

"Where?"

"Before that I was in South Carolina."

"And before that?" Balzic said. "I'll just bet you were someplace else."

"Matter of fact, I was. I was in North Carolina."

"And I'll just bet you like to travel."

"What's that s'posed to mean?"

"You know goddamn well what it means," Balzic said, leaning with his knuckles on the desk. "I've known a few of you guys who've 'always been in correctional work,' and I know why you keep moving.

"I don't know who hired you, and I don't know what they were thinking about when they did, but you can bet your ass I'm going to find out. And I'll tell you something else. This prisoner is being put here for a very short time, and then he's being transferred to a hospital. It's all a matter of paperwork. But while he's here, you better make it a personal thing to see nobody bothers him. You understand that?"

"Yessir."

Balzic straightened up and directed Tommy to a chair by the wall. Then he gave R. C. Derr the information needed to complete the admission form.

They had just finished when a back door opened and into the office, carrying a can of beer in each hand, walked Pete Muscotti. At first he walked straight, and it was hard to see that he was drunk, but the nearer he came to the group clustered around Derr's desk, the more obvious it was that he was drunk.

"What the hell's going on here?" Balzic said.

"Hey, Chiefo," Pete Muscotti sang out. "My old buddy, Chiefo Mario."

Derr sprang out of his chair and tried to turn Pete Muscotti around and head him toward the door he'd come in.

"Wait a minute, Derr. I asked you, what the hell was going on here."

Derr mumbled something about a trustee.

"Hold it right there," Balzic said. "I want to know what that man's doing here in that condition."

"What's it look like, Chiefo? You're so fuckin' smart. You tell us."

"Shut up," Derr said and tried to push Pete toward the back door

168

again. "Goddamn you, shut up and get back where you belong." He was trying to whisper, but the irritation carried his words.

"Just drinking a little beer, Chiefo. A couple beers and a couple Miltowns, put them both together they spell high, Chiefo. . . ."

"Move out, goddammit," Derr said and put his shoulder into Muscotti's chest and heaved him toward the back door.

Pete Muscotti hit the door with a thump that forced him to drop the cans of beer. One was open, and the suds erupted in a tiny geyser when it hit the floor. "Now look what you made me do, ya fuckin' rebel," Pete shouted. He bent down to pick up the cans, but Derr jerked him up by the shirt.

"Leave it," Derr said.

"Hey, ya fucker, I paid you good bread for that beer."

Derr cracked Muscotti across the face with an open hand. "One more word," he said.

Pete Muscotti opened his mouth but nothing came out. His eyes said, wait till later. He took his time turning around and opening the door, his defiance turning to a smirk, and then slammed the door behind him.

Balzic and Moyer exchanged a look that both took to mean: so this is how it is. Moyer shrugged and started for the door, leaving without a word, but Balzic was filling with a rage that came up from between his legs. He could have taken Derr's throat in his hands and crushed it like a cardboard tube, and because he knew that, he started to back away from Derr.

Derr mistook the retreat. "I think it's about time you all got out of here," he said, "and let me get on with my work."

"Your work?" Balzic said. "Your work! Why you grubbing, grafting, thieving piece of shit." He stopped backing away. He wasn't moving forward, but the way he'd stopped made it plain to Derr that he had mistaken Balzic's retreat.

"You got two things to do here, Derr. You got this boy to put in isolation, and then you got your resignation to write. And God won't help you if you don't do them both right."

Balzic waited a moment longer to see how what he'd said had registered.

Derr didn't move and he didn't speak. He looked frozen for what seemed a long time but was no more than a second or two, and then his adam's apple went up and down.

Balzic went over to Tommy and touched him on the shoulder. He told him to go with this man, that everything would be all right, and that he would see him soon. Tommy looked frantic, then bewildered, but finally he nodded.

Balzic walked out to his car without looking back at Derr.

Valcanas had fallen asleep, his mouth ajar, and Balzic drove back into town with the silence in the cruiser broken only occasionally by the calls and static coming over the radio.

Balzic started to feel the exhaustion when he dropped Moyer off at the train station. It struck him that he had been walking for a long time during a wet snowfall and that only when he'd paused was he aware how heavy the snow was. He amused himself with that idea as he drove back to Muscotti's. He roused Valcanas and got him inside and propped on a stool.

No one was in the bar except Big Henry, the bent-back janitor, and Sal Muscotti, a cousin of Dom's who long ago had indebted himself to Dom for reasons no one knew and was obliged to work the bar when Dom wanted to be other places.

"The priest here?" Balzic asked Sal.

"In the back." Sal started to get off his stool. "You want something to drink?"

"For him," Balzic said, pointing to Valcanas, who was staring quizzically at himself in a mirror beside the cash register. "Put it on my tab."

Balzic went to the back room. His legs were heavy, his feet were aching, and he wanted to sit down, but he wanted more to settle the whole business tonight. He didn't think he had enough left in him to face Mrs. Andrasko again, not even with the priest along, but he knew there was no way out of it.

He found Father Marrazo watching the card players with his hands folded behind his back and shifting impatiently from foot to foot.

"You still want to tell Mrs. Andrasko?" the priest asked.

"No. I don't want to. What I want to do is fall down someplace. Obliterated, if possible."

"If your sense of duty permits," Father Marrazo said, "I'll help you get obliterated."

"Will you see to it that I get home?"

"I'll help you get obliterated. How you get home is your business. I want to get obliterated myself."

"Fair enough," Balzic said. But when they sat at the bar, he said, "I really shouldn't be doing this. I ought to be out there telling that woman I got her son locked up."

"Then let me do my best to talk you out of it," Father Marrazo said, "I've dealt with enough grief for one night, and I know that if you go to see her, you're going to drag me along."

"Pretty rough in the hospital?"

The priest shook his head and sagged. "The family was bad enough, but Dom—Dom was unbelievable. I never knew he had it in him."

"Yeah. I thought he was going to break down here when I told him about it."

"I don't know why anybody let him into the room."

"Was he still alive when you left?"

The priest shook his head. "If ever God was merciful, He was merciful to take that man. Some would say God was too slow. I don't know. I don't think he heard me, but he was conscious for a time. He was making this terrible sound in his throat. That's when Dom came in. In time to hear that, and then it was over. Then Dom went wild."

"Wild? How do you mean? I mean, did he get calmed down?"

"No. The head nurse ordered him out, and when he wouldn't go, she called an orderly. Dom knocked him down and kicked him in the stomach. I tried to talk to him, but he told me to keep away or he'd hurt me. Then two of your men came. I had to leave. I couldn't stand to watch it. Dom is really a very powerful man. I didn't know that. It surprised me."

Balzic covered his face with his hands. "Oh, Jesus Christ, why didn't you tell me this before?" He went behind the bar and got the phone and dialed his station.

"I don't know," Father Marrazo said. "It just surprised me so much. . . ."

"Joe? Balzic. What's the story with Dom Muscotti?" Balzic listened and began to curse. "Well, where is he now?" He listened a minute longer and then slammed the receiver down. "Hey, Sal, did Dom have a bag with him when he left? A doctor's bag?"

"No. He left it here. Told me to watch it."

"Thank somebody for that," Balzic said, running for the front door. "Keep on watching it, you hear?"

"Hey, where you going for crissake?" Valcanas said as Balzic ran by.

"Where we came from," Balzic said and then he was through the door.

"Where we came from," Valcanas said to his reflection in the mirror. "Where the hell was that. . . ."

Balzic used the siren to get around the few cars on the road to Southern Regional. The exhaustion was still with him, but the fury he felt for his own men for taking Dom Muscotti to this lockup instead of to his own was greater than any exhaustion he would ever feel.

"Stupid, stupid, stupid," he kept repeating, his head racing with the idea of Tommy Parilla being so close to Pete Muscotti and Dom Muscotti and R. C. Derr. Who knew how close they were to one another? Who knew what had been said? Worse, who knew what had been guessed at, wished for, hinted at, offered, accepted? And Pete Muscotti was floating on beer and tranquilizers, and Dom Muscotti was wild with grief, wild enough to beat hell out of a hospital orderly and give two cops half his age a battle.

Balzic tried to guess when Dom had been locked up. It had to have been sometime after they'd brought Tommy Parilla, which meant Pete Muscotti would know about Tommy. And if Pete had been able to buy Derr within hours, then Dom, with his money, would be able to buy him in minutes, and Pete would be sure to get next to Dom. Who would be happier for the opportunity? What had Pete been working for, flunkeying for, sweet-talking for all these years?

It can't happen, Balzic tried to convince himself. But he knew it could, and he knew that if he didn't get Dom Muscotti out of there, it would.

He had hopes: Pete might be too fogged to know what Dom was talking about; Derr might be too scared not to do his job about isolating Tommy; Dom might not make the connection between Vitale Ducci and Tommy; Pete might not even say anything about the bloodied, thumb-sucking kid who had just been brought in. No, Balzic thought. That kind always talks, especially about the tricks the world played on them, the bad breaks, the rotten luck, the crummy abuses they didn't deserve. Oh, they'll talk, all right, Balzic thought. They'll find one another after they buy Derr, and they'll talk until their tongues hurt.

Some hopes he had. Hope. What is hope? Hope is a whore, his mother used to say. Hope goes to bed with anybody. And when you had heads like those working—Pete, Dom, and R. C. Derr, Jesus . . .

He nearly didn't get the brakes on in time at the gate. He lurched out of the car and called the administration building. The phone kept ringing. "Come on, you piece of shit, pick it up."

After more rings than Balzic thought to count, the phone was answered and a voice said: "Administration Building, Officer Derr speaking."

"Open up, Derr. This is Balzic. I'm coming in to move one of the people."

"Who?"

"Balzic. Chief in Rocksburg. I was just here twenty, thirty minutes ago."

There was a pause and Balzic could hear the receiver muffled against cloth.

"Come on, goddammit," Balzic shouted.

"Get in your car, Chief," Derr said and then hung up.

Balzic slammed down the receiver and hustled for his car. He got in, put it in gear, and sat there. The gate didn't open. Thirty seconds passed. A minute. Balzic scrambled back out and to the phone again. This time he counted the rings. Twenty-three.

"You better press a button before I get back in my car, Derr," Balzic said, "or you're going to have real problems, you hear me?"

"I hear ya, Chiefo, only this ain't Derr. He's taking a leak. How do you like them apples, Chiefo? Huh? How do you like them?"

"Where's Derr, Pete?"

"I never heard of either one of them two, Chiefo. You know anybody else up here you might wanna talk to—anybody that'd wanna talk to you?"

"Pete, you'll regret this. As God is my witness, you'll regret this."

"Come on, Chiefo. Get yourself together. This Pete, whoever he is, he ain't here right now. And you know God ain't here. Now is there anybody else?"

"Pete, so help me—"

"What, Chiefo? What you gonna do? You on the outside, Chiefo, you forget that? When you people put them fences up you was only thinking how nobody could get out. You didn't think how you couldn't get in neither if nobody didn't wanna let you. Specially when you want to, like now, huh, Chiefo? What you got to say about that? Ain't that a real bitch now?"

Balzic slammed the phone on the hook and began to pace in front of the gate.

"All right, you fuckers," he said, getting into his car, "if this is the way it's going to be, then this is the way it's going to be."

He called the state police on the car phone.

"State Police. Sergeant Rudawski speaking."

"This is Mario Balzic, Rudy. I'm at the gate of Southern Regional, and the clown on the desk in the admin building is playing games. I want you to call the warden and tell him he's got a disturbance in that building, and if he doesn't answer after twenty rings, I want every unit you got up there out here. Read me?"

"I read you. Give a minute."

Balzic sat back and lit a cigarette.

"Mario?" the voice crackled over the receiver.

"Right here. Go."

"Warden Wolman acknowledges and says he's sending people to investigate. Meantime, he's standing by the master board in his office. In the event he gets no word in five, repeat, five minutes from zero-two-seventeen hours, he will close alternate circuits to gate and alarm systems. Meantime, we are dispatching two nearest units to you and alerting other availables. Time now zero-two-eighteen."

"You're my man, Rudy. Standing by."

Balzic adjusted his watch and waited, tapping on the steering while. At two-twenty-one, the gate slid open, and Balzic called Sergeant Rudawski back.

"No alarm sounded with the gate, so Wolman must've triggered it from the master board."

"You still want the units we dispatched?"

"I can see one coming now. I'll tell him to stand by here at the gate after I go on in. How's that?"

"Roger, Mario. Out."

The younger of the two troopers in the state cruiser looked disappointed when Balzic told him that in all probability whatever had been going on was now under control. The older trooper, the driver, said, "That suits me just fine," and stretched out across the front seat.

Balzic saw the inner compound gate opening as he approached, so that he didn't have to slow to go through. He hoped the worst he'd find was a simple case of drunkenness and dereliction. What he and Moyer had seen earlier was enough for Derr's dismissal; the business with the gate was more than enough. With luck, that was all there was going to be to it, and none of the possibilities that had brought him out here had happened. But no matter what had gone on, he did not intend to leave without seeing Pete Muscotti in a cell, Dom Muscotti in a state police cruiser going to another lockup, and Tommy Parilla in his own car going to his own lockup. He was furious with himself for bringing the boy here in the first place.

When he got inside the office, he found Warden Wolman and three guards with riot guns standing around R. C. Derr, who was sitting with his head in his hands in the chair Tommy Parilla had been sitting in earlier. Wolman was wearing a raincoat over his pajamas, his face creased from sleep, and he was shaking his head in pained disbelief.

"Four years," Wolman kept saying. "Four years, and it never happened before . . ."

"What happened?" Balzic asked one of the guards.

The guard turned his back to Wolman and whispered, "He just hired this guy two days ago, and the first night he's on duty, this happens."

"What happened, man?"

"Weren't you the one trying to get in the gate?"

"Yes, but what happened?"

"Everything. Beer cans all over the place, one of the people assaulted, the gate—everything."

"Which one assaulted?"

"I don't know his name. Never saw him before. Must've been brought in today."

"No names at all?"

"Not so far. This damn guy won't open his mouth."

Balzic brushed past the guard and approached Warden Wolman.

"Warden, who's been assaulted?"

Wolman threw up his hands. "I don't know. This man won't say anything. I don't know who was here, who was answering the phones, who was fooling with the gate, never mind who got assaulted. We just got the man over to the infirmary, and the only thing I can say for certain is that he wasn't wearing our issue."

Balzic felt something cold spread over his chest.

"Derr," Wolman said, "I'm going to ask you once more to tell me what went on here tonight, and I'll tell you that no matter what you say eventually, the fact that you remained silent for this long is going to go against you. That, plus the fact that you've made a fool of me...."

"You bastards wouldn't believe me even if I did tell you."

"Well, say something, man, for God's sake," Wolman said, his face blotchy.

"I'll say something," Derr said. "The only thing I'm going to say. I want a lawyer."

"Bullshit!" Wolman bellowed, storming away from Derr. To the guards he said, "Put him in a cell. I don't want to look at him again." To Balzic he said, "I've been hiring people here for four years, but never, never, have I made such a mistake. I ought to have my head examined."

"Warden, will you allow me into the infirmary?" Balzic asked.

Wolman looked at Balzic and seemed for the first time to recognize him. "Were you the one trying to get in the gate?"

"Yes."

"Well, will you tell me what you know about this?"

"I'd be glad to if you'd just let me in the infirmary to see who got worked over."

"Better yet, I'll take you, and you can tell me on the way."

Wolman called over his shoulder to one of the guards, "Have you called that ambulance?"

"Yessir. Should be here in a few minutes."

Wolman grunted and led Balzic through the back door of the office and across the compound to an adjacent building. Balzic told him everything he could in the time it took to cover the distance, some seventy-five yards.

"Well, I'm afraid this is your man," Wolman said. "I'm not a doctor, but even I could see he's lost an awful lot of blood."

"Most of that blood isn't his," Balzic said as they entered the infirmary. "At least I hope it isn't."

"You say he murdered two men?"

"There was some doubt about the first one, but there's none about the second. But he was psycho. He didn't know he was doing it."

They went into the treatment room, and there lying motionless on a table was Tommy Parilla. The attendant standing beside the boy had his fingers on Tommy's wrist. When he heard Wolman and Balzic come in, he looked up and shook his head.

Balzic thought his legs were going to buckle.

"How bad is it?"

"I'm not a doctor," the attendant said. "All I can tell you is he's still alive—if having a pulse this weak means somebody's still alive. I just took his blood pressure, and it's dropping fast. If that ambulance don't get here pretty soon, no doctor's going to be able to do anything."

"How'd it happen?"

"He's got a puncture wound in his chest. Very little blood coming from that, so it must be going inside."

"Isn't there anything you can do?" Balzic said.

"I told you. I'm not a doc. I'm not even a nurse. And with the stuff we got here, even if I was, there isn't a hell of a lot I could do." The attendant's face was rough cut and badly pockmarked. He walked with a pronounced limp, but his voice was soft and his manner that of a man long resigned to the sort of thing he was party to now. "Pulse is just fluttering now. Barely feel it."

"You know," Balzic said, looking at the floor, "I knew this was going to happen. I knew a half-hour, forty-five minutes ago—hell, what difference does it make how long ago. But I knew it, and it was the very goddamn thing I was trying to prevent—where the fuck's that ambulance?"

"I think I see a red light coming up the drive now," the attendant said. "'Less it's a bull wagon."

"I'm going to get dressed," Wolman said. "It's going to be a long time until tomorrow." He went over and glanced down at Tommy. He said something under his breath about being just a kid, and then left the infirmary.

Balzic waited until the ambulance came—its light had been the one the attendant had seen—and the men strapped Tommy into the stretcher. He took another look at the boy as the stretcher was being wheeled out the door, and that cold spread across his chest again. He forced himself to find out who knew where Dom and Pete Muscotti were.

Halfway across the compound between the infirmary and the administration building, he went down. He sat in the grass, running his hands through the dewy grass, trying to figure whether he had fainted or whether it had just been his legs telling him they had to stop awhile or whether it was the weight he felt on the top of his head and which spread downward through his neck and outward across his shoulders that had just pushed him down. He couldn't figure it, but it took him nearly five minutes to find the will and the strength to push himself up and go on.

After much confusion in the office, trying to find the log, with Balzic trying to explain to the two guards still in the office who he was looking for, one of them found the log, and all three tried to read it at the same time. All they learned was that R. C. Derr, among his other abberations, was a terrible writer. His script was incoherent.

"No sober man writes like this," was all Warden Wolman said when he came back into the office and looked at the log. "First, this Muscotti was brought in by the state boys after arraignment, is this it, Mario?"

"Yeah. That's Pete. Sometime early yesterday."

"So we're looking in the wrong place for him. That would have been entered earlier." He thumbed back a page in the loose-leaf book and found it. "Here it is. Muscotti, Peter L. He's supposed to be in C Building. Go get him."

One of the two guards went out.

"And you say your people brought this other one—with the same last name?"

"That's right. But Derr would have made that entry, and I can't make sense of his scribbling."

"I don't know whether this is it or not, but it looks like it," Wolman said, "but it's as near as I can come to it. Try C Building," he said to the other guard. "God knows where either of them are."

The other guard left, and Wolman turned back to Balzic. "I've been in this kind of work since I was twenty-three years old, Mario, and I've seen a lot of stupid things happen. Some of them I don't repeat. Not to anybody. I swore that if I ever got to be warden, I'd do everything in my power not to let things like that happen in any institution of mine. And now look. My God, how could I have been fooled so badly by that man? Everything about him should've told me, and yet, because we needed people, I looked right past all of it. My God."

Balzic knew exactly how Wolman felt, but he was too tired to say it. He was trying to save what was left of his energy for questioning the two Muscottis.

"You plan for these things—against them," Wolman went on, talking more to himself now than to Balzic, "you plan and plan. You make contingency plans. You go over them and over them, and you think you haven't left anything out, and then one day you make a mistake, and the whole damn thing comes down. In an hour's time, everything goes to hell. . . ."

Pete Muscotti was pushed into the office then, interrupting Wolman. The expression on his face told Balzic they were in for a time of it. Pete had always been a gloater, playing his gloating out by allowing the police to know that he'd done what he'd done and then daring them with a continuous smirk to prove it.

Until now, his greatest achievements had been petty larceny and low-score frauds, all carried out with what Balzic knew to be a ridiculous belief that he was proving himself to his Uncle Dom Muscotti. For Pete Muscotti believed in the Black Hand and the Mafia and the Cosa Nostra. No matter that his belief had come mostly from watching Edward G. Robinson movies on late-night television. The belief was religious, and Balzic knew that if Dom Muscotti sat his nephew down in a sound-proof room and explained the truth about himself, Pete would refuse to give up his belief and would go out of the room thinking that the truth Dom told was only meant to goad him into trying still another scheme in the hope of making himself worthy to be accepted by his uncle and men like him.

When Dom was brought in a minute or two later, Pete's face gave him away and convinced Balzic: Pete's eyes danced with the glow of ultimate success. Dom didn't even look at him, coming instead immediately to Balzic.

"Mario," Dom said, his voice filled with injury, "what the hell's going on here? Okay, so I went a little goofy in the hospital, but listen, you know me. You know I'll take care of that kid I kicked. I mean, Jesus, Acey was my paisan. Since we were little kids. I was just mad. Goofy mad, you know how it is. You get like that yourself once in a while. Like you done with Sam Carraza. You know how you can get, but I mean, Jesus, can't a guy show a little grief without getting locked up for it? And your guys, they were pretty rough on an old man—whatta ya say? Get me out of here. I ain't used to this. Jail, Jesus . . ."

Balzic looked past Dom at Pete and knew that Pete believed it was all an act, that Dom didn't mean a word he was saying and was pretending the tone of his voice.

Balzic knew otherwise. Dom wasn't acting. Dom believed a man was entitled to display his grief in a rage and that if all the damages were taken care of, were promised to be paid, well, then, that was all there was to it. A man went goofy with grief, he saw to it that the victims were covered, and everybody went home to a hot shower and a cold glass of wine. What else did you do when somebody you loved got killed?

Warden Wolman started to say something, but Balzic gave him a look that meant, let me have first shot. Wolman consented with a shrug. He went to a desk, took out a notepad, and started writing. Though he'd dressed, he hadn't bothered with socks, and his ankles showed very white above his black shoes.

Balzic sat down and invited Dom to do the same.

"Dom, it's not as simple as you think it is."

"What ain't?"

"The whole thing, everything that happened in the last couple hours."

"So tell me what ain't simple. I'll listen. When did you know me not to listen?"

"In the first place, Dom, we had the kid that killed your paisan. Did you know that?"

"No. All you told me was Acey got hurt. Beat up. I didn't know nothing else."

Balzic glanced again at Pete who was slouched against a wall.

"We did. We caught him practically in the act. I'm just sorry for everybody we didn't use our heads a little better, maybe we could have grabbed him before. But we didn't. You know who it was?"

Dom shook his head. "How would I know?"

"It was John Andrasko's stepson."

"You mean the Parilla kid?" Dom's brow arched. "He was—"

"He was what?"

"Well, he was—he was here," Dom said. "I seen him. A little while ago. He was a mess, and I asked him what was wrong—you know, Jesus, I know the kid from . . . you mean he killed John too?" Dom's face was incredulous.

181

"You got it," Balzic said.

"But what was wrong with him? I mean, did he go goofy? He musta been goofy, Mario. Am I right?"

Balzic nodded. "I brought him out here just for safekeeping for a day or so. Then I was going to take him out to Mamont. All I had to do was get some papers from a judge. Believe me, Dom, the kid didn't know what he was doing."

Dom shook his head. "Mario, Jesus, that woman, she must be going nuts. That poor woman . . ."

"That's right, Dom. First she marries a bum, then after she had the kid, the bum takes off and sticks her with the kid. Then she meets John, and everything starts to look up, only the thing is, John won't marry her."

"John A. never married her?" Dom's face opened again in disbelief. "But he was straight arrow."

"He wasn't straight that way," Balzic said, glancing from Dom to Pete and back as he talked. "But when young Tommy killed him, he wasn't really killing him."

"I don't follow," Dom said.

"What I mean is, he was really killing Tami Parilla, his blood father. It's a long story, Dom, so you'll just have to take my word for it, but it was the same way tonight, believe me. He wasn't killing your paisan tonight. He was killing his father, his real father, all over again."

"Jesus, who'd believe it?" Dom said.

"But that doesn't mean you wouldn't take the heat about him," Balzic said. "I mean, if you didn't know anything about this, or even if you did, for a while, you'd really have the heat for whoever did it to your paisan."

"Oh, sure. You kidding? I would've killed him myself if I could've." Dom thought for a moment. "Well, you know what I'm saying now, Mario. I maybe wouldn't 've killed him, but I would've did a job on him. Ah, what am I saying? If it was the kid, how could I 've done that? I mean, I know the kid's story—not this part you're telling me now, this sickness, but even without that, I couldn't 've done nothing to him. Jesus, he's just a kid."

Balzic shot another look at Pete. He was no longer slouching. He had stiffened against the wall, and his mouth was working with his lips together as though he was trying to keep from crying out.

"How long did you see the kid tonight, Dom?"

"Oh, I don't know. Couple minutes. That guard was taking him out. Me and Petey come up here—"

"How were you able to come up here?" Wolman interrupted.

"What?"

"I said, how were you able to come to this office? You just said you came up here as though you were taking a walk on Sunday. How was that possible? How did you get out of your cell? You were in a cell?"

"Well, yeah. Sure I was in a cell. Then Petey came up to see me, and he said I could come out."

"And you just walked out? Just like that? I mean, there was a door on that cell, wasn't there?"

"Well, sure."

"Well how did it get open, man? Did it just open itself?"

"No. Petey had a key. I asked him where he got it, but I don't remember what he said. When he opened up, I just came out, that's all. How was I supposed to know—I never been locked up in my life. I just figured Petey knew somebody. What did I care? I just wanted out. It smelled in there. Like vomit."

Wolman shook his head and started writing things on the pad again.

"Was that the first time you saw Petey tonight, Dom?"

"Huh? No. I seen him earlier. When your guys brought me up."

"Where did you see him?"

"Right here. In here. I knew he got himself arrested, but to tell you the truth, I wasn't thinking about him. I see him around so much, when I seen him here, I really didn't think nothing about it. I was too busy thinking about me, and what the hell was I doing winding up in jail. The first time in my life, Mario. Jesus, I'm fifty-eight years old. And I was a little bit scared, too."

"You thinking about anything else?"

"Sure. Whatta you think? I was thinking about Acey. About his wife."

"You still mad then? You still have the heat?"

"Sure I had the heat. Whatta you think? You have the heat for five minutes over something like that and it goes away? Sure I still had the heat."

"You tell Petey about it?"

"I don't know. Maybe I did. Sure, I must've told him—hey, Mario, what is this anyway? All of a sudden, I get the feeling you're not talking to me like a friend. . . ." Dom's expression was sincere enough even for Pete.

"Shut up!" Pete shouted, lurching away from the wall. The two guards stopped him, finally getting a pair of handcuffs on him and then locking that pair of cuffs to another pair which they locked to a heavy chair.

"What's wrong with him?" Dom said, looking first at Balzic and then at his nephew. "What's wrong with you? You nuts or something? Since when do you tell me shut up, huh? Since when?"

"Since he stuck something in Tommy Parilla tonight, Dom."

"What?"

"Shut your face, you goddamn wop. You dried-up goddamn wop!" Pete shouted.

"Get him out of here," Wolman said to the guards.

"Wait a minute," Dom said. He stood and went over to Pete. "Did you do that—what Mario said? Did you hurt that kid? 'Cause of what I said to you?"

"Come on, Uncle Dom. Just a little bit closer, so I can kick you where your balls used to be."

"Mario," Dom said, his eyes wide, "tell me this ain't my nephew." He shuffled toward Balzic. "Tell me this ain't Petey. Tell me I ain't hearing what I'm hearing. Mario, for crissake, tell me something. . . ."

"I can't tell you anything, Dom. You heard it."

"Get him out of here," Wolman said. This time he said it so there could be no delay, and the two guards unlocked the cuffs which held Pete to the chair and started to take him out.

As he was going, Pete shouted, "Stones you got, you fuckin' old wop! Your eggs turned to stones!"

Dom sank into a chair and hid his face behind his hands.

Balzic went over to Wolman, who was making still another notation, and said, "I want to take this man out of here."

Wolman glared up at him. "Why?"

"Because he doesn't belong here."

"Who belongs here?" Wolman said. "I don't belong here—ah, take him. Just sign a transfer, that's all I ask. At least we can have that much order." He reached into a drawer and brought out another pad of forms. "Sign it," he said. "I'll have somebody fill in the details later. Now I have to call the state boys. They can have the rest of this." He picked up a phone, shaking his head.

Balzic signed the transfer form and took Dom by the elbow and led him out of the office. Dom didn't refuse Balzic's hand nor ask where he was being taken. Fifteen minutes later, when Balzic pulled into Dom's driveway, Dom looked as though he wanted to explain something, but when he tried, he couldn't clear his throat. He sat looking at his gray stone house for a long moment and then got out of the car and walked up the drive without saying a word to Balzic.

Balzic spun the wheels pulling away and used his siren to get through intersections on his way to the hospital.

At the emergency room admitting desk, he identified himself and said to the nurse, "That boy that was brought in. The one that was stabbed—any word on him?"

"He's still in surgery," the nurse said. "Do you want me to call up there?"

"Please."

The nurse did, and after she hung up, she said, "I'm afraid he didn't make it."

Balzic looked blankly at her for a moment. Then he asked, "Where's the lavatory?"

"Down that hall," she said, pointing. "Third door on the right."

Balzic found it and locked himself in a stall. Then he broke down. He stopped after about five minutes and went out of the stall and blew his nose in a paper towel and washed his face in cold water. He dried his face on the paper towels and started out. At the door, he hesitated. He thought he was going to be sick, but the nausea passed and he went out and back down the hall to the admitting desk.

"Anybody notify the family?" he asked the nurse.

"He didn't have any identification," she said. "We didn't know who to notify."

Balzic pinched the bridge of his nose. "Jesus," he whispered.

"I'm sorry," the nurse said. "I didn't hear you."

"Just talking to myself," he said. "Can you tell me if he ever said anything?"

"I couldn't say about that. I was busy with a little girl, so I don't know. You'd have to ask the resident or the intern."

"Wasn't anybody else here when they brought him?"

"Yes. But we had such a time of it tonight. Six or seven all in a rush. And before that, right after I came on, this man—oh, just beaten up. Terrible. And then there was the traffic accident—"

"Yeah. Okay. Thanks." Balzic started to walk away but then turned back. "All right if I use the phone?"

"Help yourself."

Balzic dialed Muscotti's and asked for Father Marrazo, and when the priest answered, he said, "Tommy didn't make it, Father."

Silence on the other end. "Mario, you've got to fill me in. The last time I saw you, you were running out the door—"

"That's right, you don't know. Well, Father, I hope you're close to some coffee, 'cause it's going to be more of the same." Balzic went on to tell him what had happened.

"I don't believe it," Father Marrazo said. "I just don't believe it."

"Better believe it, Father, 'cause it's true. How 'bout coming up here?"

"Of course. One thing, Mario. Has—does Mrs. Andrasko know?"

"What do you think I'm asking you to come up for?"

"I see. Well, give me ten minutes."

"Right," Balzic said and hung up. He paced the corridor for some minutes and then heard somebody getting off an elevator. Two doctors, followed by two nurses, all in surgical clothes, came around a bend in the hall. The nurses disappeared into a lounge, and the doctors went behind the admitting desk and poured themselves coffee.

The older of the two dropped into a chair, and the other, boyish-looking with almost pink skin, sank onto the desk. His white shoes were spotted with blood. They both sipped their black coffee, not saying anything. Balzic coughed and held out his ID case. They both looked at it and nodded.

"What can we do for you?" the younger of the two asked.

"The boy, the one that just died."

"Yes?"

"Did he say anything?"

"If he did, I didn't hear him," the older doctor said.

"The only thing I heard him say was something about his father," the younger one said. "But he wasn't conscious. I really can't say for certain what it was. Sounded like, 'Daddy did me,' but I wouldn't swear to that. Did his father do it?"

Balzic didn't answer. He asked, "There was nothing you could do?"

"We tried, but no. He was dead when he came in. What fooled me was all the blood on his clothes. Don't know why I thought it was his, but I did, didn't you, Tom?"

The older doctor nodded. "Then we got him upstairs, and it was obvious. Shouldn't even have taken him up."

"What a night," the younger one said. "For a while there I thought I was back in Korea."

"Well," the older doctor said, sighing, "you want to call the coroner, or shall I?"

"I think he's still here. He's had a night of it, too."

"I guess so. What did we have—four fatals tonight?"

Balzic said good night and went out to the parking lot to wait for Father Marrazo.

The heavy dew was everywhere, giving the macadam parking lot the look of an old blackboard that had just been washed. Balzic paced in the lot and smoked and thought about what remained to be done. There was Mrs. Andrasko to be told, and Balzic wished he could take along a doctor as well as the priest.

And then there was Marie. He would have to tell her, and he knew she wouldn't ask questions. She would just look at him, and her look would ask everything there was to ask. And Balzic knew he had none of the answers. Somehow, if he was lucky, he would be able to convince her that what happened to Tommy, what Tommy had done, would have happened whether she had refused to leave that football game or not. It was easy to think he could do that, but he knew that when Marie turned her eyes on him and asked nothing, he would have the worst possible moments.

He saw a car turn into the lot and knew it was Father Marrazo. He looked again at the macadam and was again reminded of an old blackboard recently washed. He could not shake the feeling that it was the kind of blackboard that seemed to invite people to hold the chalk at the wrong angle so that if it were possible for someone to write on it now, the chalk would squeak endlessly, and his ears would hurt and his flesh would crawl.

As the priest came toward him, Balzic wondered why he would associate the dewy macadam with an old blackboard recently washed. And then it came to him: when he was in grade school, John Andrasko's one and only prank to irritate teachers was to purposely hold the chalk at the wrong angle to make it squeak, and everybody would laugh. Everybody except the teachers and Balzic.

AFTERWORD

The good people at David R. Godine, Publisher, Inc. gave me the opportunity to write this afterword. William B. Goodman, their Editorial Director, who is also my editor, suggested that I account for the "genesis of Mario Balzic: his character, his style, his milieu." (Robin W. Winks, general editor of the Godine Double Detective series, probably egged him on in this.) Goodman also suggested that I say something about my conviction that I must write under a pseudonym. He says these two subjects would "interest readers." Well, since Goodman is one of the best readers I know (another is Robert V. Williams, and more of him later), I will go with his notions. The question-and-answer format is mine.

* * *

Q. Where did Balzic come from?

A. Immigrant parents, Serbian father, Italian mother. Born in western Pennsylvania, educated in public schools, combat veteran of World War II Pacific Theater, Marine Corps. Father killed in coal mine accident. Married, with two daughters. Mother lives with him. Never wanted to be anything but a policeman.

Q. That can be surmised from reading the books. Where did he come from?

A. He came from a news store on a Sunday morning after I'd been grumbling for days about the latest in a long line of rejection slips for what was then my most serious "straight" novel.

Q. Explain further, please.

A. I was buying a paper in a news store. While waiting for my change, I looked down. There were stacks and stacks of books by Mickey Spillane, Carter Brown, Ellery Queen, Agatha Christie, Ross MacDonald, John McDonald, Georges Simenon, et al., and I asked the owner how many of those he sold. "Can't keep 'em in stock," he said. I walked out of the store and around the corner to where my car was parked, and there, straight ahead of me, were the ruins of the local railroad station. I had to drive about a block and a half to get to the station and then had to turn away from it and go another block before I made my next turn. As I approached the station, I thought, "Now there would be a good place for somebody to get murdered." By the time I reached the second intersection, I had conjured up the basis for *The Rocksburg Railroad Murders*, i.e., a kid killing a man because he thought the man was somebody else who had deserted him when he was a toddler.

Q. And you wrote it in three days and were an overnight success.

A. I wrote it in about ten months and couldn't give it away.

Q. Aren't you leaving something out?

A. Yes, but I'm going to leave a lot out. A friend of mine, who had introduced me to literary agent Bertha Klausner, told me of a conversation he'd had with her, oh, perhaps a week before I'd walked into that store. She'd told him, "Why don't you write mysteries? They always sell," or words to that effect. So I had that in my head while I was waiting for my change.

Q. Why'd it take you ten months? Georges Simenon never takes longer than eight days, and Mickey Spillane wrote one in three days once.

A. Well, see, the thing I learned about detecs, or mysteries, or whatever you want to call them, is that plots for them are no easier to put together than plots for straight novels.

Q. Come on, man. Anybody can write a mystery.

A. That's what they all say. But I found out quickly that the problems of mysteries are no different from the ones you have in trying to write a straight novel. If you have a problem of character in a straight novel, you're going to have it in a mystery. You have to answer the same questions: Who is this person? Where did he come from? Where does he live? Where's he been? Why does he talk like that? Why is he doing this, that, or whatever? Why is he not doing this, that, or whatever? How do you present the characters in the story? What point of view? What perspective? What tone? That last one, the tone, that's the knuckle-buster. Get that one wrong, and the book's gone, the story's dead. Nobody will read it.

Q. Then how do you get it right?

A. Best question there is. Also the hardest one to answer. You do it and read it and do it again and read it again, and keep doing it until it starts to *look* like you would want to *hear* the story. Very tricky stuff, this tone business, because you're not writing it to be spoken or acted or even to be read aloud. You're writing it to be read silently. So, getting a tone that *looks* like you would want to *hear* it is a bit of a shadow dance. It's easier done than talked about, but the core is that if the tone offends your own eye and grates on your own ear, then it's probably going to offend strangers' eyes and ears, too. The tone you have to watch out for, as R. V. Williams told me often, is the one that sticks its elbow in the reader's ribs and says, "Look at me, I'm writin'!" The tendency to show off is always there. The tendency to say, in one way or another, "Christ, ain't I wonderful," has to be watched like a sick puppy. Let it get away from you and it will crawl behind the couch and choke on its own vomit. That's an unpleasant metaphor, but the ego of storytellers is no small thing and can't be ignored. Let your ego get out of control and it will crawl behind your story and throw up all over it. The hardest lesson to learn in telling stories is that the story is more important than the teller.

Q. Your digressions are almost celestial. Where did Balzic come from? And stick with it this time.

A. He came from a lifelong ambivalence about cops, ergo, authority figures, ergo, my parents and especially my mother's father.

191

Q. Lifelong? Really?

A. My earliest memories are of my mother, her father, my father, and the '36 flood. The order is significant. My grandfather was the dominant male in a small tribe. Before he died when I was twelve, I had developed a murderous hatred for him. When I learned that he had died, I asked my mother to take me to see him: I wanted to make sure he was dead. The first chance I got to be alone after seeing him laid out on his bed, I danced around, chanting, "He's dead, he's dead," until I fell down exhausted. When you hate someone and he dies, it's a wonderful feeling.

Q. Out of the wonderful feeling came Balzic?

A. When I said that the order of my memories is significant, I said it to illustrate the fact that I grew up with a profound sense of ambiguity about who was who in my family. I'm still trying to recover from that.

Q. Stay with the question, please.

A. I am. Out of the rubble of this confusion will emerge a pattern, I assure you.

Q. A pattern is not a character.

A. True. But out of the patterns of childhood come the inclinations and aversions of adulthood. Because my early family life was such a jumble, because my grandfather was such a force in my life, because my father was so much at his mercy, I had a hellish time comprehending how one gets around in this world. I'm leaving out an encyclopedia of family history (call that emotional crossfire), but my point is that for a long time I had a tough time dealing with people who thought they were supposed to tell me how to live. A slip here, a slide there, a misperception here, a miscalculation there, and I could easily have vanished into penal obscurity. I was on my way.

Q. Still no word on Balzic, eh?

A. Well, on the way I was on to, I met a few authority figures who didn't have any doubts about who they were or about what places they occupied in the social scheme. (Usually, the only place you find that kind of certitude is among professional soldiers, men who have given up their claim to assert themselves in all but a few clearly defined circumstances.) Out of those meetings came a notion of how cops ought to behave. See, when I was trying to tell the world to mind its own business, nobody had heard of Miranda, Gideon, or Escobedo. In those days (the early '50s), cops could do damn near anything. There just were no brakes, except the one on searches based on the exclusionary rule. But since Miranda, et al., the clamor for a return to "law and order" has been gaining momentum at a scary pace. It appeals to new ears every day, but what it amounts to—no matter how it's phrased—is a return to the days before Miranda, et al. The exclusionary rule is catching flak right now. There is practically a mob who would love nothing more than to break that one. They keep yammering about the "good faith" of policemen gathering evidence. But when the police break into your residence to search for contraband they think you're hiding and they're acting in good faith but without a proper warrant, who do you call? And when a cop decides to stop you and search you and he doesn't like the way you're answering him and he starts to put his billy on your back, who do you call? If you answer, "The cops," you have not seriously given any thought to what it means to return to the days before Miranda, et al.

Q. Are you saying that out of your confused emotional upbringing and your brushes with cops and your fear of people calling for law and order—are you saying Balzic comes out of that?

A. More or less. I told you there was a pattern.

Q. Christ, you ought to be handing out pamphlets on a corner somewhere. You're a closet preacher. Church of the Open Novel. By your own admission, you don't know how to deal with authority figures and here you are writing police parables.

A. Fascinating, isn't it?

Q. Do you agree you're a closet preacher?

A. No. But I will admit that it's another of the tendencies you have to guard against, another of the things that, if you're not careful, can screw the tone of a story.

Q. But you do believe that there are people out there who need to be told some things and that you're the guy to tell them, yes or no?

A. Yes *and* no. I've gone through that soap-box phase in every one of these Balzic stories. It's always there in the first draft. It's usually gone by the third draft—or at least I hope it is. When Writers are young and when they're still aiming to create Literature (observe the capitals), and when they're spending most of their time hanging out with other Writers "discussing" Literature, one of the things they talk about a lot is "having something to say." That phrase has dammed up more than a few people.

Q. Explain further, please.

A. Well, I've known people, quite capable prose writers, who, when they finally got down to pen and paper and tried to write a story or a novel, found out—if we're to take their word for it, at any rate—that they "had nothing to say." What I suspect they discovered is that they didn't know how to tell a story, but, because they have never gotten over that "having something to say" crap, they could not get on to the recognition that a story can be told about things that were said three thousand years ago. They confused the subject with the telling, in other words. A good painter can make an astonishing portrait of a dull, homely, seemingly insignificant man or woman, just as a competent storyteller ought to be able to present a good story about one, or a whole clan of them, for that matter. Witness Flannery O'Connor or Andre Dubus, among others.

Q. We're running out of space. What about the anonymity stuff? Why the alias?

A. Many reasons. I want to be able to live as normally as anybody else. I want my family to be able to do that also. I don't want to lose the protection ordinary people have because of their ordinariness. When I go out and about I don't want to waste time avoiding people who would try to make me special. I don't think my family ought to be forced to change their lives because of something I do. I also do not want to change the way I write or what I choose to write about because I have to worry about how other people may react to it. Personally, temperamentally, I am not a social person. I do not meet people easily or mix well, as they say, even with people I know. Professionally, I spend much time watching other people and eavesdropping, and I can't very well snoop in other people's lives if I have to spend time getting them to quit snooping in mine. And if you think people will not snoop in your life because they've decided you're special, then you have just never done a public thing. I had a very brief, singularly mediocre career in professional baseball. One of the things I learned from it was that some people who pay to watch you do something they think they know a lot about also think you owe them more than your work, and they try to collect at every opportunity. By the time organized baseball had retired me, I'd had all the fame I'd ever wanted.

Q. Anything else you want to say?

A. Yes. There's a canard that's been around for a long time that goes something like this: "Writing is a lonely business." It's supposed to imply some wonderfully romantic things, chief among them being, of course, that writers have no help. Well, it's partly true, and that's why it's been around for so long. But no book is ever brought before the public on a writer's work alone. In my case all of the following are involved: an agent and her staff, the publisher, editorial director, book editor, managing editor, marketing manager, copy editor, proofreader, typesetters, production manager, compositors, pressmen, binders, warehousemen, truckers, salesmen, sales clerks, publicists, reviewers, and all those secretaries and switchboard operators. I've probably left some important people out, but you get the idea. The words in the book are ultimately the storyteller's responsibility, but without the efforts of all those other people, none of those words would ever have gotten beyond the diligent folks in the Postal Service.

Q. Anything else?

A. Yes. Robert V. Williams teaches in the California State College system. Most of what I know about reading I learned from him. And about writing stories he was adamant: writing simple, solid prose is not enough; you must know how to make a box to put it in.

Q. You ever going to stop?

A. One last thing. My wife has put up with a bunch of stuff because of me and from me. Being married to me is a slippery business, and I want it in writing that I love her. Trying to juggle a marriage, a family, a job now and then, and a guy carrying fiction around in his head takes some doing. It's less trying for everybody now that I've sold a few books and gotten generally good reviews, but before, it did get harrowing. In addition to all the daily things that can cause heat within a family, having one member of it traveling in a make-believe world for much of the time takes a toll on all the other members.

Then there is the inherent nuttiness of trying to make money by writing fiction. What you're doing, after all, is telling lies, the more believable the better, in order to make enough money so that you can quit your honest, respectable job and stay home to have more time to make up even more lies. It's a dubious ambition, suspicious if not sinister, and it gets even nuttier because, when you start to achieve some success at it, then, you see, strangers begin to compliment you in print for doing a thing which, if you did it in person every day, would eventually lead to a hearing in front of the commitment committee of the county board of mental health.

K. C. Constantine

196